Alexander Milton Ross

Memoirs of a Reformer, 1832-1892

Alexander Milton Ross

Memoirs of a Reformer, 1832-1892

ISBN/EAN: 9783337295264

Printed in Europe, USA, Canada, Australia, Japan

Cover: Foto ©Raphael Reischuk / pixelio.de

More available books at **www.hansebooks.com**

"REFORM *is the wisest and most natural* PREVENTIVE OF REVOLUTION."—*Emerson.*

MEMOIRS

OF

A REFORMER.

(1832—1892.)

BY

ALEXANDER MILTON ROSS,

Author of " Recollections and Experiences of an Abolitionist "
(1872) ; Corr. Member of the British and Foreign Anti-Slavery
Society, and the Anti-Slavery of France ; Vice-President
of the National Liberty League of the U. S.; Presi-
dent of the Ontario Medical Liberty League, the .
Anti-Compulsory Vaccination League, and
the Food Reform Society of Canada,
etc., etc., etc.

"Whatsoever ye would that men should do to you, do ye even so to them."—*Jesus.*

TORONTO:

HUNTER, ROSE & COMPANY.

1893.

To the Memory

OF

JOHN BROWN,
The Martyr ;

JOSEPH GARIBALDI,
The Liberator ;

ABRAHAM LINCOLN,
The Emancipator ;

Lucretia Mott, Gerrit Smith, Wendell Phillips, Horace

Greely, William Lyon Mackenzie,

Marshal S. Bidwell, Russel T. Trall and

J. Emery Coderre,

Reformers,

This volume is reverently dedicated by

THE AUTHOR.

PREFACE.

—•••—

THESE Memoirs are given to the public in compliance with the repeated solicitations of friends and co-laborers. In their preparation I have strictly refrained from any attempt at embellishment or amplification, but have aimed at accuracy of statement, briefness of description, and simplicity of style.

TORONTO, 1893.

MEMOIRS

OF

A REFORMER.

CHAPTER I.

1849–55.

MY HERITAGE.

FROM my mother I received a heritage of qualities which have been ruling factors in all my labors for the betterment of humanity—a love of nature, and a love of freedom. From my childhood I have hated and rebelled against tyranny and oppression, under whatever form they were manifested or imposed.

EARLIEST RECOLLECTIONS.

My earliest recollections of a struggle against oppression date back to the year 1838. The Canadian Government at that time was a selfish, arrogant, oppressive Family Compact, that deserved annihilation, and would have met it, had all the Liberal leaders been animated with the zeal, energy, courage, intelligence and consistency of William Lyon Mackenzie, to whom Canadians of to-day are more than to any man indebted for the rights and liberties they now possess.

FIRST IMPRESSION OF HUMAN SLAVERY.

My first impressions of human slavery were received from my mother, to whom I am indebted for whatever I have accomplished or attained that is worthy and meritorious. Subsequent descriptions of the internal working of the institution of slavery in the slave states, were given me by fugitive slaves in Canada.

Many of these victims of "man's cruelty to man" bore ineffaceable evidence of brandings with red hot irons, scourgings, and horrible mutilations, the sight of which kindled an unquenchable flame, and clinched my determination to do what I could toward "letting the oppressed go free."

LEAVE CANADA.

In my seventeenth year I went to the United States to prepare for the battle of life. My first object was to acquire a broader and fuller knowledge of the workings of human slavery in the United States. My next object was to acquire a knowledge of medicine and surgery, which would enable me to earn the means to prosecute what was even at that early period the leading aspiration of my life—the abolition of human slavery.

I had long before determined to cast my lot with the despised and hated men and women, who were sacrificing their all to obtain freedom for the poor down-trodden slaves of the republic.

MARSHAL S. BIDWELL.

I had often heard my mother refer in kindly terms to Marshal S. Bidwell, as an old friend then residing in New York. Mr. Bidwell had occupied a prominent political position in Canada, previous to the rebellion of 1837, but becoming involved in opposition to the (Family Compact) Tory Government he was forced to leave the country, and settled in New York, where he attained high distinction as a lawyer and jurist. He was noted for his high and delicate sense of honor, as well as for intellectual refinement and culture. He received me in the kindest manner, asking many questions about old friends in Canada. I became a frequent visitor at his home, and there met many of the most worthy citizens of New York.

Through Mr. Bidwell, I became acquainted with Horace Greeley, William Cullen Bryant, and many other good men and women, whose kindly sympathy and pure lives have been a blessing to me.

DR. R. T. TRALL.

I also formed what proved a life-long friendship with Dr. Trall the Hydropathist, who at that time was actively disseminating his hydropathic and hygienic theories. I attended his evening lectures and subsequently graduated at his school. He was an active, vigorous thinker and speaker: very independent and uncompromising, and tenacious of his opinions. His life and labors were productive of great good to humanity.

DR. VALENTINE MOTT.

I also became acquainted with Dr. Mott, who at that time stood at the head of his profession in America, if not in the world.

Dr. Mott was a kind, philanthrophic man, quite simple in his manner and unconsious of his professional distinction. He rendered me great assistance in my studies, and did me many acts of true kindness at a time when I was preparing for the battle of life. I shall ever revere his memory.

FIRST VISIT TO WASHINGTON.

Mr. Greeley and other friends advised me to spend the winter in Washington. I was made acquainted with Joshua R. Giddings, of the House of Representatives, General Sam. Houston, of the Senate, and Dr. Gamaliel Bailey of the *National Era*, who secured me a good position in the office of the *Era*, where my duties were light, affording me plenty of time for study and observation. I was made a welcome visitor at the house of Dr. Bailey and his excellent wife, and participated in the delightful intellectual feasts that made their home the resort of the best and greatest men of that day. At the feet of "Gamaliel" I was happy to sit and listen to words of wisdom. Weekly and bi-weekly informal receptions were held by Mrs. Bailey, which were attended by liberals of every shade of politics and religion. There I frequently met Joshua R. Giddings, Benjamin F. Wade, Salmon P. Chase, William H. Seward, Horace Mann, Henry Wilson, Robert Rantoul, and sometimes foreign political refugees.

Congress was in session, and the city was full of gay people. General Taylor was President, and the Government was under the baneful influence of the slave-power. I spent several hours every evening at the capitol, listening to the speeches of the great men of that period, for there were intellectual giants in the Senate in those days. But, although the intellectual power of the Senate at that time undeniably surpassed that of any other period in the history of that body, there was a cringing and bowing down to the slave power, that in a great measure destroyed the usefulness of these great men.

In the Senate were Daniel Webster, Henry Clay, John C. Calhoun, Colonel Benton, General Sam. Houston, Jefferson Davis, Mason of Virginia, and Pierre Soule of Louisiana.

In the house of Representatives were Joshua R. Giddings, Salmon P. Chase, Thaddeus Stevens, Preston King, David Willmott (of Wilmott Proviso), Charles Durkee, Alexander H. Stevens, Andrew Johnson, and many other men of mark. With Mr. Giddings and General Houston I formed friendships that continued till their deaths.

I frequently heard Webster, Clay and Calhoun speak.

These three Senators formed a trio of intellectual giants, but morally they were dwarfs.

Mr. Calhoun was aged and infirm; his voice was tremulous, and his step feeble, he appeared despondent and gloomy, and no wonder, for all his plans and schemes had failed. He was wasting away with the disease that eventually terminated his life.

He was thin, pale and feeble, but his intellectual

face, and the peculiar light that flashed from his eyes while speaking, made him a very striking figure.

Daniel Webster at that time was a most majestic-looking man, physically and intellectually,

His frame was massive and lion-like, his head large, neck full and strong, his eyes the grandest and most expressive of intellectual power I ever saw. His influence for good, however, was weakened by political and pecuniary environments. He had been repeatedly thwarted in his ambition for the presidency, and the disappointment marred his life.

Henry Clay was a ready, forcible speaker, and very effective in debate ; his presence was magnetic, he was tall, slender and alert. His head was large and high, his nose prominent and inquisitive, his eyes bright and piercing, his eyebrows overhanging. Being a man of great personal magnetism, he had many personal friends who spoke of him with pride as "Harry of the West." Mr. Clay's great ability and power were rendered useless for the public good, by the evil spirit of human slavery, and by his ambition to become President, which hampered and embittered his last years.

HOUSE OF REPRESENTATIVES.

I occasionally witnessed exciting scenes in the House. The southern members were habitually

haughty and dictatorial in their manner, and in their
speeches assumed a domineering tone toward northern members, especially the Whigs. On one occasion I witnessed a very exciting conflict between
Foote of Tennessee, commonly called "Hangman
Foote," and Colonel Benton, nicknamed "Old Bul-
lion." They were both from slave states, consequently, I was neutral in my sympathy, and indifferent as to the consequences, the contest however,
ended without bloodshed. On several occasions I
witnessed brutal attacks on northern men, and
often saw bowie-knives and pistols flourished, accompanied by threats of violence. It was the cus-
tom of the slave-holders to try and accomplish by
intimidation and brute force, what they could not
meet by argument. The power and influence of
the Government at that time was wielded in the
interests of human slavery.

INTEMPERANCE AT THE CAPITAL.

The vice of intemperance was not, as now, re-
stricted to a few exceptional cases, but was fear-
fully prevalent. A glass of whiskey or brandy could
often be seen on the desk of a Senator during a debate, and the free use of intoxicating drinks by Senators was too common to provoke remark. It was
still more common in the House, and the scenes of
drunkenness and disorder in that body at times, es-

pecially during a prolonged night session, were sometimes disgusting. On these occasions large quantities of intoxicants were deposited in a room connected with the House, which was thronged by members at all hours of the night.

SLAVE COFFLES.

From my window I frequently saw gangs of slaves pass, generally chained together in coffles of ten or fifteen men and women promiscuously, and always moving in one direction—Virginia, the chief slave market of the south at that time. These sad sights intensified my hatred of that vile institution, and served to clinch my determination to "let the oppressed go free," but I must bide my time. In consequence of frequent attacks of illness, which I attributed to the unhealthy condition of the city, I was obliged to leave Washington and return north. My residence in the capital had been of great interest and value to me. The opportunities I had enjoyed of listening to the debates in Congress of the leading men of the nation, the many friendships I had formed, and the advantages improved, will never be forgotten. I returned to New York and continued my medical studies. My acquaintance with Mr. Greeley and Mr. Bryant, both of whom were very kind and solicitous for my welfare, brought me in contact with good minds, which proved a source of enjoyment and benefit.

To both these good men I am specially indebted for many kindnesses. At their homes I was always made to feel that I was a welcome guest. Mr. Greeley was a most excellent man, gentle as a woman, and overflowing with kindness and child-like simplicity and innocence, one of the gentlest men I ever met. His heart and brain were full of human sympathy and love.

Mr. Bryant was a true and intelligent friend, whose kindness and friendship will never be forgotten by me.

MY MOTHER'S ILLNESS AND DEATH.

In 1855, I was called to Canada by the serious illness of my mother, who was prostrated with congestion of the lungs, from which she died. Words are inadequate to describe my feelings at this terrible bereavement

She had always been my inspiration. Her assurance to me when I first left home in 1849, " In spirit I shall be with you, wherever you are," was an ever present support and rock of defence. How could any evil come to me when one so good was watching over—was ever with me ?

My mother had ever made the Golden Rule the standard by which she lived. She taught me that to live for one's own gratification and happiness was ignoble and unworthy. That the greatest pleasures are those which arise from devotedness to others;

that no work is more excellent than helping others to better lives.

The noblest career, in her eyes, was that which is given up to others' wants ; the successful was that which is worn out in conflict with wrong ; the only worthy ambition, to alleviate human misery, and leave the world some better than you found it.

My mother's life was not an uneventful one. Her father was connected with the commissariat service of the British army in Canada in 1812. When the war broke out between the United States and Britain, she, then a little girl, accompanied her parents to Newark, now Niagara, where the British troops were concentrating. During the frequent changes, defeats and victories that occurred she shared in the sufferings and vicissitudes consequent to a war in which Indian savages bore a part. When the town was destroyed by the enemy, she, with her mother, found a refuge in the " burial ground." On the return of the British forces, the women and children were placed on board a schooner and sent to Kingston. As the vessel was obliged to keep close to the Canadian shore, for fear of the United States' cruisers, it was five weeks before they reached Kingston. During the voyage there was much suffering for lack of clothing and food, as all they possessed had been destroyed in the fire. My mother's sufferings from cold inspired one of the sailors to cut the tops from his boots and make a pair of shoes for the protection of her feet. Many years after this she often spoke with feelings of gratitude of the kind act of this sailor. While residing with her mother (her father had died from wounds received from the enemy) on the Kingston or military road, west of Kingston, their house was broken into one night, by a band of half-drunken Mohawk Indians, who were on the war-path. After the Indians had eaten all the food in the house and broken the furniture, one of the savages seized my mother by the hair and lifting her from the floor, drew his scalping knife to kill her, when the chief, —Loft, by name—knocked the savage down and saved my mother's life. Years after this occurrence, this same savage was seriously, and it was thought at the time fatally, wounded in a fight, and my mother hearing of it drove to the Reservation with a physician, and provided such good treatment for the Indian that he finally recovered. When the cholera visited Canada, and hundreds were being slain by it, she sacrificed herself in caring for its victims. The draft on her vitality was so great that she never recovered from it. My mother's disposition was one of exceeding kindness, patience and devotion to duty. She was a lover of flowers and birds, and a sincere and active friend of the poor. The negro refugees, from the slave states, always found a faithful friend and a sincere welcome at her home.

CHAPTER II.

1855-1856.

VISIT GERRIT SMITH.

LEAVING Canada, I made my first visit to Peterboro', the home of that noble and sincere friend of the poor down-trodden slave, Gerrit Smith. He joined hands with me for the crusade against human slavery, and ever after remained my faithful and sincere friend. Through him, I became acquainted with all the active abolitionists of the time, Charles Sumner, William Lloyd Garrison, Lucretia Mott, Lydia Maria Child, Wendell Phillips and John G. Whittier. I had become an extreme abolitionist, determined to do my whole duty. I knew the risk, I knew that hatred, slander, malice, and social, relig-

13

ious and professional ostracism would be my portion. I knew that no other class of citizens were more despised by the rich, the powerful and the influential, than the despised abolitionists. I knew the path to professional preferment, success and influence was closed to me, but I felt then as I feel now, that the title of "negro thief" so often applied to me at that time was a prouder title than any conferred by monarchs. I felt then, and I feel now, after the lapse of thirty-five years, the approval of my own conscience, which is more to me than the fickle applause and approval of men.

THE OUTLOOK.

The outlook was dark and unpromising, but my faith in the justice of the cause was steadfast, and my hope in the future undimmed by the prevailing political fogs—and treachery of politicians and dough-faced friends.

In thirteen great states of the republic human slavery existed, and throughout these states men, women, and children were bought and sold, just as cattle and swine are bought and sold at the present time. They were deprived of all human rights, beaten, abused, outraged and killed at the will and pleasure of their owners. Husbands were sold and separated from their wives, and children were sold and separated from their parents. In fact, four

millions of men, women and children, in the slave
states, possessed no rights that their masters were
bound to respect. Slavery was the dominant power
before which all other interests were subordinate.
The coarsest, blackest, and most brutal tyranny
prevailed all over that vile south Sodom. No word
of pity or relief came to the oppressed. No one dare
utter a word aloud against the institution of slavery,
except at peril of life. To teach a slave to read was
punished with death. A reign of terror prevailed.
From the sanctum of the editor, the pulpit of the
preacher, the desk of the teacher, the counting-house
of the merchant, not a voice was heard on behalf of
four millions of human beings held in cruel bondage,
from which there appeared at that time no hope of
relief. The poor slaves were silent and hopeless ; if
they looked for help to the so-called free states of
the republic, they were met by the command, " Servants obey your masters." If they fled from bondage, the Federal government stood ready to act the
part of a policeman for the slave masters, and send
the fugitive back to slavery. In a majority of the
northern states a mean, cowardly, servile spirit prevailed, that bowed and cringed before the haughty
slave-masters.

All the power and influence of the national government, all the power and influence of the wealthy
classes, all the social and religious influence of the
clergy and professional classes, were enlisted in

positive or negative support of that sodomic institution, which made merchandise of the souls and
bodies of human beings. The press of the north
was muzzled. The religious Tract Societies, the
Bible Societies, the Missionary Societies from Vermont to Texas, were silent or quiescent in the face
of this giant wrong.

That was the condition of the American Republic in 1855. Its so-called banner of freedom, was a
flaunting lie, its constitution a compact with Satan,
its motto a deceitful, lying cant.

To the selfish and superficial observer of that time
it appeared as if this arrogant slave power would
last forever; entrenched in Federal and State law
sustained by the church and all the dominant and
wealthy classes of the republic, it appeared impreg-
nable and indestructable. But, wait and see what
a wonderful transformation was wrought in a few
short years through the earnest labors of a few com-
paratively insignificant men and women " who loved
their neighbors," and obeyed the golden rule. The
members of this little band of abolitionists were at
first ridiculed and despised, and treated as ignorant
fanatics and cranks.

As they increased in number and daring, they
were hated, persecuted, outraged, and in many cases
barbarously murdered. What crime had these men
committed? The crime of " doing unto others as
they would have others do unto them," the crime

of loving liberty better than slavery, the crime of teaching that every human being born into this world possesses an inalienable right to life, liberty, and the pursuit of happiness.

HUMAN SLAVERY AS IT WAS—FOUR MILLIONS OF SLAVES IN BONDAGE.

The number of slaves in the Southern States at this period (1856) exceeded four millions, distributed as follows: Alabama, 445,000; Mississippi, 486,431; South Carolina, 402,406; Louisiana, 341,726; Texas, 182.566; Virginia, 490,465; Missouri, 114,921; Arkansas, 111,115; North Carolina, 331,059; Tennessee, 275,719; Kentucky, 225,483; Georgia, 462,198; Florida, 61,745; Delaware, 1,798; Maryland, 87,189; making a total of more than four millions of human beings held in cruel bondage.

SLAVES WERE CHATTELS.

Throughout the slave states, slaves were considered chattels, and were classed with horses, mules, swine, and other domestic animals. The slave was subject to his master's disposal. He was doomed to toil that others might reap the fruits of his unrequited labor. He had no right in things real or personal: he was not ranked among sentient things, but among things. His wife and his

B

offspring belonged to his master, to do as he pleased with. There was no law for the slave but his master's whip. In fact, the slave had no right which his master was bound to respect. He was bought, sold and traded, the same as lands, cattle, and mules were bought, sold and traded. That my readers may have a clear idea of the status of the slaves, I reprint a few advertisements clipped from southern papers of that time; such advertisements were usually headed by a cut of a man or woman with a bundle on his or her back. The extent and cruelty of the inter-state slave trade is well illustrated by an extract from a report printed by the Presbyterian Synod of Kentucky in 1851 : "These horrid scenes (coffle gangs of slaves) are frequently occurring in our midst. There is not a neighborhood in the state where these heartrending scenes are not displayed; there is not a village or road that does not behold the sad procession of manacled outcasts whose chains and mournful countenances tell that they are exiled by force from all that their hearts hold dear."

Virginia, Maryland and Kentucky were the breeding states of the south. It has been truly said that "the best blood of Virginia runs in the veins of her slaves." This remark was equally true of Kentucky and Maryland.

SLAVE SALES.

(From N. O. Picayune.)

Foster's Slave Depot.

GREAT EXCITEMENT!!

FOUR HUNDRED SLAVES EXPECTED TO ARRIVE BY FIRST NOVEMBER.

My two Slave Depots are now open for the reception of traders and purchasers. From my numerous correspondents, I have reason to believe that I shall have from four to five hundred slaves, for sale, between this and the first of November, comprised of every size, age and sex, to suit the most critical observer. I am also prepared to accommodate Traders with comfortable lodgings and board at very reasonable rates. My stock of Slaves is equal if not superior to any offered in this market.

Thankful for past patronage, I earnestly solicit planters and the citizens generally, to give me a call before purchasing elsewhere.

N. B.—Slaves bought and sold on commission.

For Sale.

Just arrived, with a choice lot of VIRGINIA and CAROLINA NEGROES, consisting of Plantation hands, Blacksmiths, Carpenters, Cooks, Washers, Ironers, and Seamstresses, and will be receiving fresh supplies during the season, which I offer for sale, for cash or approved paper. I have removed my office from Esplanade to 90 Baronne-street, between Union and Perdido-streets, two blocks west of St. Charles Hotel. No brokerage paid on the sale of negroes.

JOHN B. SMITH,

90 Baronne-street,

Slave Depot.

195 Gravier and 85 Dryades-streets.

TO TRADERS, PLANTERS AND MERCHANTS.

Having opened my old stand, with considerable im-
provements, and another house added, I am prepared to
accommodate for sale from 150 to 200 slaves. Also, good
accommodation for owners. A good assortment of slaves constantly on hand for sale, consisting of Field Hands, Mechanics and
House Servants. Apply to   C. F. HATCHER,

195 Gravier and 85 Dryades-streets.

COMMUNITY OF PROPERTY—SLAVES, MULES AND LANDS.

(*N. O. Picayune, 1859.*)

Probate Sale of Negroes and Plantation

BY virtue of an Order issued from the Seventh District Court
of East Felciana in the above entitled succession, I will sell
on the premises, on TUESDAY, the 20th of December next, the
following property, belonging to said succession :—

The plantation, cultivated by the deceased as a cotton plantation, situated in the parish of Avoyelles, on the Atchafalaya
River, containing about 742½ acres, together with all the improve-
ments, consisting of 300 acres of open land, overseer's house,
quarters, cisterns, a good gin and mill—the said plantation being
composed of the tract known as the McMillan tract, and of
about 157½ acres from the tract known as the Evans tract, bound-
ed on the east by the Atchafalaya River, north by James H.
Cason, west by J. L. Delee, and south by Turner's Bayou.

Also the following negroes :

1. ZIDE, aged about 40 years.
2. MARTIN, aged about 55 years.
3. FID, aged about 16 years.
4. WINNEY, aged about 35 years.
5. EMELINE, aged about 40 years.
6. JANE, aged about 16 years.

7. ALEXANDER, aged about 45 years.
8. GEORGE, aged about 28 years.
9. ANTONY, aged about 26 years.
10. HARRY, aged about 15 years.
11. JANE, aged about 11 years.
12. MILLY, aged about 23 years; her three children—Dolly, 4 years, Abe, 2 years, Polly, 1 month.
13. ZELPHY, aged about 22 years, and her two children—Emmeline, 3 years, Tom, 1 year.
14. RHODA, aged 7 years.
15. ELLEN, aged 38 years.
16. ZACH, aged 9 years.
17. HENRY, aged 24 years.

Also 8 head of mules, stock of cattle, oxen, hogs and farming utensils on said plantations.

The said property will be sold in block, or separately, to suit purchasers.

TERMS OF SALE.

If sold in block, $6,000 cash; the balance on a credit of one, two, three and four years, the purchase price to bear 8 per cent. interest from day of sale, and to be secured by notes, with approved personal security, and a mortgage detained on the property.

If sold separately, the land on a credit of one, two, three and four years, with 8 per cent. interest from day of sale, to be secured by note, with approved personal security and mortgage on the property.

The negroes, one-third cash, the balance on one or two years, with 8 per cent. interest from the day of sale, to be secured by note; with approved personal security and mortgage on the property.

The mules, farming utensils, stock, etc., on a credit of twelve months, with 8 per cent. interest from day of sale, to be secured by note, with approved personal security, for all sums over $100; for all sums under $100, cash.

Persons desiring to examine the plantation before the sale, can do so by calling on the manager of the place, or communicating with R. J. Bowman, at Clinton, La.

Sheriff's Office, Marksville, this 21st day of October, A.D. 1859.

L. BARBIN,
Sheriff and ex-officio Public Auctioneer.

SLAVE WOMEN FOR SALE.

In the *Charleston Mercury*, the leading political paper of South Carolina, appeared the following advertisement :

" NEGROES FOR SALE.—A girl about twenty years of age, raised in Virginia, and her two female children, one four and the other two years old—is remarkably strong and healthy, never having had a day's sickness, with the exception of the small-pox, in her life. The children are fine and healthy. *She is very prolific in her generating qualities, and affords a rare opportunity to any person who wishes to raise a family of healthy servants for their own use.* Any person wishing to purchase will please leave their address at the *Mercury* office."

Another infamous advertisement, from the Richmond, Va., *Despatch*, reads as follows :

FOR SALE—An accomplished and handsome lady's maid. She is just turned 16 years of age, nearly white, was reared in a genteel family in Maryland, and is now for sale, not for any fault, but simply because the owner has no further use for her."

(*Ibid.*)

" NEGROES FOR SALE.—A negro woman, 24 years of age, and her two children, one 8 and the other 3 years old. Said negroes will be sold *separately* or together, as desired.

RUNAWAY SLAVES.
(*From N. O Picayune, 1857.*)

ONE HUNDRED DOLLARS REWARD.—Ran away from my plantation on Tensas River, in the parish of Catahoula, Louisiana, on the 22nd of September last, four negroes :

BILL PRIME, dark griff, about 25 years old, weighs about 165 pounds; speaks slowly and stammers a little when confused; hair tolerably long and straight.

RICHARD, about 26 years of age, weighs 145 pounds, of dark complexion; has a large scar on the left cheek and one on the chin, same side of face.

TOM SIMMS, about 25 years old; weighs about 150 pounds; dark complexion; when he left had a small goatee under the chin.

GUS SIMMS, about 18 years old; weighs about 120 pounds; dark complexion, slim, and rather delicate in appearance.

I will pay the above reward if the above-named slaves are lodged in jail where I can get them, or $25 for either one of them.

They may probably try to make their way to the Free States, and may state that they belong to Sam Buford, my overseer, or to W. L. Campbell, of New Orleans, from whom I bought them.

M. GILLIS,

Of the firm of Gillis & Ferguson

ONE HUNDRED DOLLARS REWARD.—Ran away from the undersigned, on or about the 18th of July, 1857, a negro man named PEYTON (calls himself Peyton Randolph), aged 26 years, five feet seven inches high, weighs 150 pounds; he is genteel in his appearance, and can read and write. The above reward will be paid to any one who will have him lodged in jail, so that he can be recovered, or who will deliver him to Mr. John Ermon, on the corner of Race and Camp streets in this city.

M. C. HALE,

Constance, near Second-street.

TWENTY-FIVE DOLLARS REWARD.—Ran away from the subscriber, on the 29th of October, MISSOURI or ANN, a very likely griffe, aged 15 years, and about 5½ feet high; figure rather slender. She was barefooted, and had on a brown calico dress. She is refined and plausible in her manner and language, and unacquainted in the city.

L. GREENLEAF,

Cor. Annunciation and Jackson streets.

(From the Richmond, Va., Whig.)

"One Hundred Dollars Reward will be given for the apprehension of my negro, Edmund Kenney. He has straight hair, and complexion so nearly white that it is believed a stranger would suppose that there was no African blood in him. He was with my boy Dick a short time since, in Norfolk, and offered him for sale, and was apprehended, but escaped under pretence of being a white man."

"Two Hundred Dollars Reward.—Ran away from the subscriber, last November, *a white negro man*, about 35 years old, hefght about five feet eight or ten inches, blue eyes, has a yellow woolly head, very fair skin.

"P.S.—Said man has a good-shaped foot and leg; and his foot is very small and hollow."

Twenty Dollars Reward.—Ran away from the subscriber, on the 14th instant, a negro girl named Molly. She is 16 or 17 years of age, slim made, *lately branded on her left cheek, thus,* "*R*," *and a piece is taken off her ear on the same side : the same letter is branded on the inside of both her legs.*

ABNER ROSS,
Fairfield District, S.C.

(From the Georgia Messenger.)

"Runaway.—My man George; has holes in his ears; is marked on the back with the whip; has been shot in the legs; has a scar on the forehead."

(From the Wilmington, N.C., Advertiser.)

"Ran away, my negro man Richard. A reward of twenty-five dollars will be paid for his apprehension, dead or alive. Satisfactory proof only will be required of his being killed. He has with him, in all probability, his wife Eliza, who ran away from Colonel Thompson.

(*From the Savannah Republican.*)

" FIFTY DOLLARS REWARD.—Ran away from the subscriber, on the 22nd ult., my negro man Albert, who is twenty-seven years old, *very white, so much so, that he would not be suspected of being a negro.* Has blue eyes, and very light hair. Wore, when he left, a long thin beard, and rode a chestnut sorrel horse, with about $70 belonging to himself.

" He is about five feet eight inches high, and weighs about 140 pounds. Has a very humble and meek appearance ; can neither read nor write, and is a very kind and amiable fellow ; speaks much like a low country negro. He has, no doubt, been led off by *some miserable wretch* during my absence in New York."

A letter in a Vicksburg, Miss., paper, of June, 1857, from a planter, contained the following passage : "I can tell you how to break a negro of running away. When I catch a runaway negro I tie him down and pull one of his toe nails out by the roots, and tell him if he ever runs away again I will pull out two of them. I never have to do it more than once. It cures them."

BLOOD HOUNDS.

Blood Hounds were used to track runaway slaves, especially in thick woods or in swamps, where the poor wretches would live in caves or among the rocks, to elude the pursuit of their cruel taskmasters. Many died of exposure and starvation, rather than return to their owners, to be whipped and branded with red-hot irons. I clipped the following advertisements from Southern papers :

" BLOOD HOUNDS.—The undersigned, having bought the entire pack of negro dogs (of the Hay & Allen stock) he now proposes to catch runaway negroes. His charges will be three dollars a day for hunting, and fifteen dollars for catching a runaway.

He resides three and one-half miles north of Livingston, near the lower Jones' Bluff Road.

"WILLIAM GAMBREL."

"NOTICE.—The subscriber, living on Carroway Lake, on Hoes' Bayou, in Carroll parish, sixteen miles on the road leading from Bayou Mason to Lake Providence, is ready with a pair of dogs to hunt runaway negroes at any time. These dogs are well trained, and are known throughout the parish. Letters addressed to me at Providence, will secure immediate attention. My terms are five dollars per day for hunting the trails, whether the negro is caught or not. Where a twelve hours' trail is shown, and the negro not taken, no charge is made. For taking a negro, twenty-five dollars, and no charge made for hunting.

"JAMES W. HALL."

VALUE OF BLOODHOUNDS.

The value of bloodhounds to the slave-hunters may be inferred from the following quotation of prices taken from a Columbia, S. C., paper:

"Mr. J. L. Bryan, of Moore county, sold at auction, on the 20th instant, a pack of ten bloodhounds, trained for hunting runaway negroes, for the sum of $1,540. The highest price paid for any one dog was $301; the lowest price, $75; average for the ten, $154."

Bloodhounds are larger and more compact than ordinary hounds, with hair straight and sleek as that of the finest race horse, colored between yellow and brown, short-eared, rather long-nosed, and built for scenting, quick action and speed. They can take a scent three days old and run it down. Their speed is about equal to, and their endurance

much greater than, a greyhound. Their bark re-
sembles neither that of a bulldog, cur, nor hound,
but is a yelp like a wolf's. Their bite is a wolf-like
snap, not the hold-fast grip of a bulldog. The
"catch dog" used in slavery times on Southern
plantations in capturing runaway slaves, looked like
a cross between a Newfoundland and bull of large
and powerful build.

DESCRIPTION OF A NEGRO HUNT.

The overseer or hunter mounts a fleet horse, holds
his "catch" dog by a chain, and turns loose the
hounds. Circling round, they strike the scent and
soon lead off, their fast receding yelps marking the
rapidity of the chase. The horseman follows over
fences through timber and swamp as best he can,
holding his "catch dog in leash." Hounds sighting
the negro, divide, form a semi-circle, and rapidly
draw it into a large circle around him. As the pursued wretch runs, the dogs in front of him fall back,
but preserve their equi-distant place in the circle
which they are gradually closing. On nearing him
they snap at his legs, but do not spring at his throat.
As the circle narrows, the hunter arrives. The
ominous sound of the chains' rattle, like the warning
note of the serpent, strikes the negro's ears. The
"catch dog" springs upon the exhausted runaway
and holds him, hounds are clubbed away, the fugitive secured, dogs leashed, and the hunt is over.

SPECIAL LAWS FOR RECAPTURING SLAVES.

Special laws existed for recapturing escaped slaves at any cost of life to the victims, by first proclaiming them outlaws. The following legal instrument, with its accompaniments, will suffice to show the way :

STATE OF NORTH CAROLINA,
LENOIR COUNTY.

Whereas complaint hath this day been made to us, two of the Justices of the Peace for the said county, by William D. Cobb, of Jones county, that two negro slaves belonging to him, named Ben (commonly known by the name of Ben Fox), and Rigden, have absented themselves from their said master's service, and are lurking about in the counties of Lenoir and Jones, committing acts of felony—these are, in the name of the state, to command the said slaves forthwith to surrender themselves and return home to their said master. And we do hereby, by virtue of an act of the Assembly of this state, concerning servants and slaves, intimate and declare if the said slaves do not surrender themselves and return home to their master immediately after the publication of these presents, that any person may kill and destroy said slaves by such means as he or they think fit, without accusation or impeachment of any crime or offence for so doing, without incurring any penalty or forfeiture thereby.

Given under our hands and seals, this 12th day of November, 1856.

B. COLEMAN, J.P. (seal.)
JAMES JONES, J.P. (seal.)

The following was the law in reference to recapturing slaves in Mississippi, Alabama, Georgia, Arkansas, and Louisiana : " If any slave shall happen to be slain for refusing to surrender him or herself, or in resisting any person who shall endeavor to apprehend such slave or slaves, such person so killing such slave as aforesaid making resistance, shall be and is by this Act indemnified from any prosecution for such killing."

FIENDISH BRUTALITIES TOWARDS SLAVES.

The newspapers of the slave states in 1855-6-7 teemed with advertisements descriptive of runaway slaves. One had been " lacerated with a whip "— another, " severely bruised "—another, " a great many scars from the lash "—another, " several large scars on his back from severe whipping "—another " had an iron collar on his neck with a prong turned down—another has a " drawing chain fastened around his ankle "—another " was much marked with a branding iron"—another, a negress, " had an iron band around her neck," &c., &c.   All these brutalities were permitted, if not authorized, by the slave code.   Then came another class, which, if not -authorized by law, were frequent and not prohibited : " Mary has a sore on her back and right arm, caused by a rifle ball "—another, " branded on the left jaw "—another, " has a soar across his breast and each arm, made by a knife ; loves to talk of the

goodness of God"—" Sam has a sword cut lately
received on his left arm "—Fanny has a scar on her
left eye; a good many teeth missing; the letter ' A '
branded with red-hot iron on her left cheek and
forehead "—another, " scarred with the bites of
dogs." " Runaway—A negro woman and two children. A few days before she went off I burnt her
with a hot iron on the left side of her face—I tried
to make the letter ' M.' Rachel had three toe nails
pulled out."

I could fill many pages with similar extracts from
advertisements in papers and from handbills, in circulation in the slave states, in the old dark days.
One case that came under my personal observation
in Alabama, is only a specimen of many others that
I could mention of a similar nature.

A Methodist local preacher, a slave owner, proposed illicit intercourse with a young female slave.
She refused, he sent her to the overseer to be whipped, again she refused, and he sent her again to be
whipped, again she refused, and again was whipped.
He then ordered her to be branded on the cheek,
with a red-hot iron, then she yielded to this adul-
terous wretch, who had not overstepped the limits
of the slave laws of Alabama. In fact, the poor
downtrodden slaves suffered all that wanton, grasp-
ing avarice, brutal lust, malignant spite, and insane
anger, could inflict. Their happiness was the sport
of every whim, and the prey of every passion.

Slavery was the cause of more suffering, than has followed from any other cause since the world began.

I was present at the burial of a female slave in Mississippi, who had been whipped to death by her master, for some trifling offence. While she was undergoing the punishment, she gave birth to a dead child, and mother and child were wrapped in old linen bagging and laid in the same grave—free at last !

OPINIONS OF JEFFERSON AND RANDOLPH—BOTH SLAVE-HOLDERS.

Thomas Jefferson, the author of the "Declaration of Independence," made a clause to his last will, conferring freedom on his own slave offspring, as far as the Slave Code of Virginia permitted him to do it, supplying the lack of power by "humbly imploring the Legislature of Virginia to confirm the bequests with permission to remain in the state, where their families and connections are." Two of his daughters by an octoroon female slave were taken from Virginia to New Orleans, after Jefferson's death, and sold in the slave market at $1,500 each, to be used for unmentionable purposes. Both these unfortunate children of the author of the Declaration of Independence were quite white, their eyes blue and their hair long, soft, and auburn in color.

Both were highly educated and accomplished. The youngest daughter escaped from her master and committed suicide by drowning herself to escape the horrors of her position.

A land of liberty for white people, for slave-holders, was it, where Jefferson could not bequeath liberty to his own children ? In Georgia, had he lived and died there, the " attempt " would have been an " offence " for which his estate would have been subjected to a fine of one thousand dollars, and each of his executors, if accepting the trust, a thousand more. In one of his letters Jefferson says, " when the measure of the slaves' tears, is full, when their groans have involved heaven itself in darkness, doubtless a God of justice will listen to their distress."

JOHN RANDOLPH OF ROANOKE.

John Randolph of Roanoke, one of the signers of the Declaration of Independence, and a native of Virginia, says :—"Avarice alone can drive, as it does drive, this infernal traffic, and the wretched victims of it, like so many post-horses, whipped to death in a mail-coach."

" Ambition has its cover-sluts in the pride, pomp, and circumstance of glorious war, but where are the trophies of avarice ? The handcuff, the manacle the blood-stained cowhide ! What man is worse received in society for being a hard master ? Who denies the right of a daughter or sister to such monsters ? " (Speech in Congress.)

Study this picture. Wholesale murder, barbarism and cruelty. The general prevalence of these in the highest circles, and no one regarding the perpetrators the worse for it, or shrinking back from the closest family affinity with the monsters !

THE CLERGY OF THE SLAVE STATES.

Every clergyman in the Slave States, either openly or passively, upheld human slavery. They maintained that slavery was a wise and beneficent institution devised by God for the protection and welfare of the negro race. These reverend pro-slavery champions resembled the priests of Juggernaut recommending the worship of their god by pointing to the wretches writhing and shrieking and expiring under his car. From a pro-slavery pamphlet, published by the Reverend James Smiley of the Amita Presbytery, Mississippi, I extract the following: "If slavery be a sin, and if the buying, selling and holding a slave be a sin, then three-fourths of all the Episcopalians, Methodists, Baptists and Presbyterians of eleven states of this union are of the devil. They not only buy and sell slaves, but they arrest and restore runaway slaves, and justify their conduct by the Bible."

C

A SABBATH SCENE IN THE SOUTH.

Scarce had the solemn Sabbath bell
　Ceased quivering in the steeple ;
Scarce had the parson to the desk
　Walked stately through his people,

When down the summer shaded street
　A wasted female figure,
With dusky brow and naked feet,
　Came rushing wild and eager.

She saw the white spire through the trees,
　She-heard the sweet hymn swelling ;
O, pitying Christ ! a refuge give,
　That poor one in Thy dwelling.

Like a scared fawn before the hounds
　Right up the aisle she glided ;
While close behind her, whip in hand,
　A lank-haired hunter glided.

She raised a keen and bitter cry,
　To Heaven and Earth appealing ;
Were manhood's generous pulses dead ?
　Had woman's heart no feeling ?

" Who dares profane this hour and day ? "
　Cried out the angry pastor ;
" Why, bless your soul, the wench's a slave,
　And I'm her lord and master !

" I've law and gospel on my side,
　And who shall dare refuse me ? "
Down came the parson, bowing low,
　" My good sir, pray, excuse me !

"Of course I know your right divine,
  To own, and work, and whip her;
Quick, deacon, throw that Polyglot
  Before the wench, and trip her!"

Plump dropped the holy tome, and o'er
  Its sacred pages stumbling;
Bound hand and foot, a slave once more,
  The hapless wretch lay trembling.

I saw the parson tie the knot,
  The while his flock addressing;
The Scriptural claims of slavery,
  With text on text impressing.

Shriek rose on shriek—the Sabbath air
  Her wild cries tore asunder;
I listened with hushed breath to hear
  God answer with His thunder.

All still!—the very altar's cloth
  Had smothered down her shrieking;
I saw her dragged along the aisle,
  Her shackles loudly clanking.

My brain took fire; "Is this," I cried,
  The end of prayer and preaching?
Then down with pulpit; down with priest,
  And give us Nature's teaching!

WHITTIER.

THE NATIONAL SACRIFICE.

No wonder it required an army of two millions
of men (half of whom were slain) to rid the land
of such a monstrous curse as human slavery. From
the torture dens of the outraged, bruised and

beaten slaves the prayer for justice had reached the "god of battles," and the command had gone forth to that vile South Sodom to "let the oppressed go free," and slavery with its whips, fetters, chains, bloodhounds and red-hot branding irons, was swept away in rivers of blood.

SOME OF THE DANGERS ATTENDING MY CRUSADE.

In all the Slave States there were laws for the enforcement of severe penalties for interference with the institution of slavery. Senator Preston of Virginia declared in his place in the U. S. Senate that "any person uttering abolition sentiments in the Slave States would be hanged." In Louisiana the laws read as follows: "If any person shall in any language hold any conversation tending to promote discontent among the slaves, he may be imprisoned from three to twenty years; or he may suffer death at the direction of the court." In Georgia, Alabama and Mississippi the same laws existed. In North Carolina, the pillory and whipping for the first offence, and death for the second offence. In Virginia, for the first offence, thirty-nine lashes; the second offence, death.

From Gerrit Smith I obtained much valuable and interesting information as to the workings of the different organizations having for their object the liberation from bondage of the slaves of the

South. He accompanied me to Boston, New York. Philadelphia and Longwood, the home of Hannah Cox, whose house was always open to the poor slaves flying from their pursuers, and whose heart warmly sympathised with every means for the liberation of the oppressed.

During these visits I became acquainted with many liberty-loving men and women, whose time, talents, and means were devoted to the cause of freedom. The contact with such earnest minds, imbued with an undying hatred and detestation of that foul blot on the escutchon of their country, served to strengthen my resolution and fortify me for the labor before me. I was initiated into a knowledge of the methods to circulate information among the slaves of the South; the routes to be taken, after reaching the so-called Free States, and the relief posts, where shelter and aid for transportation could be obtained. My excellent friend also accompanied me to Ohio and Indiana, where I made the personal acquaintance of friends in those states who at risk of life and property gave shelter to the fugitives, and assisted them to reach Canada.

The Rev. O. B. Frothingham, in his life of Gerrit Smith, says:

"Alexander M. Ross, of Canada, whose remarkable exploits in running off slaves caused such consternation in the southern states, was in communication with Gerrit Smith from first to last, was aided by him in his preparation with information and counsel, and had a close understanding with him in regard to his course of procedure. Both these men made the rescue of slaves a personal matter."

FUGITIVE SLAVE LAW.

The poor fugitive who had run the gauntlet of slave hunters and bloodhounds, was not safe even after he had crossed the boundary line between the Slave and the Free States, for the slave drivers of the South and their allies, the democrats of the North, controlled the United States Government at that time, and under the provisions of the iniquitous "Fugitive Slave law," the North was compelled to act as a police officer, for the capture and return to slavery of fugitives from the Slave States.

DIFFERENT VIEWS AMONG ABOLITIONISTS.

While there existed among all true abolitionists a sincere desire to aid the oppressed people of the Slave States, there was much diversity of opinion as to the means to be adopted for their liberation from bondage.

Garrison, Whittier, Lucretia Mott, and all the members of the Society of Friends, were opposed to violent measures, such as would result in bloodshed. Their efforts were confined to the public discussion of the wrongs of the slave, and the iniquity and injustice of human slavery. On the other hand, Gerrit Smith, Theodore Parker, Joshua R. Giddings,

John Brown, and many others, equally sincere and
noble men and women, actively or passively aided
and abetted every effort to liberate the slaves from
their bondage. It is almost needless for me to say
that, while I sympathized with every man and
woman who desired the freedom of the slave, my
views accorded with those who believed human
slavery to be such a monstrous wrong and injustice,
that any measure, no matter how violent, was justifiable in so holy a cause as the liberation of those
held in bondage.

MY ANTI-SLAVERY PRINCIPLES.

The principles that animated, impelled, and controlled my actions as an abolitionist, may briefly be
summed up as follows:—

1. That every innocent human being has an inalienable right to life, liberty, and the pursuit of
happiness.

2. That no government, nation, or individual, has
any right to deprive an innocent human being of
his or her inalienable rights.

3. That a man held against his will as a slave has
a natural right to kill every one who seeks to prevent his enjoyment of liberty.

4. That it is the natural right of a slave to de-
velop this right in a practical manner, and actually
kill all those who seek to prevent his enjoyment of
liberty.

5. That the freeman has a natural right to help the slaves to recover their liberty, and in that enterprise to do for them all which they have a right to do for themselves.

6. That it is the natural duty of a freeman to help the slaves to the enjoyment of this liberty, and as a means to that end, to aid them in killing all such as oppose their natural right to freedom.

7. That the performance of this duty is to be controlled only by the freeman's power and opportunity to help the slaves.

" Remember them in bonds."

CHAPTER III.

1856-59.

UNDERGROUND RAILWAY.

In Philadelphia I made the necessary preparations
for my work in the Southern States. My good
friend Gerrit Smith was my faithful and principal
supporter in this my first effort to help the slaves
to freedom.

In undertaking this mission I did not disguise
from myself the dangers I would most certainly
have to encounter, and the certainty that a speedy
and perhaps cruel death would be my lot, in case
my plans and purposes were discovered. And not

41

only would my life be exposed, but the lives of those
I sought to help. My anti-slavery friends in Boston
and Philadelphia warned me of the dangers that
were in my path and some of them urged me to
seek other and less dangerous channels wherein to
aid the oppressed.

I felt convinced, however, that the only effectual
way to help the slaves was to aid them to escape
from bondage. To accomplish that it was necessary
to go to them, advise them, and give them practical
assistance. For, with but few exceptions, the slaves
were in absolute ignorance of everything beyond
the boundary of their plantation or town. The circulation of information among the oppressed would
also tend to excite a spirit of inquiry and create a
feeling of independence which ultimately might
lead to insurrection, and the destruction of the institution of slavery in the United States. Before
leaving Philadelphia, it was mutually arranged between my friends and myself, in respect to confiden-
tial correspondence, that the term "hardware" was
to signify males and "dry goods" females. I was
to notify my friend in Philadelphia (if possible)
whenever a package of "hardware" or of "dry
goods" was started for freedom, and he in turn
warned the friends in Ohio and Pennsylvania to be
on the lookout for runaways. My name was dropped, and others assumed to meet the emergency of
the occasion. My communications with the outside

world were in cipher and confined to one individual with many names. These precautions were deemed absolutely necessary for my personal safety and success in my hazardous task. My appearances and disappearances were so uncertain and mysterious that my northern friends were accustomed to call me the "Man of Mystery," while in the south a much more sulphurous title was accorded me.

INTO THE LAND OF BONDAGE.

Fully equipped, I crossed the Potomac and entered the land of bondage. On my arrival in Richmond I went to the house of a gentleman to whom I had been directed and who was known at the north to be an abolitionist.

I spent a few days in quietly determining upon the best plans to adopt.

THE WORK BEGUN.

Having finally decided upon my course, I invited a number of the most intelligent, active, and reliable slaves to meet me at the house of a colored preacher, on a Sunday evening.

TALK TO FORTY-TWO SLAVES.

On the night appointed, forty-two slaves came to hear what prospect there was for their escape from bondage. I took each by the hand, asked their name, age and whether married or single.*

I had never before at one time seen so many colored men together, and I was struck with their individuality and general kindness and consideration for each other. I explained to them my object and purpose in visiting the Slave States, the various routes from Virginia to Ohio and Pennsylvania, and the names of friends in border towns who would help them on to Canada. I requested them to circulate this information discreetly among all upon whom they could rely. Thus each of my hearers went forth an agent in the good work. I then told them that if any of their number desired to make the attempt to gain their freedom, in the face of all the obstacles and dangers in their path, to come to the same house on the following Sunday evening, prepared to take the " underground railroad " to Canada.

NINE FUGITIVES FROM BONDAGE.

On the evening appointed, nine stout, intelligent young men had declared their determination to gain their freedom or die in the attempt. I carefully explained to them the route and the names of friends along the border upon whom they could rely for shelter and assistance. I never met more apt students than these poor fellows, and their " yes

massa, I know it now " was assurance that they did.
They were only to travel by night, resting in some
secure spot during the day.

Their route was to be through Pennsylvania or
Ohio, to Erie, or Cleveland, on Lake Erie, and from
thence across the Lake to Canada. I bid them good-
bye with an anxious heart, for well I knew the
dangers they would have to encounter. I learned
many months after that they all had arrived safely
in Canada. Three of these brave fellows enlisted in
a colored regiment, for service in the war that gave
freedom to their race. Two of my Richmond pupils
were married men, and left behind wives and children. The wife of one made her escape, and reached
Canada within six months after her husband gained
his liberty.

AT WORK IN NASHVILLE.

The day following the departure of my little band
of fugitives from Richmond, I left for Nashville, in
the State of Tennessee, which I decided should be
my next field of labor. On arriving in Nashville
I went direct to the residence of a Quaker lady
well-known for her humane and charitable disposition toward the colored people. When I informed
her of my success in Richmond, and that I intended
to pursue the same course in Nashville, she expressed great anxiety for my safety, but finding that I
was determined to make the attempt, she sent for

an old free negro and advised me to trust him implicitly. This good man was nearly eighty years of age, and had the confidence of all the colored people for miles around Nashville. He lived a short distance outside the city limits. At his house he preached to such of the slaves as were disposed and could attend every Sunday evening. I requested him to invite as many reliable and intelligent slaves as he could to meet at his house on the next Sunday evening. On the evening appointed, thirteen fine able-bodied men assembled to see and hear an abolitionist. Never have I met more intelligent looking colored men than those that composed my little audience on that occasion: their ages ranged from eighteen to thirty. Some were very black, while others were mulattoes, and two of them had straight hair and were light-coloured.

ON GUARD.

My host volunteered to stand guard outside the house to prevent interruption and to intercept any unfriendly or evil-minded callers. I talked to my hearers earnestly and practically, explaining the condition and prospects of the colored people in Canada, and the obstacles and dangers they would have to encounter on the way to that land of refuge. No lecturer ever had a more intensely earnest audience than I had that evening. I gathered the brave fel-

lows around me so that I could look each in the
face and give emphasis to my instructions. In conclusion I told them that I should remain in Nashville until after the following Sunday evening, when
as many as felt disposed to make the attempt to
gain their freedom would find me at the same house
at 9 p.m. I requested those who decided to leave
on that night to inform their old friends before the
next Friday, that I might make some necessary
provision for their long and perilous journey.

Early in the week I received word from five, and
by Friday evening two more had decided to make
the attempt to obtain the precious boon of liberty.
At nine o'clock on the Sunday evening appointed I
was promptly at the house of my friend. He again
stood guard. It was nearly 10 o'clock when I heard
the signal agreed upon, " scratching upon the door,"
I unlocked the door, when in stepped four men, followed soon after by three others: they were all
married. I asked each if he had fully determined to
make the attempt, and receiving an affirmative reply I again carefully explained to them the routes
to be taken, the dangers they might expect to encounter, and the friends upon whom they could call
for aid.

SEVEN CANDIDATES FOR FREEDOM.

At midnight I bade them good-bye and these
brave-hearted fellows with tears in their eyes and

hearts swelling with hope, started for the land of freedom. I advised them to travel by night only, and to keep together if possible.

Next morning I called upon my Quaker friend, and informed her of the result of my labors in Nashville. She expressed her delight and satisfaction. But feared for my safety if I remained in the city after the escape of the slaves became known.

STARTLING NEWS.

As I was passing the post office a man handed me a small printed bill which announced the escape of thirteen slaves from Richmond, but nine only were described, together with the names of their owners. A reward of $1000 was offered for their capture and return to Richmond. I now thought it time to leave for other fields of labor.

Early next day I bade farewell to my kind Quaker friend and started for Memphis. On my arrival there I sought the house of an anti-slavery man to whom I had been directed. He was absent from home, but his good wife received me kindly and urged me to make her house my home during my stay in the city. I felt, however, that I had no right to expose the family to trouble and suspicion in case I got into difficulty. I consequently went to a hotel; being tired and weary laid down on a couch to rest, and must have fallen asleep, for I was aroused by the shouting of a newsboy under my window. The burthen of his cry was the escape of several slaves from Nashville in one night. I raised the window and told the boy to bring a paper to my room. It contained the following item of interest to me :—

"TWELVE HUNDRED DOLLARS REWARD.

"Great excitement in Nashville; escape of seven first-class slave men by the aid of an abolitionist, who has been seen in the city for several days. Three hundred dollars reward is offered for the capture and return of each of the slaves, and twelve hundred dollars for the apprehension of the 'accursed abolitionist.'" Then followed a description of the slaves, and a very good description of myself, considering that I kept very close during my stay in Nashville. At a glance I saw the danger of my position, and determined to leave the hotel at once. Returning to the house I had first visited, I made enquiries for the residence of a colored-man upon whom my colored friend in Nashville told me I could rely. Having received the proper direction, I went to his humble dwelling and was cordially welcomed on mentioning the name of his old friend at Nashville.

D

A NOBLE MAN.

He was a fine-looking man, with honest eyes, open countenance, and of more than ordinary intelligence for one of his race. I handed him the paper and pointed to the reward for my apprehension. When he read it, he grasped my hand, and said, " Massa, I'll die for you; what shall we do ? "

The paper which contained the exciting news also contained the announcement that a steamer would leave for St. Louis that night at nine o'clock. It was now three. Six long hours to remain in the very jaws of death !

I determined to leave, if possible, on that steamer, and asked permission to remain in his house until the arrival of the boat. The noble fellow placed his house and all he possessed at my command.

A POOR NEGRO SPURNS THE REWARD.

This poor despised negro held in his hand a paper offering a reward of $1,200 for my capture. He was a laboring man, earning his bread by the sweat of his brow, and yet I felt perfectly safe, and implicitly trusted this poor negro with my life. In fact, I felt safer in his house than I should have felt in the house of a certain vice-president of the United States, who in more recent times sold himself for a similar amount. This poor oppressed negro had everything to gain by surrendering me into the hands of the slave-masters, and yet he spurned the reward, and was faithful to the trust I reposed in him. On many occasions I have placed my life in the hands of colored men without the slightest hesitation or fear of betrayal.

A FEMALE FUGITIVE.

Night was approaching and my friend suggested the propriety of changing my dress. While engaged making these alterations, I overheard an animated conversation in an adjoining room between my host and a female. The woman earnestly begged him to ask me to take her to Canada where her husband then was. The poor man told her my life was already in great danger, and if she was seen with me it would render my escape more difficult, but still she continued to beg. When I had completed my change of appearance, he came into the room and told me that a slave woman who had lately fled from her master on account of his cruelty to her was in the house and wished to speak to me. She was a light mulatto of bright, intelligent appearance. She told me of the escape of her husband to Canada about two years previously and her master's cruelty in beating her because she refused. to marry a negro whom he had selected for her

She showed me her back which was still raw and
seamed with gashes where the lash of her cruel
master's whip had ploughed up her flesh. She
earnestly besought me to take her to Canada. I
determined to make the attempt, and told my
host to dress her in male attire, that she might
accompany me in the capacity of valet. The poor
woman was soon ready for the journey. I named
her "Sam," and myself Mr. Smith, of Kentucky.
At half past eight, p.m., we left the house of my
faithful friend for the boat, "Sam" walking behind
me and carrying my valise. Through some cause
or other, the boat was detained until near eleven
o'clock. Oh what hours of misery! Every minute
filled with apprehensions of disaster not only to
myself but to the poor fugitive depending on me.
No one not similarly placed can imagine the
anxiety and dread that filled my mind during this
long delay. The moments passed so slowly that
they seemed hours. "Sam" stood near me looking
as anxious as I felt. At length we got aboard the
boat. I secured tickets for myself and servant for
St. Louis, and when the boat left the levee I
breathed freer than I had done for several hours.
I reached St. Louis without the occurrence of any
incident of importance and sent a telegram to my
friend in Philadelphia to be on the lookout for
"hardware" from Tennessee. Resting in St. Louis
for a few hours I left for Chicago, accompanied

by my happy valet whose frequent question, "Massa, is we near Canada yet?" kept me continually on the alert to prevent our exposure.

ARRIVAL IN CHICAGO WITH A CHATTEL.

When we reached Chicago I took my servant to the house of an abolitionist, where she was properly cared for. It was deemed prudent that she should wear male attire until she reached Canada, for it occasionally happened that fugitives were caught in Detroit, and taken back to bondage after having come in sight of the land of promise. Their proximity to a safe refuge from their taskmasters, and from the operations of the infamous Fugitive Slave Law, rendered them careless in their manner, and so happy in appearance, that they were frequently arrested on suspicion by the minions of the United States Government, ever on the watch to obey the behests of the slave power. After a few hours' rest in Chicago, I left with my charge for Detroit, where I arrived in due time on the following day, and taking a hack, drove to a friend's house in the suburbs of the city. Here I made arrangements to be rowed across the river to Canada, as soon as darkness would render the passage safe. I also sent telegrams to friends in London, Chatham, and Amherstburg, to ascertain the whereabouts of her husband, and finally heard that he was living in London.

SAFE ON THE SOIL OF CANADA.

At night the poor fugitive and myself were taken silently across the river that separated the land of freedom from the land of slavery. Not a word was spoken until we reached the soil of Canada. I then told her that she was a free woman, that no one could now deprive her of her right to " life, liberty, and the pursuit of happiness." I conveyed her to the house of a friend, and on the following day she went to London, where she and her husband were re-united after a separation of two years. Returning to Detroit, I took the train for Cleveland. There I received a telegram from Boston stating that Capt. John Brown of Kansas would meet me in Cleveland in a day or two, and that he desired to confer with me on a subject connected with the anti-slavery cause.

INTERVIEW WITH JOHN BROWN.

On the evening of my third day in Cleveland, whilst seated in my room at the hotel, a gentle tap at my door aroused me. I said, "Come in." The door opened, and a plain, farmer-like man, with a countenance strongly indicative of intelligence, coolness, tenacity of purpose and honesty, entered the room. He appeared about five feet ten inches in height,

of slender but wiry and tough frame; his glance
was keen, steady and honest; his step lithe and
firm. He was, although simply and plainly dressed,
a man of remarkable appearance. He introduced
himself as "John Brown, of Kansas," and handed
me letters from friends in Boston. Captain Brown
remained with me nearly all night, eagerly listening to a narrative of my trip through Virginia and
Tennessee, and in relating incidents connected with
his labors in Kansas. His manner and conversation
had a magnetic influence, which rendered him very
attractive and stamped him as a man of more than
ordinary coolness, tenacity of purpose, and devotion
to what he considered right. No idle, profane, or
immodest word fell from his lips. During our interview he related many incidents of his life bearing upon the subject of slavery. He said he had
for many years been studying the guerilla system
of warfare adopted in the mountainous portions
of Europe, and by that system he could, with a
small body of picked men, inaugurate and maintain
a guerilla war in the mountains of the slave states
which would cause so much annoyance to the
United States Government, and create such a feeling of dread and insecurity in the minds of slaveholders, that they would ultimately be glad to "let
the oppressed go free." He maintained that the
only way to successfully attack the institution of
slavery was, by conveying to the slaves such in-

formation as would aid them in making their escape to Canada, and by exciting in their minds a
desire for knowledge, which would enable them to
combine in a struggle for freedom. He had little
faith in the efficacy of moral suasion with slaveholders. He very properly placed them in the same
catogory with thieves and murderers.

DISAPPOINTMENT.

John Brown was now returning to the west, from
the eastern states, where he had been for several
weeks trying to collect means to carry on the
struggle for freedom in Kansas. He had met with
disappointment, and felt it most keenly. He had
sacrificed his own peace and comfort, and the peace
and comfort of his family, in obedience to his sincere
convictions of duty toward the oppressed people of
the south, while those who had the means to help
him make war upon the oppressors, were lukewarm
or declined to aid him in his warfare. During our
conversation he handed me a piece of paper, on
which he had written the following, which he said
he indited with the object of having it published
before leaving Boston, but had been persuaded not
to do it :—

"OLD BROWN'S FAREWELL."

"To the Plymouth Rocks, Bunker Hill 'Monuments, Charter Oaks and Uncle Tom's Cabin.

"He has left for Kansas. Has been trying since he came out of the Territory to secure an outfit, or, in other words, the means of arming and thoroughly equipping his regular minute men, who are mixed up with the people of Kansas, and he leaves the States with a feeling of deepest sadness, that after exhausting his own small means, and, with his family and his brave men, suffered hunger, cold, nakedness, and some of them sickness, wounds, imprisonment in irons with extreme cruel treatment, and others death; that after lying on the ground for months, in the most sickly, unwholesome and uncomfortable places, some of the time sick and wounded, destitute of any shelter, and hunted like wolves, sustained in part by Indians, that after all this, in order to sustain a cause which every man in this ' glorious republic ' (?) is under equal moral obligations to do, and for the neglect of which he will be held accountable to God ; a cause in which every man woman and child of the entire human family has a deep, awful interest ; that when no wages are asked or expected, he cannot secure amidst all the wealth, luxury and extravagance of this ' Heaven exalted people,' even the necessary supplies of the common soldier. ' How are the mighty fallen !' "

To George L. Stearns of Boston, and his noble wife, are due the honor and glory of having supplied the financial wants of John Brown, which enabled him to make his heroic onslaught, that kindled the flame which devoured the institution of slavery and gave freedom to millions of slaves.

CHARACTER OF JOHN BROWN.

I have been in the presence of many men called great and distinguished, but never have I met a more remarkable man than Captain John Brown. There was manifest in all he said and did an absorbing intensity of purpose controlled by lofty moral principles. He was not a religionist, but he was a Christian.

JOHN BROWN'S ANCESTRY.

The following items I gathered during our interesting interview. John Brown was born in Torrington, Conn., on the 9th of May, 1800. He was by occupation a farmer, and the fifth by descent from Peter Brown, one of the brave exiles, who, on the 22nd of December, 1660, knelt at Plymouth Rock and expressed gratitude and joy for their preservation from the dangers of the deep, during their passage from England in the Mayflower.

It was in 1839 that John Brown first-conceived the idea of becoming a liberator of the southern slaves; he had seen every right of the colored people in the south ruthlessly trodden under the feet of the tyrannical Slave Power. He saw slavery blighting and blasting the manhood of the nation, and he listened to the voice of the poor that cried. He heard Washington loudly praised, but he saw no

helper of the bondman. He saw the people building the sepulchres of the fathers of '76, but lynch-
ing and murdering the prophets that were sent unto them. He believed that "Who would be free
themselves must strike the blow." But the slaves
were scattered, closely watched, and prevented from
assembling to conspire, without arms, apparently
overpowered, at the mercy of every traitor, knowing
the white man only as their foe. Seeing everywhere
and always that the negroes, in order to arise and
strike a blow for liberty, needed a positive sign
that they had friends among the dominant race,
who sympathized with them, believed in their right
to freedom, and were ready to aid them in their attempt to obtain it, John Brown determined to let
them know that they had friends, and prepared
himself to lead them to liberty.

NEWS FROM THE SOUTH.

The excitement in Richmond and Nashville consequent upon the escape of so many valuable slaves
extended to all the surrounding country. In the
reading-room of the hotel at Cleveland, Ohio, I
picked up a Richmond paper, which contained a lengthy account of the escape of slaves from Richmond,
Nashville, and other parts of the south. The writer
stated that a general impression prevailed in that
community that a regularly organized band of abo-

litionists existed in the south, which supplied the negroes with information and means of escape to Canada. The authorities were urged to offer a large reward for the apprehension of the " cursed negro thieves " that infested the south, and that an example be made of those who were caught, that would forever deter others from interference with their constitutional rights.

KEEPING QUIET.

I concluded it was better for the cause I was trying to serve that no further attempt should be made until the present excitement in the south quieted down. So I went to Philadelphia. .

During my stay in that city, I was busily occupied in collecting statistics of the slave populations of particular locations in the Cotton States, and in consulting with friends and acquaintances as to the best methods of circulating information among the slaves in that region.

Any one acquainted with the institution of slavery as it existed in the Gulf States, will fully appreciate the difficulties that environed such a crusade as I now contemplated—that of conveying directly to the slaves a knowledge of the best routes, the distances to be traversed, difficulties to be overcome, and the fact that they had friends in the border states to whom they could apply for aid, and on

whom they could implicity rely for aid to forward
them to Canada. Of all the dangers to myself that
loomed up before my mind, the last and least was
the fear of betrayal by the slaves.

Once they became assured of your friendship and
your desire to help them to escape from bondage,
they would willingly suffer torture or death to save
you. Such at least has been my experience with
the negroes of the Slave States.

OFF TO NEW ORLEANS.

My preparations being now completed, I engaged
passage by steamer to New Orleans, on a mission
the subject and details of which had occupied my
mind exclusively for many weeks. I was accompanied to the steamer by two steadfast friends of
freedom. One of these friends, Gerrit Smith, had
been my principal supporter and active and unflinch-
ing friend from the commencement of my career
as an abolitionist. In many parts of Ohio, Michigan, Indiana and Pennsylvania, we had fast friends,
in the majority of cases, belonging to the Society of
Friends, whose doors were always open to the poor
fugitive from bondage, and whose hearts were open
to the fugitive's appeal for help.

SLAVE AUCTIONS.

During my stay in New Orleans I occasionally
attended the slave auctions. The scenes I witnessed

there will never be effaced from my memory. The
cries and heart-rending agonies of the poor creatures
as they were sold, and separated from parents, husbands, children or wives, will never cease to ring in
my ears. Babes were torn from the arms of their
mothers and sold, while parents were separated and
sent to distant parts of the country. Tired and
overworked women were cruelly beaten because
they refused the outrageous demands of their wicked
overseers. The brutal and obscene examinations of
female slaves by lecherous and base men, while the
poor victims dare not raise a hand to resist, was
not the worst that transpired in the slave pens.
The horrid traffic in human beings, many of them
much whiter and more intelligent than the cruel
men who bought and sold them, was, without exception, the most monstrous outrage on the rights
of human beings that could possibly be imagined.

> A Christian : going, gone :
> Who bids for God's own image ?—for His grace
> Which that poor victim of the market place
> Hath in her suffering won ?
>
> My God ! can such things be ?
> Hast Thou not said whatso'er is done
> Unto Thy weakest and Thy humblest one,
> Is even done to Thee ?
>
> In that sad victim, then,
> Child of Thy pitying love, I see Thee stand—
> Once more the jest-word of a mocking band,
> Bound, sold, and scourged again.

A Christian up for sale !
Wet with her blood your whips—o'ertask her frame,
Make her life loathsome with your wrong and shame,
Her patience shall not fail !

God of all right ! how long
Shall priestly robbers at Thy altar stand,
Lifting in prayer to Thee, the bloody hand
And haughty brow of wrong?

Oh, from the fields of cane,
From the low rice-swamp, from the trader's cell—
From the black slave-ship's foul and loathsome hell,
And coffle's weary chain,—

Hoarse, horrible, and strong,
Rises to Heaven that agonizing cry,
Filling the arches of the hollow sky,
How LONG, O GOD, HOW LONG ?

WHITTIER, *the Quaker Poet.*

AT WORK IN THE GULF STATES.

Finally my preparations were completed, and I began my journey into the dark land. The route decided upon was from New Orleans to Vicksburg, and thence through the interior of Mississippi, Alabama, Georgia, South Carolina, North Carolina and Florida. I had never before visited that portion of the United States, and my field of labor was consequently surrounded by difficulties not experienced during my visit to Virginia and Tennesee, from the fact that I had not a single friend in the Cotton States on whom I could rely.

AT WORK NEAR VICKSBURG.

From Vicksburg I made frequent visits to the surrounding plantations, seizing every favorable opportunity to converse with the more intelligent of the slaves. Many of these negroes had heard of Canada from the negroes brought from Virginia and the border Slave States, but the impression they had was that Canada was so far away it would be useless to try and reach it. On these excursions I was usually accompanied by one or two smart, intelligent slaves, to whom I felt I could entrust the secret of my visit. In this way I succeeded in circulating a knowledge of Canada, and the best means of reaching that country, to all the plantations for many miles around Vicksburg. I was often surprised at the rapidity with which information was conveyed to the slaves of distant plantations. Thus on every plantation I had missionaries who were secretly conveying intelligence to the poor down-trodden slaves of that benighted region, that in Canada there were hundreds of negroes who had through the aid of friends along the border escaped from slavery, and were now free men and women. No one but a slave can fully appreciate the true meaning of the word " freedom." I continued my labors in the vicinity of Vicksburg for several weeks and then went to Selma, Alabama.

SOWING SEED AT SELMA.

I made this place my base for extensive incursions to the surrounding country. There was not a plantation within fifteen miles of Selma that I did not visit successfully.

IN A DANGEROUS POSITION.

Having completed my labors at Selma, I selected a small town in Mississippi, for my next field of labor. I had been at work about two weeks, when a difficulty occurred which, but for the faithfulness of a negro, would have ended in my death, at the hands of an infuriated mob. During one of my visits to a plantation I met a negro slave of more than ordinary intelligence. His master was a man of coarse and brutal instincts, who had burned the initials of his name into the flesh of several of his slaves, to render their capture more certain in case they attempted to run away from this merciless wretch. I saw several of the victims of his cruelty, whose backs would forever bear the marks of his branding iron and lash. He was a veritable " Legree."

On one of my excursions over his plantation, I was accompanied by the slave mentioned. During our rambles he gave me a history of his life and sufferings, and expressed an earnest desire to gain his

E

freedom. I felt that he could be relied upon, and imparted to him the secret object of my visit to the South. He listened with absorbing interest, whilst I explained to him the difficulties and dangers he would have to encounter on so long and perilous a journey. He, however, declared his determination to make the attempt, saying that death itself was preferable to his present existence. On the following day (Saturday) I again visited the plantation, and selected this slave for my companion. He informed me he had decided to start for Canada as soon as he could communicate with a brother who was a slave on a plantation a few miles distant. He wished to take his brother with him, if possible. I gave him instructions for his guidance after he should cross the Ohio, and the names of friends at Evansville, Ind., and Cleveland, Ohio, to whom he could apply for assistance. I directed him to travel by night only until he reached friends north of the Ohio river.

INTO THE JAWS OF DEATH.

On the following Monday evening, whilst seated at the supper table of the hotel at which I was stopping, I heard loud and excited talking in the adjoining room. In a few minutes the landlord came to me and said, " Col. —— wishes to speak with you. You had better go and meet him." I immediately

rose and went into the room from which the loud
talking emanated. As I entered, the Colonel, in a
loud and brutal tone, said, "That's him, arrest him."
Upon which a man stepped up and said, "You are
my prisoner." I demanded the reason why I was
arrested, whereupon the doughty Colonel strode toward me, with his fist clenched, and charged me
with being a d——d abolitionist. He said he would
have my heart's blood ; that I had enticed away his
nigger "Joe," for the nigger had not been seen since
he went out with me on the previous Saturday. The
room was filled with an excited crowd of men, who
glared upon me with fierce and fiendish looks. I
tried to keep cool, but I confess I felt that my
labors were ended. I knew the character of the
Colonel, and also knew that he possessed much influence with the worst class of Southerners of that
section.

MANACLED AND IN PRISON.

In the meantime the constable had produced a
pair of iron handcuffs, and fastened them around
my wrists. After the Colonel had exhausted his
supply of curses and coarse abuse upon me—for
the purpose of inciting the crowd to hang me—I
quietly asked if they would allow me to say a few
words, at the same time making a Masonic sign of
distress in hope that there might be a Mason in the
crowd with sufficient courage to sustain my request.

I had no sooner made "the sign of distress" than a voice near me said, "Yes, let's hear what he has. got to say. He ought to be allowed to speak." I was encouraged, and very quietly said, "Gentlemen, I am a stranger here, without friends. I am your prisoner in irons. The Colonel has charged me with violating your laws, will you act the part of cowards by allowing this man to incite you to commit a murder? Or will you, like brave men grant the only request I have to make, that is, a fair trial before your magistrates?" Several persons at once spoke up in my favor.

A DESPERATE SITUATION.

A crowd of people had gathered to see an abolitionist have the mockery of a trial. "Col. Legree" was asked by the Justice to state his case, which he did in true slave-driving style, as if determined to force his case against me. My case seemed hopeless. I saw no way of escape from my desperate situation. I was surrounded on every side by men thirsting for my blood, and anxious to vindicate the outraged laws of the State of Mississippi. At length the Colonel finished his statement, which, reduced to simple facts, was that I had called at his residence on Saturday last, and requested permission to roam over his plantation, that he had given me permission, and allowed his servant "Joe" to accompany me, that "Joe" had not returned nor could he be found, that he was sure I had aided him to escape, and demanded of the Justice that I should be punished as a " negro thief " deserved. His remarks were loudly applauded by the slave-hounds that surrounded him. The Justice turned to me, and in a loud voice said, "; Have you anything to say ?" At this moment a voice outside the room shouted, " Here's Joe, here's Joe," and a rush was made toward the door.

FIDELITY OF A SLAVE.

" Joe " was ushered into the court-room and fell on his knees before the Colonel asking his forgiveness for leaving the plantation without permission. He said he wanted to see his brother "powerful bad," and had gone to the plantation on which his brother was living, about eight miles distant, on Saturday night, expecting to return by Sunday evening, but having sprained his ankle he could not move until Monday evening, when he started for home, travelling nearly all night. As soon as he reached the Colonel's he was told of my arrest, and early that morning he had come into town to save me. The Justice ordered the constable to release me and expressed his regret that I had been subjected to so much annoyance.

RELEASED.

The Colonel was completely chopfallen at the turn affairs had taken. I was surrounded by sev-

eral good Masonic friends, who expressed their gratification at my release. I addressed the Colonel,
saying, that as he had put me to much inconvenience
and trouble, I claimed a favor of him. He asked
what it was. I begged him not to punish "Joe"
for what he had done, and to allow me to present
the brave fellow with a gift as a mark of gratitude
for his fidelity to me. As these favors were asked
in the presence of the crowd, he could not very well
refuse my request. He sulkily promised that "Joe"
should not be punished, and said if I pleased I might
make him a present. I then handed "Joe" some
money, for which he looked a thousand thanks. I
was thus able to evince my gratitude for what he
had done for me, and at the same time present him
with the means to aid him in escaping from bondage.

Two years after this occurrence, while dining at
the American Hotel in Boston, I observed a colored
waiter eyeing me very closely ; at length he recognized me and asked if I remembered him. It was
"Joe," my saviour, the former slave of "Colonel Legree." I grasped the noble fellow's hand, and con-
gratulated him upon his escape from bondage. In
the evening I invited him into the parlour and introduced him to several anti-slavery friends, to whom
I narrated the incidents above related. "Joe" subsequently gave me the following particulars of his
escape from slavery :

On the Sunday evening following my arrest and

acquittal, his brother joined him in a piece of woods near the Colonel's plantation, where he had secreted sufficient food to last them several days.

TWO PASSENGERS BY THE UNDERGROUND RAILWAY.

At midnight they started together, moving as rapidly as they could through the fields and woods, keeping the north star in front of them. Whenever it was possible, they walked in the creeks and marshy grounds, to throw the slave-hunters off their tracks. Thus night after night they kept on their way weary, hungry, and sore-footed. On the morning of the seventeenth day of their freedom, they reached the Ohio river, nearly opposite a large town; all day they lay secreted in the bushes, at night they crossed the river in a small boat and travelled rapidly, taking a north-easterly course. After enduring many hardships they reached Cleveland, Ohio, and went to the house of a friend whose name I had given "Joe." They were kindly received and supplied with clothing and other comforts. Resting a week, they were sent to Canada, where "Joe's" brother still lives (1890).

LEAVE FOR OTHER FIELDS.

On the day following my release from peril I was conveyed to Iuka, a station on the Charleston and Memphis railroad. There I purchased a through

ticket for New York, which I took pains to exhibit
to the landlord of the hotel, so that in case I was
pursued (as I certainly would be, if "Joe" and his
brother succeeded in escaping), he would state the
fact that I had bought tickets for New York, which
would probably check their pursuit. From Iuka
I went to Huntsville, Alabama, where for a short
time I was busy circulating information among the
slaves.

AT WORK IN AUGUSTA, GEORGIA.

Learning that Augusta was favorably situated
for my work, and that the slaves in that section were sharp and intelligent, I determined to
make that city my next field of labor. Having
secured a home with a Quaker family, I was soon
actively engaged in becoming acquainted with the
more intelligent colored people of that section.

FIDELITY OF THE QUAKERS.

Among the religious denominations of the south,
none were more faithful to the principles of freedom,
or to the dictates of humanity in respect to slavery,
than the friends called "Quakers." Wherever I
have met the members of that society, whether in
the north or south, they have always proved themselves friends in deed as well as in name. They
could always be implicitly trusted by the poor fugitives from bondage. I know of many instances

where at great sacrifice and risk they have shielded the outcasts from their pursuers—the slave-hunters and United States marshals.   Hundreds of the negroes of Canada will bear testimony to the unfailing fidelity of the peaceful and worthy Quakers.

ELEVEN FOLLOWERS OF THE NORTH STAR.

In Augusta I succeeded in equipping a party of eleven fine, active, intelligent slaves for the long, dangerous and weary journey to the north.   No one, unless engaged in similar work, can appreciate the extreme delicacy of my position.   There was not a day, in fact scarcely an hour, that I did not live in expectation of exposure and death.   The system of keen and constant espionage in practice throughout the slave states, rendered it exceedingly necessary to exercise the greatest prudence in approaching the slaves.   If a stranger was seen in conversation with a slave he became at once an object of suspicion. I found by experience that a frank, bold, and straightforward course was the safest and best.   I was greatly aided in my work here by a remarkably intelligent mulatto, the son of a U.S. Senator by a female slave.   This man was chosen leader of the band of fugitives from Augusta, and under his leadership the whole party arrived safely in Canada in less than two months from the time they escaped from bondage.   Two members of the party are now living in Canada, and in good circumstances.   Im-

mediately after the exodus of these brave fellows, I
quietly left the scene of my labors and went to
Charleston, S.C.

EXCITING NEWS.

A few days after my arrival, one of the Charleston papers contained a despatch from Augusta,
which stated that several first-class negro men had
disappeared from that place within a week, and that
a very general impression prevailed that abolitionists were at work exciting negroes to escape from
their masters. I left Charleston that evening and
went to Raleigh, N.C. While at breakfast next
morning two gentlemen seated near me entered into
conversation relative to the escape of slaves from
Augusta. One of them remarked that an English-
man who had been stopping in Augusta for several weeks was suspected of doing the mischief, and
that it was supposed he had gone with the fugitives,
as he had not been seen since the slaves were miss-
ed ; but if he should be caught, no mercy would be
shown him, as it was time to make an example of
the nigger-thieves that infested the south. I lost
no time, obviously, and left by the first train for
Washington.

IN WASHINGTON.

During my stay in Washington I was the guest
of Charles Sumner, at whose house I met many dis-

tinguished people, who evinced a warm and appreciative interest in my labors. The slave-holders at
that period held the balance of power in the United
States, and the northern Democrats were used by
them to tighten the bonds that bound the colored
people of the south in the chains of slavery. The
slave-masters were not satisfied with the recognized
boundaries of their institution, and sought by every
device to obtain some portion of the new territories
of the south-west to which they could carry their
vile institution. Northern men of the Douglas and
Seymour stamp were willing to yield to the slave
lords, and even sacrifice the dearest interests of their
country, providing they could advance their individual claims to the presidency. The haughty and
outrageous demands of Davis, Mason and Toombs
were abetted by the cowardly Democratic politicians of the north. Towering above these contemptible political demagogues stood Charles Sumner, the
brave champion of freedom. No prospect of political advancement could tempt him from the path of
duty, nor could the brutal threats and assaults of
his cowardly opponents, cause him to halt in his
warfare for the rights of man.

On my arrival in Philadelphia I laid before my
anti-slavery friends a report of my work. One
venerable and talented Quaker lady, at whose house
our reunion took place, and whose name has long
been identified with the cause of human freedom,

tendered me the congratulations of the society on my safe return from the land of darkness and despair.

FUGITIVES FROM HUNTSVILLE, ALABAMA.

While in Philadelphia a telegram was received from a friend in Evansville, Ind., informing me that two fugitives had arrived there in a most pitiable condition, their emaciated bodies bearing the marks of many a bruise. I at once went to Evansville to render them such aid as I could. They were delighted to meet me again, and recalled an interview they had with me at Huntsville, Alabama. The poor fellows were kindly cared for, and after a few days' rest, continued their journey to Canada, prepared to defend their right to own themselves against whoever might dispute it. The route travelled by these fugitives from Huntsville to the Ohio river was marked with their blood. Their escape was soon discovered and persistent efforts were made to capture them. They were followed for two days by bloodhounds that were placed on their tracks, but which they succeeded in eluding by wading in the creeks and marshes; for forty-eight hours the deep baying of the hounds was frequently heard. They travelled by night only, taking the north star for their guide, and by day rested in secluded places. Their sufferings from hunger were very severe, which they were often obliged to relieve by eating frogs and other reptiles. Occasionally, however, they succeeded in confiscating poultry from the hen-houses of the slaveholders on their route.

" In dark fens of the Dismal Swamp,
  The hunted negro lay ;
He saw the fire of the midnight camp,
And heard at times a horse's tramp,
  And a bloodhound's distant bay.

Where will-o'-the wisps and glow-worms shine
  In bulrush and in brake ;
Where waving mosses shroud the pine,
And the cedar grows, and the poisonous vine
  Is spotted like the snake ;

Where hardly a human foot could pass,
  Or a human heart would dare,
On the quaking turf of the green morass,
He crouched in the rank and tangled grass,
  Like a wild beast in its lair.

All things above were bright and fair,
  All things were glad and free ;
Lithe squirrels darted here and there,
And wild birds filled the echoing air
  With songs of liberty.

On him alone was the doom of pain,
  From the morning of his birth ;
On him alone the crime of Cain
Fell, like a flail on the garnered grain,
  And struck him to the earth."

                              LONGFELLOW.

My experience in the Cotton States served to intensify my abhorrence and hatred of slavery, and to

nerve me for the work I was engaged in. On several
occasions while in the slave states I attended church
service, and invariably observed that whenever the
subject of slavery was mentioned it was referred to
as a wise, beneficent institution, and one minister
declared that " the institution of slavery was devised
by God, for the especial benefit of the colored race."

" Just God !—and these are they
Who minister at Thine altar, God of Right !
Men who their hands, with prayer and blessing, lay
　　On Israel's Ark of light !

What ! preach and kidnap men ?
Give thanks—and rob Thy own afflicted poor ?
Talk of Thy glorious liberty, and then
　　Bolt hard the captive's door ?

What ! servants of Thy own
Merciful Son, who came to seek and save
The homeless and the outcast,—fettering down
　　The tasked and plundered slave !

Pilate and Herod, friends !
Chief priests and rulers, as of old, combine !
Just God and holy ! is that church, which lends
　　Strength to the spoiler, Thine ?

Paid hypocrites, who turn
Judgment aside, and rob the Holy Book
Of those high words of truth which search and burn
　　In warning and rebuke :

Feed fat, ye locusts, feed !
And in your tasselled pulpits, thank the Lord
That, from the toiling bondman's utter need,
　　Ye pile your own full board.

How long, O Lord ! how long
Shall such a priesthood barter truth away,
And, in Thy name, for robbery and wrong
    At Thy own altars pray ?

Woe to the priesthood ! woe
To those whose hire is with the price of blood—
Perverting, darkening, changing as they go,
    The searching truths of God !

Their glory and their might
Shall perish ; and their names shall be
Vile before all the people, in the light
    Of a world's liberty.

Oh ! speed the moment on
When Wrong shall cease—and Liberty, and Love,
And Truth, and Right, throughout the earth be known
    As in their home above."

             WHITTIER, *the Quaker Poet.*

CHAPTER IV.

1859-1861.

LEAVE FOR BOSTON.

FROM Evansville I returned to Philadelphia, and
after a short stay in that city left for Boston, via
Springfield.

MEET WITH AN OLD FRIEND.

At Springfield, Mass., the train stopped a few
minutes for refreshments. As I took my seat at
the table, I observed an elderly gentleman looking
very earnestly at me. At length he recognized me,
and taking a seat near me said in a whisper,
"How is the hardware business?" The moment

80

he spoke I recognized Capt. John Brown, of Kansas. He was much changed in appearance, looked older and more careworn, but there was no change in his voice or eye, both were indicative of strength, honesty and tenacity of purpose. Learning that I was on my way to Boston, whither he was going on the following day, he urged me to remain in Springfield over night and accompany him to Boston. In the evening we retired to a private parlor, and he asked me to tell him about my trip through Mississippi and Alabama. He listened intently to the recital of my narrative, from the time I left New Orleans until my arrest in Mississippi, with great earnestness and without speaking, until I described my arrest and imprisonment; then his countenance changed, his eyes flashed, he paced the room in silent wrath. I never witnessed a more intense manifestation of indignation and scorn. Coming up to me, he took my wrists in his hands and said, "God alone brought you out of that hell; and these wrists have been ironed and you have been imprisoned for doing your duty. I vow that I will not rest from my labor until I have discharged my whole duty towards God and towards my brother in bondage." When he ceased speaking, he sat down and buried his face in his hands, in which position he sat for some minutes as if overcome by his feelings. At length, arousing himself, he asked me to continue my narrative, to which he listened patiently during its recital.

F

He said, "You have been permitted to do a work that falls to the lot of few." Taking a small Bible or Testament from his pocket, he said, "The good book says, 'Whatsoever ye would that men should do to you, do ye even so to them;' it teaches us, further, to remember them in bonds as bound with them." He continued, "I have devoted the last twenty years of my life to preparation for the work which I believe God has given me to do, and while I live, I will not cease my labors." He then gave me some details of a campaign which he was then actually preparing for, and which he said had occupied his mind for many years. He intended to establish himself in the mountains of Virginia with a small body of picked men. He felt confident that the negroes would flock to him in large numbers, and that the slave-holders would soon be glad to let the oppressed go free; that the dread of a negro insurrection would produce fear and trembling in all the slave states; that the presence in the mountains of an armed body of liberators would cause a general insurrection among the slaves, which would end in their freedom. He said he had about twenty-two Kansas men undergoing a course of military instruction; these men would form a nucleus, around which he would soon gather a force sufficiently large and effective to strike terror through the slave states. His present difficulty was a deficiency of ready money. He had been

promised support to help the cause of freedom—
which was not forthcoming now that he was preparing to carry the war into the South. Some of
his friends were disinclined to aid offensive operations. During this interview he informed me that
he intended to call a convention at Chatham, Canada, for the purpose of effecting an organization
composed of men who were willing to aid . him in
his purpose of invading the slave states. He said
he had rifles and ammunition sufficient to equip
two hundred men ; that he had made a contract for
a large number of pikes, with which he intended to
arm the negroes ; that the object of his present trip
to the East was to raise funds to keep this contract,
and perfect his arrangements for an attack upon the
slave states. He accompanied me on the following
day to Boston. During our journey, he informed
me that he required a thousand dollars at least to
complete his preparations, and that he needed
money at once to enable him to fulfil a contract for
arms with a manufacturer in Connecticut. He also
needed money to bring his men from Iowa to
Canada. He met with but little success in Boston.
It appeared that such friends of the cause of freedom as had an inkling of his project, were not disposed to advance money for warlike purposes, except for the defence of free territory. Many of his
sincere friends feared that the persecution of himself and family by the pro-slavery border ruffians

would provoke him to engage in some enterprise
which might result in the destruction of himself
and his followers. I am persuaded that there was
no reason for any such apprehension. I never
heard him express any feeling of personal resent-
ment towards any one, not even border ruffians.
He appeared to me to be under the influence of
broad, enlightened, and humane views, and a fixed
determination to do his duty towards the oppressed.

Next morning Capt. Brown departed from Boston. I accompanied him to the depôt, and bade
him farewell.

CAPTAIN BROWN CALLS A CONVENTION.

The following invitation from Capt. Brown to attend a convention "of true friends of freedom," to
be held in Chatham, Canada, I did not receive until
the 13th of May—three days after the time appointed for holding the convention:

CHATHAM, CANADA,
May 5th, 1858.

MY DEAR FRIEND:

I have called a quiet convention in this town of the true
friends of freedom. Your attendance is earnestly requested
on the 10th inst.

Your friend,

John Brown

REFUGEES IN CANADA.

During the following summer I visited Canada, and had great pleasure in meeting many of those who had, under my auspices, escaped from the land of bondage. In Hamilton I was welcomed by a man who had escaped from Augusta. The meeting with so many of my former pupils, and the knowledge that they were happy, thriving, and industrious, gave me great satisfaction. The trials and dangers I had endured in their behalf were rendered pleasing reminiscences.

The information obtained from these refugees relative to the experiences while *en route* to Canada enabled me subsequently to render valuable aid to other fugitives from the land of bondage.

AT WORK IN DELAWARE.

On one occasion I visited Wilmington, Delaware, for the purpose of liberating the young wife of a refugee, who the year previous had made his escape to Canada, from the little town of Dover. I learned that the object of my visit was owned by a widow lady, who had but recently purchased the slave, paying the sum of twelve hundred dollars for her. I also learned that the widow was disposed to sell the girl, in fact that it was her intention to take her to New Orleans in the fall, for the purpose of offering her for sale in the market, where prices ranged in proportion to the beauty and personal charms possessed by these victims of man's inhumanity.

After a few hours' consideration I decided upon a plan which ultimately interfered with the widow's project. In the morning I called at the house of the widow, ostensibly to purchase her slave woman. The bell was answered by an octoroon woman, whom from the description I had received of her, I knew to be the object of my visit. I enquired whether her mistress was at home. She replied that her mistress had gone to market, and would not be home for an hour or two ; further, that she was the only person in the house. I asked her name, and other questions, which proved that she was Martha Bennett, the wife of the Canadian refugee. I then told her my object in calling, that I had recently seen her husband, and that if she desired to go to him, I would endeavor to take her to Canada. I gave her a few lines written by her husband, begging her to come to him. She read the paper with deep feeling, trembling from head to foot, the tears falling fast upon the paper. She said, " Massa, I will do just what you tell me. I wish I could get to Canada. Missis is going to take me to New Orleans this fall, and then I shall never see my husband again." I told her to leave the house at midnight, or as soon after as possible, prepared to accompany me ; that I would have a conveyance ready not far from the house to carry her out of the state to a place of safety; that she must attend to her duties during the day as usual, and not excite, by any unusual appearance or conduct, the suspicions of her mistress. I then left, and made preparations to convey her to the house of Hannah Cox, near Kennett Square, Pennsylvania.

DEPOT OF THE UNDERGROUND RAILWAY.

The house of this noble woman had for years been one of the depôts of the "underground railroad" (the rendezvous of fugitive slaves from Maryland and Delaware), where many poor fugitives have come with bleeding feet and tattered garments, relying upon the humanity of this noble woman, who shielded the outcasts from their pursuers. Hannah Cox was a worthy member of the Society of Friends. She possessed great sweetness of disposition, combined with energy, courage and tried sympathies, a highly cultivated mind and the ease and grace of a queen. Mrs. Cox, like all other outspoken abolitionists, was at that period outlawed from public respect, scorned and hated by the Church and State, and despised by the rich. There never lived a purer or more noble woman than Hannah Cox. She outlived the institution of slavery, and received the homage and respect of those who in other days persecuted and despised her.

Returning to the house of my friend, I obtained a horse and small waggon, and at twelve o'clock that night drove down the street on which the house of the widow was situated. At last I caught sight of the object of my search. Taking her into the carriage, I drove rapidly away on the road to Kennet Square, Penn. I kept the horse at a rapid gait, until I got out of sight of Wilmington. About four o'clock in the morning I heard the sound of a carriage rapidly following me. Upon reaching the top of a small hill I looked back and saw a horse coming at full gallop—behind him a buggy with two men in it. I directed the girl to crouch down in the bottom of the vehicle, I then put my horse to its utmost speed, hoping to cross the Pennsylvania line before my pursuers came up to me. The stifled cries of the poor slave at my feet made me resolve to defend her to the last extremity. I had two good navy revolvers with me, and got them ready for action. Looking back, I saw that my pursuers were gaining upon me. They were not more than two hundred yards distant, and I could hear shouts for me to stop; in another moment I heard the report of a pistol and the whizzing sound of a bullet. I then drew my revolver and fired four times in rapid succession at the horse of my pursuers. I saw the animal stagger and fall to the ground. One of my pursuers then fired several times at me without effect. I was soon out of danger from them, and safe with my charge at the house of good Hannah Cox.

I went on to Philadelphia, where I remained until the excitement had quieted down. I then returned and conveyed the poor fugitive to Clifton, Canada; from thence she went to Chatham, where she found her husband.

JOHN BROWN READY TO MOVE.

On the 9th of October, 1859, I was somewhat surprised to receive the following brief letter from Captain Brown, announcing his intention to make an attack on the Slave States in the course of a few weeks:

CHAMBERSBURG, PENN.,
October 6th, 1859.

DEAR FRIEND,— * * * I shall move about the last of this month. Can you help the cause in the way promised? Address your reply to Isaac Smith, Chambersburg, Penn.

Your friend,
JOHN BROWN.

IN RICHMOND.

I had promised Captain Brown, during our interview at Springfield, Mass., that when he was ready to make his attack on the Slave States, I would, if possible, go to Richmond, and await the result. In case he should be successful in his attack; I would be in a position to watch the course of events, and enlighten the slaves as to his purposes. It might also be possible for me to aid the cause in other respects. Accordingly, I was in Richmond on the 15th (the day before the raid), prepared to remain there and await the course of events.

CAPTAIN BROWN ATTACKS HARPER'S FERRY.

On the morning of Monday, the 17th of October, wild rumours were in circulation about the streets of Richmond, that Harper's Ferry had been captured by a band of robbers; and again that an army of abolitionists under the command of a desperado by the name of Smith, was murdering the inhabitants of that village and carrying off the negroes. Throughout the day groups of excited men gathered about the newspaper offices to hear the news from Harper's Ferry.

OFFICIAL REPORTS.

On the following morning (Tuesday) an official report was received which stated that a large force of abolitionists under Old Osawatomie Brown had taken possession of the U. S. armory at the ferry, and had entrenched themselves. An aged negro whom I met in the street seemed completely bewildered with the excitement, and military preparations going on around him. As I approached him he raised his hat and said, " Please massa, what's

the matter ? what's the soldiers out for ?" I told their
a band of abolitionists had seized Harper's Ferri-
and liberated many of the slaves of that section ;
and that they intended to free all the slaves in the
South if they could. " Can da do it, massa ?" he
asked, while his countenance brightened up. I replied, perhaps so, and asked him if he would like to
be free ? He said, " O yes, massa ; I'se prayed for
dat dese forty years. My two boys are away off in
Canada. Do you know where dat is, massa ?"

BLOW FELT THROUGH THE SLAVE STATES.

That John Brown had struck a blow that was
felt throughout the Slave States, was evident from
the number of telegraph despatches from the South,
offering aid to crush the invasion.

DEFEAT OF CAPTAIN BROWN.

The people of Richmond were frantic with rage
at this daring interference with their cherished institution, which gave them the right to buy, beat,
work and sell their fellow men. Crowds of rough
excited men filled with whiskey and wickedness
stood for hours together in front of the offices of
the *Dispatch* and *Enquirer*, listening to the reports,
as they were announced from within. When the
news of Brown's defeat and capture, and the destruction of his little band, was read from the win-

poses. the *Dispatch* office, the vast crowds set up a caɴ oniac yell of delight, which to me sounded like a death knell to all my hopes for the freedom of the enslaved. As the excitement was hourly increasing, and threats made to search the city for abolitionists, I felt that nothing could be gained by remaining in Richmond.

I left for Washington, almost crushed in spirit at the destruction of Capt. Brown and his brave little band. On the train were Southerners from several of the Slave States, who boldly expressed their views of Northern abolitionists, in the most emphatic slave-driving language. The excitement was intense, every stranger, especially if he looked like a Northerner, was closely watched, and in some instances subjected to inquisition.

DOUGH-FACED NORTHERNERS.

The attitude of many of the leading Northern politicians and so-called statesmen of Washington, was simply disgusting. These weak-kneed and craven creatures, were profuse in their apologies for Brown's assault, and hastened to divest themselves of what little manhood they possessed, while in the presence of the women-whippers of the South. " What can we do to conciliate the Slave States ?" was the leading question of the day. Such men as Crittenden and Douglas were ready to compromise with the slave-holders, even at the sacrifice of their avowed principles. While Toombs, Davis, Mason, Slidell and the rest of the slave-driving crew, haughtily demanded further guarantees for the protection of their "institution;" and had it not been for the stand taken by the people of the Northern States at that time, their political leaders would have bound the North hand and foot, to do the bidding of the slave-holders. But, on that occasion, the people of the North showed themselves worthy descendents of their revolutionary sires.

EFFECTS OF JOHN BROWN'S ATTACK.

The blow struck at Harper's Ferry, which the democratic leaders affected to ridicule, had startled the slave-holders from their dreams of security, and sent fear and trembling into every home in the Slave States. The poor oppressed slave as he laid down on his pallet of straw, weary from his enforced labors, offered up a prayer for the safety of the grand old captain, who was a prisoner in the hands of merciless foes, thirsting for his blood.

BRAVERY OF CAPTAIN BROWN.

How bravely John Brown bore himself in the presence of the human wolves that surrounded him, as he lay mangled and torn in front of the engine-house at Harper's Ferry! Mason, of Virginia, and

that Northern renegade, Vallandigham, interrogated
the apparently dying man, trying artfully, but in
vain, to get him to implicate leading Northern men.
In the history of modern times there is not recorded
another instance of such rare heroic valour as John
Brown displayed in the presence of Governor Wise,
of Virginia. How contemptible Mason, Wise, and
Vallandigham appear when compared with the
wounded old liberator, who lay weltering in his
blood, shed in behalf of the oppressed. Mason,
Wise and Vallandigham died with the stain of treason on their heads.

CAPTAIN JOHN BROWN.

To superficial observers, Brown's attack on Virginia with so small a force, looked like the act of a
madman; but those who knew John Brown, and

the men under his command, are satisfied that if he
had carried out his original plans, and retreated
with his force to the mountains, after he had captured the arms in the arsenal, he could have baffled
any force sent against him. The slaves would have
flocked to his standard by thousands, and the slaveholders would have trembled with fear for the
safety of their families.

JOHN BROWN VICTORIOUS.

John Brown in prison, surrounded by his captors,
won greater victories than if he had conquered the
South by force of arms. His courage, truthfulness,
humanity, and self-sacrificing devotion to the cause
of the poor downtrodden slaves, shamed the cowardly, weak-kneed, and truculent Northern politicians into opposition to the haughty demands of
the despots of the South. The crack of his rifle at
Harper's Ferry suddenly confronted every man in
America, with his traditional cowardice, moral,
political, or physical. There was a moment of
timid deprecation or hasty denial: "We know not
the man;"—the million eyes met, the explosion of
long-pent fires, the nation is rent, the lie dragged to
judgment, the laws re-constructed, and the people
of the Free States confess that John Brown, the
"outlaw," the "lunatic," the spurned of all sections
to an ignominious death, was not prophet only, but

the very cry that was rising in every true heart in America.

I esteem it a great privilege to have known John Brown, and to have had the opportunity of aiding him in his great purpose.

AN EFFORT TO SEE JOHN BROWN.

December the 2nd, 1859, was the day appointed for the execution of Captain Brown. I determined to make an effort to see him once more if possible. Taking the cars at Baltimore, on November 26th, I went to Harper's Ferry, and applied to the military officer in command for permission to go to Charlestown. He enquired my object in wishing to go there at that time, while so much excitement existed. I replied, that I had a desire to see John Brown once more before his death. Without replying to me, he called an officer in the room and directed him to place me in close confinement until the arrival of the train for Baltimore and then to place me on the train, and command the conductor to take me to Baltimore. Then, raising his voice, he said, "Captain, if he (myself) returns to Harper's Ferry, shoot him at once." I was placed under guard until the train came in, when, in spite of my protests, I was taken to Baltimore. Determined to make one more attempt, I went to Richmond to try and obtain permission from the Governor. After much difficulty I obtained an

INTERVIEW WITH GOVERNOR WISE.

I told the Governor that I had a strong desire to see John Brown before his execution; that I had some acquaintance with him, and had formed a very high estimate of him as a man. I asked him to allow me to go to Charlestown (under *surveillance* if he pleased), and bid the old Captain "goodbye." The Governor made many inquiries to ascertain my views of Brown, and finally asked whether I justified his attack on Virginia. I replied, that from childhood I had been an ardent admirer of Washington, Jefferson and Madison, and that all these great and good men deplored the existence of slavery in the Republic. That my admiration and friendship for John Brown was owing to his holding similar views and his earnest desire to abolish the evil. The Governor looked amazed at my pertinacity, and for a moment made no reply. At length he straightened himself up, and, assuming a dignified air, said, "My family motto is, '*sapere aude.*' I am *wise* enough to understand your object in wishing to go to Charlestown, and I *dare* you to go. If you attempt it I will have you shot. It is such men as you who have urged Brown to make his crazy attack upon our constitutional rights and privileges. You shall not leave Richmond until after the execution of Brown. I would like to hang a dozen of your leading abolitionists."

G

GOVERNOR WISE WOULD LIKE TO BAG GIDDINGS AND GERRIT SMITH, AND HANG THEM !

"If I could *bag* old Giddings and Gerrit Smith, I would hang them without trial."

The Governor became excited, and paced the floor angrily, saying, "No, sir! you shall not leave Richmond. You shall go to prison, and remain there until next Monday; then you may go North, and slander the State which ought to have hanged you!" I replied, that as he refused me permission to see Captain Brown, I would leave Virginia at once, and thus save the State any trouble or expense on my account. I said this very quietly, while his eyes were riveted on me. In reply, he said, "Did I not tell you that you should remain a prisoner here until Monday?" I replied, "Yes, Governor, you did; but I am sure the executive of this great State is too *wise* to fear one unarmed man." For a moment he tapped the table with his fingers, then shaking his fore-finger, said : "Well, you may go, and I would advise you to tell your Giddings, Greeleys, Smiths and Garrisons, cowards that they are, to lead the next raid on Virginia themselves."

Fearing that obstacles might be thrown in my way, which would cause detention and trouble, I requested the Governor to give me a permit to leave the State of Virginia. Without making reply, he picked up a blank card, and wrote as follows :—

" The bearer is hereby ordered to leave the State of Virginia within twenty-four hours."

Henry A. Wise

This he handed me, saying, " The sooner you go, the better for you ; our people are greatly excited, and you may regret this visit if you stay another hour."

On returning to Philadelphia I wrote to Captain Brown, bidding him a last farewell. Several days after his execution I received from the sheriff of Jefferson County, Virginia, the following letter, written by the captain the day before his execution :—

CAPTAIN BROWN'S FAREWELL LETTER TO THE AUTHOR.

" JAIL, CHARLESTOWN, VA., December, 1st, 1859.

"MY DEAR FRIEND :—Captain Avis, my jailor, has just handed me your most kind and affectionate letter. I am sorry your efforts to reach this place have been unavailing, I thank you for your faithfulness, and the assurance you give me that my poor and deeply afflicted family will be provided for. It takes from my mind the greatest cause of sadness I have experienced since my imprisonment. In a few hours, through infinite grace in ' Christ Jesus, my Lord,' I shall be in another and better state of existence. I feel quite cheerful and ready to die,

My dear friend, do not give up your labors for the ' poor that cry, and them that are in bonds.' "

(Fac-simile of the three last lines.)

Farewell God bless you
Your Friend
John Brown

EXECUTION OF JOHN BROWN.

On the morning of his execution, an ordinary furniture waggon, containing a plain coffin, was brought to the door of the jail, soon after which the door opened, and John Brown appeared, followed by Sheriff Campbell and John Avis, the jailer. As John Brown passed out he said, "Good-bye " to several whom he recognized, and some of whom had done him little acts of kindness during his imprisonment. To one of the guards he handed a slip of paper on which he had written the following prophetic words :—

"CHARLESTOWN JAIL, December 2nd, 1859.
" I, John Brown, am now quite certain that the crimes of this guilty land will never be washed away except with blood. I had, as I now think, vainly flattered myself that without much bloodshed it might be done."

These, his last written words, were sent to me by John Avis, his jailor. John Brown quickly mounted the waggon, and seated himself on the coffin which was soon to contain his lifeless remains. The pretty story of his kissing a negro child as he was leaving the jail, has no foundation in fact. The only remarks he made while being driven to the field where the execution took place, were in reference to the natural beauty of the surrounding country. From the jail to the scaffold he was closely surrounded by soldiers. When the procession reached the scaffold, John Brown stepped from the waggon and was the first to mount the steps, followed by the sheriff and jailor. John Brown's step was firm, his bearing solemn, cool and brave. Around him were hundreds of Virginians in warlike array, the forms of many men who were soon to die violent deaths as traitors to their country. Near the gallows stood Stonewall Jackson in command of his cadets, with John Wilkes Booth (the assassin of President Lincoln) as one of his volunteers. Jackson was killed while fighting against his country. Seated on a beautiful horse was General Ashby— he too died a violent death in the rebel ranks, Near by stood the contemptible Jeff Thompson, who had brought from Missouri a rope with which to hang John Brown. He too served and survived the rebellion to endure poverty and contempt. Gov. Wise, who signed John Brown's death warrant, fought as a rebel against his country, and survived to see a daughter of John Brown teaching the children of Freedmen in his home. Nearly all the rank and file that surrounded that scaffold died violent deaths in the battles of the slaveholders' rebellion, and the few who survive live to see John Brown vindicated in every slave that now receives wages for his labor.

When John Brown ascended the gallows he stood erect, cool and steady. He wore a broad-brimmed felt hat. His clothing was plain and scrupulously clean. His white beard had been cut somewhat shorter than usually worn. His every movement was grave, gentle and dignified. The sheriff approached him and covered his face. When he was placed upon the trap he said, "Be quick; do not keep me waiting." Then began a series of fussy movements by the military, which occupied fully ten minutes, after which the trap fell, and the spirit of John Brown joined his comrades in the spirit land. There were few, we fancy, of those who that day witnessed the death of John Brown, who imagined that his name would outlive the name of the politicians and so-called statesmen of that day. Virginia, in her pride and strength, judicially murdered John Brown; but the day is not far distant when the freedmen and freemen of the South will erect a monument on the spot where he gave up his life, a willing sacrifice for the cause of human freedom.

The memory of John Brown will grow brighter

and brighter through all coming ages, and long after the Southern statesmen who shouted for his death are mouldering in the silent dust forgotten, or unpleasantly remembered, the name of John Brown, of Osawatomie, will be a household word with millions yet unborn.

LETTERS TO THE AUTHOR FROM CAPTAIN JOHN BROWN'S WIDOW AND CHILDREN.

From Mary A. Brown, Widow of Capt. John Brown, the Martyr.

DEAR FRIEND,—* * * My husband often spoke of you as being one of his most faithful and sincere friends. Your tender and kindly sympathy for his afflicted family in those terrible days of '59 will never be forgotten by me. I send you a lock of his hair in remembrance of your friendship. * * *

———

From John Brown, Jr., Son of Capt. John Brown, the Martyr.

MY DEAR FRIEND,—All honor to you for the courage and devotion to the cause of liberty which led you to peril your life again and again for those who had no other claim on you than that of common humanity. You may indeed feel gratified by the medals, diplomas of honor and royal decorations conferred on you by the learned societies and crowned heads of Europe, yet these are toys compared with that which entitles you to be known as *the tried and true friend of mankind.* * * *

———

From Owen Brown, son of Capt. John Brown, the Martyr.

* * * I shall hold you in lasting remembrance for your fidelity to father, and the cause he died in serving. You have my earnest hopes for your success, though any one of your stamp who will exercise such unfaltering persistance against so many kinds of difficulties will surely succeed.

From Ruth Brown, Eldest Daughter of Capt. John Brown, the Martyr.

* * * I wish every person in our land knew how noble and self-sacrificing you have been. * * * I wish you could have seen father when you went to Virginia. To have seen you again would have done him more good than all the prayers of all the pro-slavery ministers in the world.

From Annie Brown, youngest daughter of Capt. John Brown, the Martyr.

I wish to express my unbounded gratitude to you for placing my father before the world in his true light. You *comprehended* him, you *knew* him. * * *

THE JOHN BROWN SONG.

BY EDNA A. PROCTOR.

John Brown died on the scaffold for the slave ;
Dark was the hour when we dug his hallowed grave ;
Now God avenges the life he gladly gave—
    Freedom reigns to-day !
      Glory, glory, hallelujah,
      Glory, glory, hallelujah,
      Glory, glory, hallelujah,
    Freedom reigns to-day !

John Brown sowed, and his harvesters are we ;
Honor to him who has made the bondmen free !
Loved evermore shall our noble ruler be ;
    Freedom reigns to-day !
      Glory, glory, hallelujah, &c.

John Brown's body lies mouldering in the grave ;
Bright o'er the sod let the starry banner wave ;
Lo ! for the millions he perilled all to save,
    Freedom reigns to-day !
      Glory, &c.

John Brown's soul through the world is marching on ;
Hail to the hour when oppression shall be gone !
All men will sing in the better ages' dawn,
    Freedom reigns to-day !
      Glory, etc.

John Brown dwells where the battle strife is o'er ;
Hate cannot harm him, nor sorrow stir him more ;
Earth will remember the martyrdom he bore ;
    Freedom reigns to-day !
      Glory, &c.

John Brown's body lies mouldering in the grave ;
John Brown lives in the triumphs of the brave ;
John Brown's soul not a higher joy can crave ;
    Freedom reigns to-day !
      Glory, glory, hallelujah !
      Glory, glory, hallelujah !
      Glory, glory, hallelujah !
    Freedom reigns to-day !

JOHN BROWN'S MEN AT HARPER'S FERRY.

The men that John Brown gathered about him
for his last fight with slavery were men like himself of heroic mould. They were young men in the
full morning of life. They were each attached to
him by the subtle magnetism that attracts the
lesser to the greater. Like John Brown, they were
earnest men, haters of tyranny and injustice, and
lovers of freedom. They were each and all God-
fearing men, of staunch moral character, temperate,
truthful, sincere and brave. No profane word or
jest was heard from their lips. In their devotion,

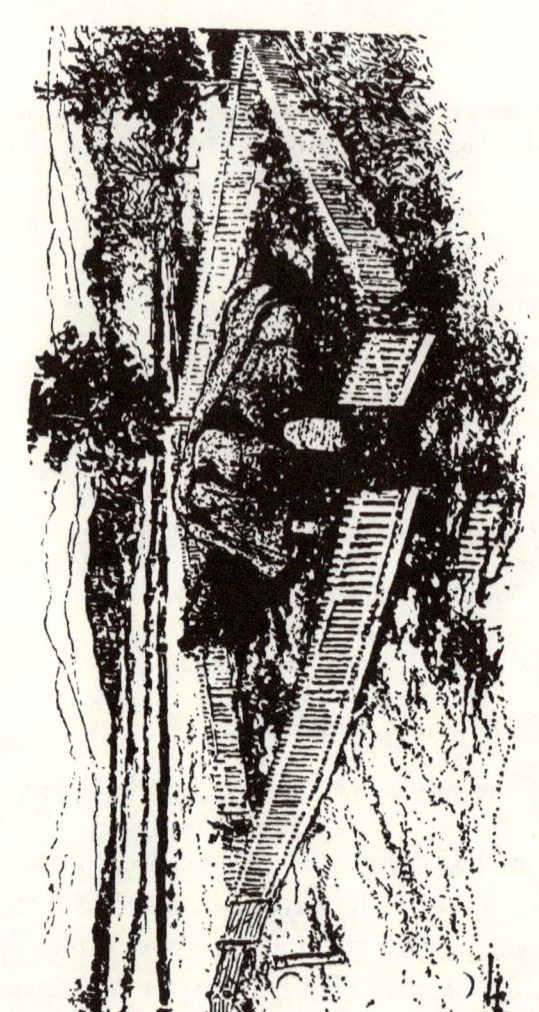

JOHN BROWN'S GRAVE AT NORTH ELBA, N. Y.

fidelity and self-sacrifice, they resembled the "Iron-sides" of Cromwell. Their faith and confidence in their strong old captain was such that they would, as they did, follow him without a murmur into the very "jaws of death." It is meet, right, and just that these heroic men should have a place in history, by the side of their fearless old leader.

CASUALTIES AT HARPER'S FERRY.

Aaron D. Stevens and John H. Kagi were Capt. Brown's right-hand men during the Kansas war for freedom, and at Harper's Ferry, Stevens was wounded, taken prisoner and executed. Kagi was driven into the river by a score of assailants, and cowardly murdered. Owen Brown escaped and is still living (1892). Oliver and Watson Brown were killed in the fight. John E. Cook escaped, was captured, and executed. Edwin Coppic, Albert Hazlett, John Copeland, Shields Green, and Dangerfield Newby were taken prisoners and executed. Stuart Taylor, William Lehman, Louis Leary, William and Dauphin Thompson, and Jeremiah Anderson were killed in the fight. Barclay Coppic, Frank J Merriam, Charles Plummer Tidd, and O. P. Anderson escaped,

Names and rank of John Brown's men at Harper's Ferry.

MUSTER ROLL.

Aaron Dwight Stevens .... Captain
John Henry Kagi .... "

Owen Brown (son of John Brown)....................Captain
Oliver Brown   "   "   ....   "
Watson Brown   "   "   ....   "
John F. Cook ....   "
Edwin Coppic........................ ....Lieutenant
Albert Hazlett.......... ....   "
William Lehman......... ....   "

PRIVATES.

Barclay Coppic, Stuart Taylor, Frank J. Merriman, Louis
Leary, Shields Green, Dangerfield Newby, Jeremiah Anderson,
O. P. Anderson, John Copeland, Charles Plummer Tidd, William
Thompson (son-in-law of John Brown), Dauphin Thompson (son-
in-law of John Brown).

Captain Brown expected the slaves would flock
to his standard in hundreds in case he was successful, hence the disproportionate number of commissioned officers in his force.   These officers had been
thoroughly drilled by Colonel Forbes, formerly an
officer of Garibaldi's army, and it was Captain
Brown's purpose to organize his colored recruits
into companies under these officers.

Never in the history of the world, did mightier
results follow the actions of a like number of men.

JOHN BROWN'S "PROVISIONAL CONSTITUTION."

On page 84 the reader will find a call from John
Brown for a convention to be held in Chatham,
Canada, in May, 1858.   The convention met on the
day appointed and formed a " Provisional Constitution," and elected a president and other civil officers.

John Brown was appointed Commander-in-Chief, John Henry Kagi, Secretary of War, and Owen Brown, Treasurer of the military forces. This "Provisional Constitution" was to be John Brown's shield and authority as Commander-in-Chief, and it was by virtue of this authority that his officers were commissioned.

Copy of Brown's commission to his Officers.

Headquarters, War Dept.,

Near Harper's Ferry, Md.,

· October 15th, 1859.

GREETING :

Whereas, *Owen Brown* has been nominated a captain in the army, established under the provisional constitution.

Now, therefore, in pursuance of the authority vested in us by said constitution, we do hereby appoint and commission the said *Owen Brown,* a captain.

Given at the office of the Secretary of War, this October 15th, 1859.

John Brown

Commander in-Chief.

J. H. KAGI,

    Secretary of War.

(The original is printed except the words in italics, which are in the writing of Kagi.)

CHAPTER V.

1860-61.

Number of Refugees in Canada—Negro Slave's Escape to Canada—Cruelty and Injustice of the Fugitive Slave Law—Presidential Election, 1860.

NUMBER OF REFUGEES IN CANADA.

I spent the next three months in Canada, visiting those refugees in whom I had taken a personal interest. I found six in Chatham, two in London, four in Hamilton, two in Amherstburgh, and one in Toronto—fifteen in all; while several had gone from Canada to New England. It afforded me great satisfaction to find them sober, industrious members of society. It has often been remarked by both Canadians and visitors from the States, that the negro refugees in Canada were superior specimens of their race. The observation is true; for none but those possessing superior qualities could hope to reach Canada. The difficulties and dangers of the route, and the fact that they were often closely pursued for weeks by human foes and by bloodhounds, required the exercise of rare qualities of mind and body. Their route would often lay through dismal swamps inhabited only by wild animals and poisonous reptiles. Sometimes the distance between the land of bondage and freedom was several hundreds of miles, every mile of which had to be traversed on foot. It is, indeed, surprising that so large a number of fugitives succeeded in reaching Canada, considering the obstacles they had to contend with on their long and dangerous journey.

The number of refugee negroes in Canada at the outbreak of the Slaveholders' Rebellion, was not far short of forty thousand. Probably more than half of them were manumitted slaves who, in consequence of unjust laws, were compelled to leave the States where they were manumitted. Many of these negroes settled in the Northern States, but the greater portion of them came to Canada.

The following simple lines were familiar to most of the fugitives in Canada thirty years ago:—

THE NEGRO SLAVE'S ESCAPE TO CANADA.

" I'm on my way to Canada, that free and happy land,
The cruelty of slavery I can no longer stand.
My soul is grieved within me to think that I'm a slave,
And I'm resolved to strike a blow for freedom or the grave.
Farewell, farewell, old master, I'm on my way to Canada,
　　　Where colored men are free."

" I heard old master pray last night, I heard him pray for me,
That God would come with might and power and me from
　　Satan free.

So I from Satan would be free and flee the wrath to come,
But if Satan is in human form, old master's surely one.
Farewell, farewell, old master, I'm on the road to Canada,
        Dear land of liberty."

" I've heard that Queen Victoria, if we would all forsake
Our native land of slavery and come across the lake,
That she was waiting on the shore with arms extended wide,
To give us all a peaceful home in Canada by her side.
Farewell, farewell, old master, that's good enough for me,
        I'm on my way to Canada, dear land of liberty."

" The hounds are baying on my track and master's close behind,
Resolved that he will take me back before I cross the line.
I no more dread the auctioneer, nor fear the master's frown,
I no more tremble when I hear the baying of the hound.
Farewell, farewell, old master, I've just arrived in Canada,
        Where every man is free ; God bless Canada ! "

CRUELTY AND INJUSTICE OF THE FUGITIVE SLAVE LAW.

When the Fugitive Slave Law was enacted in 1850, it carried terror to every person of African blood in the Free States. Stung with hopeless despair, more than six thousand Christian men and women fled from their homes, and sought refuge under the flag of Britain in Canada. In the words of Charles Sumner :—

"The Free States became little better than a huge outlying plantation, quivering under the lash of the overseer; or rather they were a diversified hunting ground for the flying bondman, resounding always with the 'halloo' of the huntsman. There seemed to be no rest. The chase was hardly finished at Boston, before it broke out at Philadelphia, Syracuse or Buffalo, and then again raged furiously over the prairies of the west. Not a case occurred which did not shock the conscience of the country, and sting it with anger. The records of the time attest the accuracy of this statement."

Perhaps there is no instance in history where human passion showed itself in grander forms of expression, or where eloquence lent all her gifts more completely to the demands of liberty, than the speech of Theodore Parker (now dead and buried in a foreign land), denouncing the capture of Thos. Simms, at Boston, and invoking the judgment of God and man upon the agents in this wickedness. This great effort cannot be forgotten in the history of humanity. But every case pleaded with an eloquence of its own, until at last one of these tragedies occurred which darken the heavens, and cry out with a voice that will be heard. It was the voice of a mother standing over her murdered child. Margaret Garner had escaped from slavery' with three children, but she was overtaken at Cincinnati. Unwilling to see her offspring returned to the shambles of the South, this unhappy mother, described in the testimony as "a womanly, amiable, affectionate mother," determined to save them in the only way within her power. With a butcher knife, coolly and deliberately, she took the life of one of the children, described as " almost white, and a little girl of rare beauty," and attempt-

H

ed, without success, to take the life of the other two. To the preacher who interrogated her, she exclaimed, "The child is my own, given me of God to do the best a mother could in its behalf. I have done the best I could; I would have done more and better for the rest; I knew it was better for them to go home to God than back to slavery." But she was restrained in her purpose. The Fugitive Slave Act triumphed, and after the determination of sundry questions of jurisdiction, this devoted historic mother, with the two children that remained to her, and the dead body of the little one just emancipated, was escorted by a national guard of armed men to the doom of slavery. But her case did not end with this revolting sacrifice. So long as the human heart is moved by human suffering, the story of this mother will be read with alternate anger and grief, while it is studied as a perpetual witness to the slaveholding tyranny which then ruled the Republic with execrable exactions, destined at last to break out in war, as the sacrifice of Virginia by her father is a perpetual witness to the decemviral tyranny which ruled Rome. But liberty is always priceless. There are other instances less known, in which kindred wrong has been done. Every case was a tragedy—under the forms of law. Worse than poisoned bowl or dagger was the certificate of a United States Commissioner—who was allowed, without interruption, to continue his dreadful trade.

THE PRESIDENTIAL ELECTION OF 1860.

During no previous Presidential election (except that of 1856, when Fremont and Buchanan were the candidates), was there so much excitement on the slavery question as that of 1860, when Lincoln Breckenridge, Bell, and Douglas, were the candidates.

To enable my readers to form a correct opinion of the political position occupied by the republican candidate toward the institution of slavery, I give below the "Republican Platform," on which President Lincoln went before the people for their suffrages :—

REPUBLICAN NATIONAL (LINCOLN) PLATFORM.

ADOPTED AT CHICAGO, 1860.

Resolved,—That we, the delegated representatives of the Republican electors of the United States, in Convention assembled, in discharge of the duty we owe to our constituents and our country, unite in the following declarations :

1. That the history of the nation, during the last four years, has fully established the propriety and necessity of the organization and perpetuation of the Republican party, and that the causes which called it into existence are permanent in their nature, and now, more than ever before, demand its peaceful and constitutional triumph.

2. That the maintenance of the principles promulgated in the Declaration of Independence and embodied in the Federal Constitution, "That all men are created equal; that they are endowed by their Creator with certain inalienable rights; that among these are life, liberty, and the pursuit of happiness; that

to secure these rights, governments are instituted among men, deriving their just powers from the consent of the governed," is essential to the preservation of our Republican institutions ; and that the Federal Constitution, the Rights of the States, and the Union of the States, must and shall be preserved.

7. That the new dogma, that the Constitution of its own force, carries Slavery into any or all of the Territories of the United States, is a dangerous political heresy, at variance with the explicit provisions of that instrument itself, with contemporaneous exposition, and with legislative and judicial precedent ; is revolutionary in its tendency, and subversive of the peace and harmony of the country.

8. That the normal condition of all the territory of the United States is that of freedom ; That as our Republican fathers, when they had abolished Slavery in all our national territory, ordained that "no person should be deprived of life, liberty, or property, without due process of law," it becomes our duty, by legislation, whenever such legislation is necessary, to maintain this provision of the Constitution against all attempts to violate it ; and we deny the authority of Congress, of a territorial legislature, or of any individuals, to give legal existence to Slavery in any Territory of the United States.

9. That we brand the recent re-opening of the African slave-trade, under the cover of our national flag, aided by perversions of judicial power, as a crime against humanity and a burning shame to our country and age ; and we call upon Congress to take prompt and efficient measures for the total and final suppression of that execrable traffic.

Dr. Ross

For his steadfast strength & courage
   in a dark & evil time,
When the Golden Rule was treason,
   And to feed the hungry crime,
For the poor slave's hope & refuge
   When the hounds were on his track,
And scent & sennin State & Church
   joined hands to send him back,
Blessings upon him! What he did
   For each sad, suffering one
Chained, hunted scourged & bleeding,
   unto our Lord was done!

                    John G. Whittier
                Secretary of the Convention
Oak Knoll   in 1833 which formed
              the American Anti Slavery
Danvers Mass   Society,
12th Mo. 1879

CHAPTER VI.

1861–1865.

THE SLAVEHOLDERS' REBELLION.

For many weeks after the death of Capt. Brown, I felt that the defeat of his plans at Harper's Ferry was a great calamity to the enslaved. I saw nothing in store for the poor slaves but toil and bondage for another generation. For who, at that time, foresaw the mighty conflict that was soon to be inaugurated

117

by the haughty slaveholders, by which they and their cherished institution were to be completely overthrown.

The brave and noble words and conduct of John Brown, while in the hands of his murderers, shook the institution of slavery to its very foundation. The slaveholders fully comprehended that unless they could obtain from the North further guarantees for the protection of the institution of slavery—that secession from the Free States was their only salvation. Their insolent demands upon the North were met by a quiet determination that not another foot of the public domain should be given up to slavery. Northern politicians had become so accustomed to yielding obedience to the commands of the slave-drivers, that strong efforts were made to effect a compromise with the pro-slavery leaders in Congress.

But the patience of the peace-loving people of the Free States was at length exhausted ; they had submitted to the outrageous provisions of the Fugitive Slave Law ; they had looked on while the champions of freedom in Congress were insulted and assaulted by the slave-drivers of the South ; they had borne for years the taunts and sneers of the Southern chivalry ; and now they resolved to assert their just rights and privileges as citizens of a free country.

The threats and demands of the slaveholders were treated with the contempt they deserved.

CONFIDENTIAL SERVICE IN CANADA.

A few months after the inauguration of President Lincoln, I received a letter from the Hon. Charles Sumner, requesting me to come to Washington at my earliest convenience.

INTERVIEW WITH PRESIDENT LINCOLN.

The day after my arrival in Washington, I was introduced to the President. Mr. Lincoln received me very cordially, and invited me to dine with him. Assembled at the President's table were several prominent gentlemen, to whom Mr. Lincoln introduced me as " a red-hot abolitionist from Canada." One of the guests, a prominent member of Congress, from Indiana (severely injured in after years by the *Credit Mobilier*), said in a slurring manner, " I wish the negroes of the United States would emigrate to Canada, as the Canadians are so fond of their company." Mr. Lincoln said, "It would be better for the negroes, that's certain." " Yes," I replied, a little warmly, " it would be better for the negroes; for, under our flag, the blackest negro is entitled to, and freely accorded, every right and privilege enjoyed by native Canadians. We make no distinction in respect to the colour of a man's skin. It is true, we live under a monarchial form of government; but every man and woman, white, black or brown, have equal rights

under our laws." Mr. Lincoln, in a jocular way, said
to the member of Congress, " If you are not careful,
you will bring on a war with Canada.   I think we
have a big enough job on hand now."

The conversation then turned on the attitude of
England toward the Free States in their contest
with the slaveholders.   One gentleman remarked
that he was surprised to see so many manifestations
of unfriendliness on the part of the English and
Canadian people, and asked me how I accounted for
it.   I replied, " How can you expect it otherwise,
when there exists in your Northern States so much
diversity of opinion as to the justness of your cause ?
The unfriendly expressions of an English statesman,
or the avowed hostility of a few English and Canadian papers, are noted by you with painful surprise,
while the treasonable utterances and acts of some of
your own political leaders and people are quite over-
looked.   Besides, you cannot expect the sympathy
of Canadians in your behalf, while you display such
an utter disregard for the rights and liberties of
your own citizens, as I witnessed in this city yesterday."

Mr. Lincoln asked to what I alluded ?   I replied,
" A United States Marshal passed through Washington, yesterday, having in his charge a coloured man,
whom he was taking back to Virginia under your
Fugitive Slave Law.   The man had escaped from his
master—who is an open rebel—and fled to Wilming-

ton, Delaware, where he was arrested, and taken
back into slavery."

After dinner, Mr. Lincoln led me to a window,
distant from the rest of the party, and said, " Mr.
Sumner sent for you at my request. We need a
faithful friend in Canada to look after our interests, and keep us posted as to the schemes of the
Confederates in Canada. You have been strongly
recommended to me for the position. Your communications may be sent direct to me. Think it
over to-night; and if you can accept the mission,
come up and see me at nine o'clock to-morrow morning." When I took my leave of him, he said, " I
hope you will decide to serve us." I concluded to
accept the responsibilities of the mission, being persuaded to this conclusion by the wishes of the President and my friend Mr. Sumner.

THE PRESIDENT AN ABOLITIONIST.

At nine o'clock next morning, I waited upon the
President, and announced my decision. He grasped
my hand in a hearty manner, and said. "Thank
you ; thank you ; I am glad of it." I said, "Mr.
Lincoln, if the purpose of your Government is the
liberation from bondage of the poor slaves of the
South, I shall feel justified in accepting any position where I could best serve you ; but when I see
so much tenderness for that vile institution and for

the interests of slaveholders, I question whether
your efforts to crush the rebellion will meet with
the favour of Heaven." He replied, "I sincerely
wish that all men were free ; and I especially wish
for the complete abolition of slavery in this country ; but my private wishes and feelings must yield
to the duties of my position. My first duty is, to
maintain the integrity of the Union. With that
object in view, I shall endeavour to save it, either
with or without slavery. I have always been an
anti-slavery man. Away back in 1839, when I was
a member of the Legislature of Illinois, I presented
a resolution asking for the emancipation of slavery
in the District of Columbia, when, with but few exceptions, the popular mind of my State was opposed
to it. If the institution of slavery is destroyed, and
the slaves set free, as a result of this conflict which
the slaveholders have forced upon us, I shall rejoice
as heartily as you. In the meantime, help us to
circumvent the machinations of the rebel agents in
Canada. There is no doubt they will use your
country as a communicating link with Europe, and
also with their friends in New York. It is quite
possible also that they may make Canada a base,
to harass and annoy our people along the frontier."

After a lengthy conversation relative to private
matters connected with my mission, I rose to leave,
when he said, "I'll walk down to 'Willard's' with
you : the hotel is on my way to the Capitol, where
I have an engagement at noon."

OFFICE SEEKERS.

Before we reached the hotel, a man approached the President, and thrust a letter into his hand, at the same time applying for some office in Wisconsin. I saw that the President was offended at the rudeness, for he passed the letter back without looking at it, saying emphatically, "No, sir! I am not going to open shop here." This was said in a most emphatic manner, but accompanied by a comical gesture, which caused the rejected applicant to smile. As we continued our walk, the President spoke of the annoyances incident to his position, saying, "These office-seekers are a curse to this country. No sooner was my election certain, than I became the prey of hundreds of hungry, persistent applicants for office, whose highest ambition is to feed at the government crib." When he bid me good-bye, he said, "Let me hear from you once a week at least." As he turned to leave me, a young army officer stopped him, and made some request, to which the President replied with a good deal of humour: "No; I can't do that. I must not interfere; they would scratch my eyes out, if I did. You must go to the proper department."

As I watched the President wending his way towards the Capitol, I was deeply impressed with the dreadful responsibility that rested upon him! The hopes of millions of Republicans throughout the world were fixed upon him; while twenty millions of his own people looked to him for the salvation of the Republic, and four millions of poor down-trodden slaves in the South looked to him for freedom.

Mr. Lincoln was no ordinary man. He had a quick and ready perception of facts, a retentive memory, and a logical turn of mind, which patiently and unwaveringly followed every link in the chain of thought on every subject which he investigated. He was honest, temperate, and forgiving. He was a good man—a man of noble and kindly heart. I never heard him speak unkindly of any man; even the rebels received no word of anger from him.

CONFEDERATES IN CANADA.

On my return to Montreal, I sought opportunities to become acquainted with the names, habits, and occupations of the various Confederates in Canada.

The principal Confederate agent in Canada at that time was Jacob Thompson, an ex-member of Buchanan's administration, whose contemptible conduct, while a member of the Government, in warning the rebels of Charleston of the sailing of the steamer "Star of the West" with provisions for the besieged garrison at Fort Sumpter, furnishes a good index to his character. The plots and schemes devised by him and his subordinates to furnish the rebels with clothing, boots and shoes, etc.; *via* Nassau, Cuba, and to keep open a channel of communication with the Confederate States, kept me continually on the *qui vive* to frustrate their designs.

There prevailed in Canada at this period a very strong and active sympathy for the Confederates. Indeed, I may say, that among the wealthy and influential classes there were few but what wished for the success of the slaveholders, and the consequent disruption of the Union. This was not from any love for slavery, but rather a reflex of the sympathy manifestsd by the higher classes in England for the Confederacy. To overcome this prejudice against the Northern cause, and awaken kindly sympathies for the people of the Free States in the contest with slavery, was the object of my earnest efforts. To assist me in accomplishing that purpose, I brought before the Canadian people the claims of the Sanitary Commission of the United States Army, an organization that excited the generous impulses of Christians of all denominations and classes.

The Montreal *Daily Witness,* in alluding to this subject at the time, said :—

"The United States Sanitary Commission has opened branches in three of the European capitals, London, Paris and Berlin;

and from the London branch alone a large amount of pecuniary
aid has been remitted. Dr. A. M. Ross has opened another
branch in this city. We know of no agency more likely to
awaken kindly feelings here, towards the United States, than
this. Dr. Ross informs us, indeed, that this is the object of the
Commission in forming their foreign offices, which give an
opportunity of circulating information which may remove prejudice, and of receiving benefits and awakening kindly sympathies
for the sick and wounded soldiers."

REBEL POSTAL SERVICE.

Toward the close of 1862, I discovered that a
regular system of postal service was in operation
between the Confederate States and Europe, *via*
Detroit, Montreal and Boston. After weeks of diligent search, the detectives arrested a woman who
regularly passed between Detroit and Boston, *via*
Montreal and Rouse's Point, N.Y., once a fortnight.
She was despoiled of her *mail*, and placed in prison.
I carried the " mail" to Washington, arriving there
at midnight, and went direct to the White House
and sent my card to the President, who had retired
to bed. In a few minutes the porter returned and
requested me to accompany him to the President's
room, when the President would soon join me.
The room into which I was ushered was the same
in which I had spent several hours with the President on the occasion of my first interview with
him. Scattered about the floor, and lying open on
the table, were several military maps and documents indicating recent use. On the wall hung a

picture of that noble friend of freedom, John Bright, of England.

WITH PRESIDENT LINCOLN.

In a few minutes, the President came in, and welcomed me in the most friendly manner. I expressed my regret at disturbing him at such an hour. He replied in a good-humoured manner, saying, " No, no; you did right; you may waken me whenever you please. I have slept with one eye open ever since I came to Washington : I never close both, except when an office-seeker is looking for me." " I am glad (referring to a letter I had sent him) you are pleased with the Emancipation Proclamation; but there is work before us yet. We must make that Proclamation effective by victories over our enemies. It is a paper bullet after all, and of no account, except we can sustain it." I expressed my belief that the cause of the Union would prosper now that justice had been done to the poor negro. He replied, " I hope so! The suffering and misery that attends this conflict is killing me by inches. I wish it was over!"

REBEL DESPATCHES.

I then laid before the President the " rebel mail." He carefully examined the address of each letter, making occasional remarks. At length he found one addressed to Franklin Pierce, ex-President of the United States, then residing in New Hampshire, and another to ex-Attorney General Cushing, a resident of Massachusetts. He appeared much surprised, and remarked with a sigh, but, without the slightest tone of asperity, " I will have these letters enclosed in official envelopes, and sent to these parties." When he had finished examining the addresses, he tied up all those addressed to private individuals, saying, " I won't bother with them ; but these look like official letters: I guess I'll go through them now." He then opened them, and read their contents slowly and carefully.

While he was thus occupied reading the letters I had brought him I had an excellent opportunity of studying this extraordinary man. A marked change had taken place in his countenance since my first interview with him. He looked much older, and bore traces of having passed through months of painful anxiety and trouble. There was a sad, serious look in his eyes that spoke louder than words, of disappointments, trials, and discouragements he had encountered since the war began. The wrinkles about the eyes and forehead were deeper ; the lips were firmer, but indicative of kindness and forbearance. The great struggle had brought out the hidden riches of his noble nature, and developed virtues and capacities which surprised his oldest and most intimate friends. He was simple, but astute ; he possessed the rare faculty of seeing things just as they are; he was a just, charitable, and honest man.

MR. LINCOLN'S MISSION.

If ever an individual was specially fitted and ordained to perform a special service, that individual was Abraham Lincoln. No parent could evince a warmer interest in the welfare of his family than he did for the safety and welfare of his country. Every faculty he possessed was devoted to the salvation of the Union.

" How humble, yet how hopeful he could be ;
  How in good fortune and in ill, the same ;
Nor bitter in success, nor boastful he,
  Thirsty for gold, nor feverish for fame.

He went about his work, such work as few
  Ever had laid on head, and heart, and hand,
As one who knows, where there's a task to do,
  Man's honest will must heaven's good grace command.

So he went forth to battle, on the side
  That he felt clear was Liberty's and Right's,
As in his peasant boyhood he had plied
  His warfare with rude nature's thwarting mights.

So he grew up a destined work to do ;
  And lived to do it : four long, suffering years,
Ill fate, ill feeling, ill report, lived through,
  And then he heard the hisses change to cheers.

The taunts to tributes, the abuse to praise,
  And took both with the same unwavering mood."

Taylor.

I

REBELS IN NEW BRUNSWICK.

Having finished reading a letter, he said, " Read this (handing me a letter signed by the Confederate Secretary of State), and tell me what you think of it." The letter was addressed to the rebel envoy at the French Court, and stated that preparations were being made to invade the Eastern frontier of the United States in the vicinity of Calais, Maine. It also expressed the opinion that an attack in so unexpected a quarter would dishearten the Northern people and encourage the Democrats to oppose the continuation of the war.

I told the President that this confirmed the truth of information I had communicated to him several weeks previously, that the rebels were preparing to raid on some of the Eastern States from the British Provinces. He replied, " That's so ! You had better go down to New Brunswick, and see what the rebels are up to. The information contained in the despatches I have read is of great importance. There are two despatches which I cannot read, as they are in cipher : but I'll find some way to get at their contents."

I then rose to go, saying that I would go to " Willard's " and have a rest. " No, no," said the President, " it is now three o'clock, you shall stay with me while you are in town ; I'll find you a bed," and leading the way he entered a bedroom, saying, "Take a good sleep; you shall not be disturbed." Bidding me "Good night," he left, to return to his investigation of the rebel letters.

HOSPITALITIES OF THE WHITE HOUSE.

I did not awake from my sleep until eleven o'clock in the forenoon, soon after which Mr. Lincoln came into my room, and laughingly said, "When you are ready, I'll pilot you down to breakfast," which he did, and, seating himself at the table near me, expressed his fears that trouble was brewing on the New Brunswick border; that he had gathered further information on that point from the correspondence, which convinced him that such was the case. He was here interrupted by a servant, who handed him a card, upon reading which he arose, saying, "The Secretary of War has received' important tidings; I must leave you for the present. Come to my room after breakfast, and we'll talk over this New Brunswick affair."

On entering his room, I found him busily engaged in writing, at the same time repeating in a low voice the words of a poem, which I remembered reading many years before. When he stopped writing, I asked him who was the author of that poem. He replied, " I do not know. I have written the verses down from memory, at the request of a

lady who is much pleased with them." He passed
the sheet, on which he had written the verses, to
me, saying, "Have you ever read them?" I replied that I had many years previously, and that I
should be pleased to have a copy of them in his
handwriting, when he had time and inclination for
such work. He said, "Well, you may keep that
copy, if you wish."

The following is the poem, as written down by
Mr. Lincoln :—

OH ! WHY SHOULD THE SPIRIT OF MORTAL BE PROUD?

Oh ! why should the spirit of mortal be proud ?
Like a swift-fleeting meteor, a fast-flying cloud,
A flash of the lightning, a break of the wave,
He passeth from life to his rest in the grave.

The leaves of the oak and the willow shall fade,
Be scattered around and together be laid ;
As the young and the old, the low and the high,
Shall crumble to dust, and together shall lie.

The infant a mother attended and loved ;
The mother that infant's affection who proved ;
The father, that mother and infant who blest—
Each, all are away to that dwelling of rest.

The maid, on whose brow, on whose cheek, in whose eye,
Shone beauty and pleasure—her triumphs are by ;
And alike from the minds of the living erased,
Are the memories of mortals that loved her and praised.

The hand of the king that the sceptre hath borne ;
The brow of the priest that the mitre hath worn ;
The eye of the sage, the heart of the brave,
Are hidden and lost in the depths of the grave.

The peasant, whose lot was to sow and to reap,
The herdsman, who climbed with his goats up the steep,
The beggar, who wandered in search of his bread,
Have faded away like the grass which we tread.

So the multitude goes, like the flower or the weed,
That withers away to let others succeed ;
So the multitude comes, even those we behold,
To repeat every tale that has often been told.

For we are the same our fathers have been ;
We see the same sights they often have seen ;
We drink the same stream, we see the same sun,
And run the same course our fathers have run.

The thoughts we are thinking our fathers did think ;
From the death we are shrinking our fathers did shrink ;
To the life we are clinging, our fathers did cling,
But it speeds from us all like the bird on the wing.

They loved—but the story we cannot unfold ;
They scorned—but the heart of the haughty is cold ;
They grieved—but no wail from their slumbers will come ;
They joyed—but the tongue of their gladness is dumb.

They died : ah, they died. We, things that are now,
That walk on the turf that lies over their brow,
And make in their dwelling a transient abode,
Meet the things that they met on their pilgrimage road.

Yea, hope and despondency, pleasure and pain,
Are mingled together in sunshine and rain ;
And the smile and the tear, and the song and the dirge,
Still follow each other like surge upon surge.

'Tis the wink of an eye, the draught of a breath,
From the blossom of health to the paleness of death;
From the gilded saloon to the bier and the shroud.
Oh ! why should the spirit of mortal be proud ?

"*Presented to Dr. Ross by*
"A LINCOLN."

LEAVE FOR NEW BRUNSWICK.

The rebel documents contained abundant evidence that the Confederates were organizing a band in Canada to raid upon the United States frontier, and the President was anxious that I should go to New Brunswick and, if possible, ascertain what the rebels were up to in that quarter.

I left Washington that night, and arrived in Boston in time to take the steamer for St. John, N.B. The boat was crowded with passengers, and I had to share my stateroom with a gentleman who came aboard at Portland. The features of my room companion were dark and coarse; his hair, black and long. He was about six feet in height, of tough and wiry frame. His language and general appearance were strikingly Southern. I selected the top berth, and retired before him, so that I might the more readily observe him : for I had strong suspicions that he was a Confederate, which he proved to be.

OCCUPY A ROOM WITH A REBEL.

When he entered the stateroom, he introduced himself as the owner of one of the berths, and said: "I am glad you are not a Yankee." "How do you know?" I asked. "The clerk told me you were a Canadian, and the Canadians are all on our side." I easily engaged him in talking; he was a boastful braggart, fond of whiskey, of which he drank freely. I remarked that I was tired of hearing threats and boasts of what they, "the Confederates were going to do." This nettled my companion, and he exclaimed, "Well, sir! you'll soon hear that we *have* done something. We have many picked men in St. Andrews and St. John, New Brunswick, and we have a good supply of stores on Grand Menan Island. I expect thirty men from Canada next week. As soon as they arrive we will prepare for an attack on Eastport; and, by ——, we intend to wipe it out. And then we will attack Calais in the rear, and, if hard pressed, retreat into New Brunswick."

This astounding news corroborated the information obtained from the captured letters.

ARREST OF THE REBEL OFFICER.

On the arrival of the steamer at Eastport, my new acquaintance was arrested, and I telegraphed to Mr. Lincoln the information obtained. A revenue cutter was immediately sent to Eastport. The Provincial authorities were warned, and prompt steps taken to prevent any infraction of the Neutrality Laws on the New Brunswick border.

MISSION TO RICHMOND.

Several weeks after my return from New Brunswick, I was requested by the President to come to Washington. On reporting to him, he said, "Doctor, I want you to go to Richmond, and endeavour to obtain the consent of the confederate authorities to treat our colored soldiers, now prisoners in their hands, as prisoners of war subject to exchange. As you are a Canadian, you will have more influence than any one I can think of," adding, "Of course you go simply as a friend of the colored race, and entirely on your own hook. You will be carried to the front, and turned loose to find your way to Richmond as best you can."

BETWEEN THE TWO ARMIES.

On the following day I reached the confederate lines. After perceiving a rebel soldier, I waved a handkerchief and approached him. When within several yards of him, he ordered me to halt, and asked who I was, and where from. Having satisfied him, he led me to his commander, who forwarded me to General Lee's headquarters.

INTERVIEW WITH GENERAL R. E. LEE.

I was taken into a large room, where there were many officers in uniform, some writing, others examining maps and in conversation. The officer with me announced my name, when an elderly gentleman approached me, saying, " I am General Lee; I am told you desire to go to Richmond. What is the business that takes you there?" This was said in a quiet, gentlemanly manner, which, together with his form and bearing, favorably impressed me. I regretted that so noble a man should be engaged in so unrighteous a cause. He listened respectfully to what I had to say, and then directed an officer to accompany me to Richmond.

INTERVIEW WITH JEFFERSON DAVIS AND SECRETARY BENJAMIN.

On the day following I was introduced to Mr. Benjamin. On being brought face to face with him my impression was, here is a smooth, oily, cunning, treacherous and deceitful man. He asked me to be seated and, seating himself, said, " Please state your business with the Government." While I was talking a door opened behind me and some person quietly entered the room and appeared to be listening to my intercession for the colored soldiers. When I had concluded, Mr. Benjamin said, " We cannot for one minute entertain such a proposition, and Lincoln knew it before you left Washington." At this point a pale, thin, bilious-looking man approached me and in a quick, nervous voice said, "Tell Mr. Lincoln that we will not accord the right of exchange to our fugitive slaves whom he has armed and sent out to assasinate us. We will treat every colored soldier we capture as a fugitive slave. It is useless to discuss this matter." Jefferson Davis (for it was he who had spoken) had changed greatly in appearance since I first saw him in 1850. He was much thinner, and had a careworn look. He spoke slowly, but the tone indicated bitterness and hate towards the North. Early next morning I was conveyed to the outposts opposite Fortress Monroe, and from thence to Washington.

RETURN TO WASHINGTON.

Mr. Lincoln cordially welcomed me back and expressed his gratitude for my services. When I informed him of the result of my mission he said, " Well, I did not expect any other result; if that is their determination we shall have to wait until they become more reasonable. It's bad for our colored boys. They must take care and not get captured." During my stay in Washington I was the guest of Mr. Lincoln and enjoyed many opportunities for studying the character of this extraordinary man.

MR. LINCOLN'S PATIENCE AND JUSTICE.

Many complaints had reached the President of the disloyalty of two prominent federal officers of the civil service in Baltimore. The President wrote to me as follows:—" I am in doubt as to the justice of the complaints made against them. Will you, please, satisfy yourself as to the matter, and inform me? Take sufficient time to be well satisfied."

Both of the officials were found to be traitors, using their official position to injure the government that fed them. Both made their escape to the confederacy, and to my chagrin the President expressed himself as *glad* that he was well rid of them.

PERSECUTION OF JOSHUA R. GIDDINGS.

The cruel and unnecessary arrest of the Hon. Joshua R. Giddings, Consul-General of the United States, at Montreal, for the alleged connivance at the kidnapping of one Redpath, was incited by the Confederate agents. Redpath had fled to Canada to escape punishment for murder committed during the draft riots in New York. A United States detective followed Redpath to Montreal, and arrested him. He was ironed, placed in a close carriage, and driven to the depot, where he was guarded by an assistant, while the detective went to the United States Consulate, and told Mr. Giddings that he had arrested a man charged with murder in New York : that he had complied with the requirements of the extradition treaty, and requested Mr. Giddings to give him a letter to General Dix, advising compensation for the services of an assistant to convey Redpath to New York. Mr. Giddings, without ascertaining (for which he was in fault) whether all the formalities of the extradition treaty had been complied with, gave the detective a note to General Dix, in which he simply requested the General to remunerate the detective for the service of an assistant.

When the detective reached New York with his prisoner, Redpath obtained legal assistance, . the result of which was, that the Canadian authorities demanded the return of Redpath to Canada. He was brought back and liberated. Then the Southern agents in Montreal took charge of this murderer, and induced him to prosecute Mr. Giddings. This was done to gratify their feelings of hatred toward a man who had for thirty years fought for the cause of human freedom.

HIS ARREST.

Mr. Giddings was arrested on Sunday evening, while dining at the house of a friend. The arrest was made on a day and at an hour when it was hoped he would be unable to obtain bail, and consequently would have to lie in jail over night. Two prominent and wealthy citizens of Montreal, Harrison Stephens and Ira Gould, gave bonds for *thirty thousand dollars* for Mr. Giddings's appearance at the trial of the cause. Thus his enemies were baulked in their despicable attempt to throw an innocent old man into prison. Mr. Giddings was in poor health at the time this outrage was perpetrated; and he fretted and grieved over it continually.

After the rebel agents had used Redpath for their purpose, they cast him off. I concluded it was a propitious time to rid Mr. Giddings of Redpath and this vindictive persecution. I found the miserable creature, after considerable search, and prevailed upon him to withdraw the suit. He confessed that the Confederate agents in Montreal had instigated him to bring the action against Mr. Giddings. The anxiety and annoyance incident to this persecution hastened the death of this noble old standard-bearer of liberty.

In reference to this trouble, Mr. Giddings sent me the following letter from his home in Ohio, where he had gone for a brief rest :—

From the Hon. Joshua R. Giddings.

My very dear friend,—How can I ever repay you for this great act of friendship? That miserable wretch Redpath is not so

much to blame as Jacob Thompson, whose wicked brain concocted
the persecution, and used Redpath as his instrument of torture.
I am in constant dread that you will be assassinated by these
rebel mercenaries, who are capable of any crime.   Heaven protect you, my dear friend.

Yours devotedly,

Joshua R. Giddings

Ashtabula, Ohio, April 16th, 1864.

DEATH OF MR. GIDDINGS.

He died suddenly while amusing himself with a
game of billiards in the St. Lawrence Hall.

The Montreal *Daily Witness* of that time, in
speaking of the death of Mr. Giddings, said :

"One of the few men of any generation who are an object of
attention to millions, has just passed away from among us, full
of years and of the respect of all who appreciate unwavering
principle and courageous perseverance.   Mr. Giddings was quite
convinced of his dissolution on Saturday last, when he handed
to Dr. A. M. Ross, of this city, letters addressed to several officers of the government, that to Mr. Lincoln being very affectionate.   That evening he spoke of a presentiment that impressed
him that his death was near, and added that he had no fear of
death.   During the week he received from Mr. Secretary Chase
a request that he would prepare an essay on the right of citizens
to recover from the Government damages for property destroyed
in war.   He wrote one paper taking strong grounds against the
acknowledgment of such claims.   This paper he requested Dr.
Ross to read yesterday morning, that he might correct it, and
see that the infirmities of age were not visible in it."

EFFORTS TO AWAKEN KINDLY FEELINGS IN CANADA
TOWARD THE UNITED STATES.

While engaged in circulating information as to the objects and purposes of the U. S. Government in the conduct of the war, and to remove prejudice and awaken kindly feelings towards the United States, I was subjected to the vilest abuse from confederate agents and their Canadian abettors. My life was often threatened, and a newspaper published in Montreal in the interest of the slaveholders, persistently assailed me and incited the enemies of freedom to acts of personal violence. I was usually referred to as the "nigger thief," " damned Yankee," or other expressive names.

When the enemies of freedom had succeeded in hounding Mr. Giddings to death, they opened their floodgates of abuse and slander upon me. So outrageous did their conduct become at last, that as an act of simple justice, the following was presented to me by the Mayor of Montreal, signed by distinguished Canadians of different religious and political creeds:

"The undersigned citizens of Montreal cheerfully bear testimony to the honorable and upright character and gentlemanly deportment of Dr. Alexander M. Ross, of this city."
Signed by the Honorable J. L. Beaudry, Mayor of Montreal ; Hon. Thomas D'Arcy McGee, M.P. ; Hon. George E. Cartier, Ex-Prime Minister of Canada ; Hon. Luther H. Holton, Minister

of Finance ; Hon. Charles S. Rodier, Ex-Mayor of Montreal ;
William Molson, Esq., President Molson's Bank, and Harrison
Stephens, Ira Gould and Edwin Atwater, Esqs., the most promi-
nent and wealthy commercial men of the city.

FAVORITE REBEL RESORT.

During the Slaveholders' rebellion, the Donagana
Hotel, Montreal, was the favorite resort of rebel
emissarries of both sexes.   Here I frequently saw
Col. Magruder, Bennet Young, Dr. Harold, Dr. Black-
burn, Jacob Thompson, " Mrs. Williams," " Belle
Brunette," and many others of rebel proclivities.
Jacob Thompson (formerly a member of Buchanan's
cabinet) was a commissioner of the Confederacy, and
had charge of the rebel funds in Canada.

SOUTHERN SCHEMES.

With Jacob Thompson, the rebel commissioner, I
formed an acquaintance and found him an intelligent and agreeable man of ultra democratic views.
He frankly told me that the Confederate scheme
was much broader and more comprehensive than
was generally known.   He said, in substance, that
when their (the rebel) independence was established, that a scheme of annexation by peaceful or
forcible means would be inaugurated, by which
Mexico and the Central and South-American Re-
publics would be annexed to the Confederacy, thus
forming an immense Empire " with human slavery

for its base." That, finally, this Confederacy would become so powerful as to overshadow the Free States and compel them to unite with their Slave Empire. Such was the infernal scheme, as unfolded to me by Jacob Thompson, who spoke of it as one of the certainties of the future. What a blessing to the world that their barbarous scheme was crushed by the armies of freedom.

WITH THE ARMY OF THE POTOMAC.

On several occasions, during the progress of the war, I visited the army of the Potomac, and witnessed reviews of tens of thousands of soldiers. I felt that the spirit of John Brown was looking on the mighty hosts with gratifying approval and delight, as the Union soldiers marched proudly in review singing the John Brown song; and as regiment after regiment caught up the inspiring words, the air for miles around was filled with the shout, that " John Brown's soul through the world is marching on," I felt that " John Brown's soul not a higher joy could crave " than the success of the armies of freedom in their contest with the slaveholders.

STEPS TOWARD EMANCIPATION.

The following Acts and Proclamations illustrate the progressive steps by which, in the end, complete emancipation was reached :—

J

Attention is hereby called to an Act of Congress, entitled
" An Act to make an additional article of war," approved March
13, 1862, and which Act is in the words and figures following :—
*Be it enacted by the Senate and House of Representatives of the
United States of America in Congress assembled :* That hereafter
the following shall be promulgated as an additional article of
war, for the government of the army of the United States, and
shall be obeyed and observed as such :

Article. All officers or persons in the military or naval service
of the United States are prohibited from employing any of the
forces under their respective commands for the purpose of returning fugitives from service of labor, who may have escaped
from any persons to whom such labor is claimed to be due, and
any officer who shall be found guilty by a court-martial of violating this article, shall be dismissed from the service.

SEC. 2. *And be it further enacted,* That this Act shall take effect
from and after its passage.

Also, to the ninth and tenth sections of an Act entitled, " An
Act to suppress insurrection, to punish treason and rebellion, to
seize and confiscate the property of rebels, and for other purposes," approved July 17, 1862, and which sections are in the
words and figures following :

SEC. 9. *And be it further enacted,* That all slaves of persons who
shall hereafter be engaged in rebellion against the Government
of the United States, or who shall in any way give aid or comfort thereto, escaping from such persons, and taking refuge
within the lines of the army ; and all slaves captured from such
persons, or deserted by them, and coming under the control of
the Government of the United States ; and all slaves of such persons found on (or being within) any place occupied by rebel
forces, and afterward occupied by the forces of the United States,
shall be deemed captives of war, and shall be forever free of their
servitude, and not again held as slaves.

SEC. 10. *And be it further enacted,* That no slave escaping into
any State, territory, or the District of Columbia, from any of
the States, shall be delivered up, or in any way impeded or hin-

dered of his liberty, except for crime or some offence against the laws, unless the person claiming said fugitive shall first make oath that the person to whom the labor or service of such fugitive is alleged to be due, is his lawful owner, and has not been in arms against the United States in the present rebellion, nor in any way given aid and comfort thereto ; and no person engaged in the military or naval service of the United States shall, under any pretence whatsoever, assume to decide on the validity of the claim of any person to the service or labor of any other person, or surrender up any such person to the claimant, on pain of being dismissed from the service.

THE EMANCIPATION PROCLAMATION.

By the President of the United States of America.

Whereas, on the twenty-second day of September, in the year of our Lord one thousand eight hundred and sixty-two, a Proclamation was issued by the President of the United States, containing, among other things, the following, to wit :

"That on the first day of January, in the year of our Lord one thousand eight hundred and sixty-three, all persons held as slaves within any State, or designated part of a State, the people whereof shall then be in rebellion against the United States, shall be then, thenceforth, and *forever free*, and the Executive Government of the United States, including the military and naval authorities thereof, will recognize and maintain the freedom of such persons, and will do no act or acts to repress such persons, or any of them, in any efforts they make for their actual freedom.

"That the Executive will, on the first day of January aforesaid, by proclamation, designate the States and parts of States, if any, in which the people thereof respectively shall then be in rebellion against the United States, and the fact that any State, or the people thereof, shall on that day be in good faith represented in the Congress of the United States by members chosen thereto at elections wherein a majority of the qualified voters of such State shall have participated, shall, in the absence of strong countervailing testimony, be deemed conclusive evidence that such State and the people thereof are not then in rebellion against the United States."

Now, therefore, I, ABRAHAM LINCOLN, President of the United States, by virtue of the power in me vested as Commander-in-Chief of the Army and Navy of the United States in time of actual armed Rebellion against the authority and government of the United States, and as a fit and necessary war measure for suppressing said Rebellion, do, on this first day of January, in the year of our Lord one thousand eight hundred and sixty-three, and in accordance with my purpose so to do, publicly proclaim for the full period of one hundred days from the day of the first above-mentioned order, and designate, as the States and part of States wherein the people thereof respectively are this day in rebellion against the United States, the following, to wit : ARKANSAS, TEXAS, LOUISIANA (except the Parishes of St. Bernard, Palquemines, Jefferson, St. John, St. Charles, St. James, Ascension, Assumption, Terre Bonne, Lafourche, St. Mary, St. Martin, an Orleans, (including the City of Orleans), MISSISSIPPI, ALABAMA, FLORIDA, GEORGIA, SOUTH CAROLINA, NORTH CAROLINA, and VIRGINIA (except the forty-eight counties designated as West Virginia, and also the counties of Berkeley, Acconac, Northampton, Elizabeth City, York, Princess Ann, and Norfolk, including the cities of Norfolk and Portsmouth), and which excepted parts are, for the present, left precisely as if this Proclamation had not been issued.

And by virtue of the power, and for the purpose aforesaid, I do order and declare that *all persons held as slaves* within said designated States and parts of States *are and henceforward* SHALL BE FREE! and that the Executive Government of the United States, including the Military and Naval authorities thereof, will recognize and maintain the freedom of said persons.

And I hereby enjoin upon the people so declared to be free, to abstain from all violence, unless in necessary self-defence, and I recommend to them that in all cases, when allowed, they labor faithfully for reasonable wages.

And I further declare and make known that such persons of suitable condition will be received into the armed service of the United States to garrison forts, positions, stations, and other places, and to man vessels of all sorts in said service.

And upon this act, sincerely believed to be an act of justice, warranted by the Constitution, upon military necessity, I invoke the considerate judgment of mankind and the gracious favour of Almighty God.

In testimony whereof I have hereunto set my name, and caused the seal of the United States to be affixed.

Done at the City of Washington, this first day of January, in the year of our Lord one thousand eight [L.S.] hundred and sixty-three, and of the Independence of the United States the eighty-seventh.

ABRAHAM LINCOLN.

By the President.—WILLIAM H. SEWARD,
Secretary of State.

RATIFICATION OF THE CONSTITUTIONAL AMENDMENT AND PROCLAMATION OF FREEDOM.

On the 18th of December, 1865, Secretary Seward officially announced to the world the glad tidings that the Constitutional Amendment abolished slavery and involuntary servitude throughout the United States, or any place subject to their jurisdiction, as follows :—

To all to whom these presents may come, Greeting:

Know ye, That whereas the Congress of the United States, on the 1st of February last, passed a resolution, which is in words following, namely :

"A resolution submitting to the Legislatures of the several States a proposition to amend the Constitution of the United States."

Resolved. By the Senate and House of Representatives of the United States of America in Congress assembled, two-thirds of both Houses concurring that the following article be proposed to the Legislatures of the several States as an Amendment to the Constitution of the United States, which, when ratified by three-fourths of said Legislatures, shall be valid to all intents and proposes as a part of said Constitution, namely :

" " Article XIII.

" 'SECTION 1. Neither slavery nor involuntary servitude, except as a punishment for crime, whereof the party shall have been duly convicted, shall exist within the United States, or any place subject to their jurisdiction.

" 'SECTION 2. Congress shall have power to enforce this article, by appropriate legislation.' "

And whereas, It appears from official documents on file of this Department, that the Amendment to the Constitution in the United States proposed as aforesaid, has been ratified by the Legislatures of the States of Illinois, Rhode Island, Michigan, Maryland, New York, West Virginia, Maine, Kansas, Massachusetts, Pennsylvania, Virginia, Ohio, Missouri, Nevada, Indiana, Louisiana, Minnesota, Wisconsin, Vermont, Tennessee, Arkansas, Connecticut, New Hampshire, South Carolina, Alabama, North Carolina, and Georgia, in all 27 States.

And whereas, The whole number of States in the United States is 36.

And whereas, The before specially named States, whose Legislatures have ratified the said proposed Amendment, constitute three-fourths of the whole number of States in the United States ;

Now, therefore, be it known that I, William H. Seward, Secretary of State of the United States, by virtue and in pursuance of the second section of the act of Congress, approved the 20th of April, 1818, entitled "An Act to provide for the publication of the laws of the United States, and for other purposes," do hereby certify that the Amendment aforsaid has become valid to all intents and purposes as a part of the Constitution of the United States.

In testimony whereof, I have hereunto set my hand, and caused the seal of the Department of State to be affixed.

Done at the City of Washington, this 18th day of December, in the year of our Lord 1865, and of the Independence of the United States of America the 90th.

WM. H. SEWARD, Secretary of State.

Thus terminated the great struggle between Freedom and Slavery in the United States.

LAUS DEO.

ON HEARING THE BELLS RING FOR THE CONSTITUTIONAL AMENDMENT ABOLISHING SLAVERY IN THE UNITED STATES.

"It is done!
Clang of bell and roar of gun;
Send the tidings up and down.
How the belfries rock and reel,
How the great guns, peal on peal,
Fling the joy from town to town!

Ring, O bells!
Every stroke exulting tells
Of the burial hour of crime.
Loud and long, that all may hear,
Ring for every listening ear
Of eternity and time!

Let us kneel:
God's own voice is in that peal,
And this spot is holy ground.
Lord forgive us! What are we,
That our eyes this glory see,
That our ears have heard the sound!

Loud and long,
Lift the old, exultant song ;
Sing with Miriam by the sea ;
He has cast the mighty down ;
Horse and rider sink and drown ;
He has triumphed gloriously.

Blotted out !
All within, and all about
Shall a purer life begin ;
Freer breathe the universe
As it rolls its heavy curse
On the dead and buried sin.

Ring and swing
Bells of joy ! on morning's wing
Send the song of praise abroad ;
With a sound of broken chains,
Tell the nations that He reigns
Who alone is Lord and God ! "

WHITTIER, *the Quaker Poet.*

Complimentary letters from President Lincoln, Governor Fenton and Charles Sumner.

From President Lincoln :—

EXECUTIVE MANSION, WASHINGTON,
March 9th, 1865.

To Dr. A. M. Ross, Montreal :

DEAR DOCTOR :—The terrible war is rapidly approaching its end.   I write now to tender you my warmest thanks for the many valuable services you have rendered me since 1861.   Your ability, zeal and fidelity merits and receives my sincere gratitude. * * * Accept my best wishes for your future happiness and prosperity.

Yours sincerely,

A. Lincoln

From Governor Fenton :—

EXECUTIVE DEPARTMENT,
STATE OF NEW YORK.
Albany, April 11th, 1865.

MY DEAR SIR:

On behalf of the loyal people of this State, I thank you for your patriotic services during the war ; your active interest in our cause, I assure you, is highly appreciated.

Yours very truly,
R. E. FENTON,
Governor.

Dr. Ross, Montreal.

From Senator Sumner :—

SENATE CHAMBER, WASHINGTON,
January 31st, 1865.

Dr. A. M. Ross :

MY DEAR FRIEND :— * * * You deserve the thanks of this nation for your generous and patriotic labors in our behalf. * * * You have done a noble work, and I congratulate you on your record. May God bless you, is the prayer of your friend,

Charles Sumner

MEXICO.

When the slaveholders' rebellion broke out the Emperor Napoleon seized the occasion to invade Mexico and overthrow the Republic. He took this step, no doubt, in confident expectation that the slaveholders would succeed in establishing an empire on this continent. When, after four years of terrible war, the U. S. Government crushed the rebellion and established its supremacy over the whole country, the Mexican people made a determined effort to drive out their oppressors. I then offered my services as surgeon to President Juarez, who promptly accepted my offer as follows:

MEXICAN LEGATION, WASHINGTON, August 1st, 1865.

DR. ALEXANDER M. ROSS, Montreal.

DEAR SIR,—I am instructed by President Juarez to accept your services as Army Surgeon, and to convey to you his high appreciation of your patriotic offer in this the darkest hour in the history of Mexico. With sentiments of high esteem, I remain,
Yours faithfully,
M. ROMERO,
Mexican Minister.

Many of my friends urged me not to risk my life in a struggle so unequal as that between the French Empire and poor down-trodden Mexico.

WENDELL PHILLIPS wrote me :—" In the present condition of affairs in Mexico, it is time, perhaps life, thrown away to endeavor to aid the Republicans. Take my advice, refrain from going —your wish to aid an oppressed race will, I am sure, find ample and honorable field and more effectual channels in our still distracted country. Save yourself for that, there is more to be done here than in Mexico in your day or mine, I am sure."

HORACE GREELEY wrote :—" Max. will root out Juarez and the Republicans, to be rooted out himself in turn, by the next move of revolution, and whether by the Clerical or Liberal party I cannot now guess. Max. will stand as long as Napoleon sends him troops and fools lend him money ; when these resources fail, he goes down. It is not yet time for you to go to Mexico to help the Republic."

WILLIAM CULLEN BRYANT wrote :—" I see by the *Tribune* that you are going to Mexico to help the Republicans. While I cannot but applaud your motives, I fear your life will be sacrificed in the unequal struggle. The pride of Napoleon is at stake, and the wretched demoralized Mexicans are no match for the legions of France. I hope you will not place your life in jeopardy for such a worthless race as the modern Mexicans appear to be."

In the meantime Mr. Seward, the U. S. Secretary of State, had informed the French Government that the invasion of Mexico, and the establishing of a government there inimical to the Republic, could not be viewed with friendly feelings by the U. S. The French army returned to France, and in a few months the Empire of Mexico collapsed, its Emperor, poor Max. the tool of Napoleon, was executed, and Juarez became President of the Republic of Mexico.

PRESIDENT JUAREZ OF MEXICO.

Like President Lincoln, Benito Juarez was the leader of his people in the hour of their greatest

stress and, like him, died in the Presidential office.
In many ways this Indian of Oajaca merits all the
floral, oratorical, and other tributes which have
just been again, in annual commemoration, bestowed
at his tomb. Whether as Governor of his native
State, exile under Santa Anna's dictatorship, Minister under Alvarez, President of the Supreme Court,
the relentless opponent of Miramon and the Clerical Party, or as the unfaltering head of the republic
against French domination and Maximilian, Juarez
was always of, and for, and with the people. Marks
of his handiwork and that of his party are seen in
the famous Constitution of 1857, under which it
was possible to destroy the class legislation that
had prevailed in the interest of the ecclesiastical
and military parties, and to give greater freedom
of speech and of the press, and greater political
equality.

NATURAL HISTORY LABORS.

When the dreadful war was over, and the fight
for the Union ended by the downfall of the Confederacy and the emancipation of the slaves, I made my
home in Toronto, and began a labor which I had
often contemplated with pleasurable feelings and
promised myself, when my labor as an abolitionist
was completed.

I have mentioned in the first pages of these memoirs that in my boyhood I was extremely fond of

natural history studies, and imbibed a desire to perform a labor for my own country, which had never before been attempted. This labor was the collection and classification of the *Flora* and *Fauna* of Canada. For several years I pursued this labor with all my energy, and with what success I leave to others more competent to judge, who make the testimonial record of my natural history labors. (See Appendix).

CHAPTER VII.

1851 - 1885.

Reminiscences :—Second Visit to Washington—Andrew Johnson in the Senate—Inauguration of President Lincoln—The
President's Prospects—Of Abraham Lincoln, Horace Greeley,
Lucretia Mott, the Poet Longfellow, William Lloyd Garrison,
Wendell Phillips, Joshua R. Giddings, William Lyon Mackenzie, Ralph Waldo Emerson, R. T. Trall, J. Emery Coderre, Senator Ben. Wade, Gen. Garibaldi, Gen. Houston,
Gen. Walker—Inter-State Slave Trade—Republican Refugees
in New York—Gerrit Smith.

SECOND VISIT TO WASHINGTON.

I WAS in Washington during the first week in
March, 1861, and occupied a seat in the Reporters'
Gallery of the Senate during the exciting debate
which took place on the night of the 3rd of March.
A resolution which had previously passed by a two-
thirds vote was the subject of debate. The resolution read as follows :—

" That no amendment shall be made to the Constitution
which will authorize or give Congress power to abolish or interfere within any State with the domestic institutions thereof,
including that of persons held to labor or servitude by the laws
of said State."

It was quite evident that the Senate was not disposed to adopt the Crittenden resolutions or any

other denying the right of secession. It was obvious from the speeches I heard that the utmost that could be extorted from the Senators was the passage of the above resolution, and even that appeared doubtful. Very few Senators were willing to place themselves on record as affirming the right of Congress to interfere with slavery in the States, but three-fourths of them were anxious to see it defeated,—the Republicans, because it looked like compromise; the Democrats, because it had a tendency to strengthen the Union sentiment in the democratic States.

The first thing that struck me, as I took my seat in the Reporters' Gallery, from which I had an excellent view of all the Senators, was the great change in the *personnel* of the Senate since I first visited it, in 1850-51. On looking down upon the group I observed several that occupied seats there twelve years before, but the "giants" were gone—Webster, Clay, Calhoun and Benton were no more, and their places were occupied by a very different type of men. The men from the North I could easily perceive to be men of much power, stern and inflexible in principle,—there was Sumner, Seward, Chase, Fessenden, brave "Old Ben Wade," Trumbull and Chandler, the acknowledged leaders of the Republican party. The men from the Slave States were arrogant and domineering, as of old,—there sat Mason, of Virginia, one of the most insolent and overbearing men that slavery produced; Wigfall, of Texas, a brilliant speaker; Jefferson Davis, Clingman, of North Carolina; Yancy, of Florida; John C. Breakenridge, and other men of minor importance and ability. Then there was a third or intervening party, whose mission appeared to be to compromise between the extremes. The head of this party was Stephen Arnold Douglass, the so-called Little Giant of Illinois. He was a man of marked ability, a strong and forcible speaker, patient, firm, and untiring. Senators Crittenden, Doolittle, and Andrew Johnson acted with, rather than followed, Douglass.

The debate on the Revolution waxed hot and furious, all the prominent men taking part in the discussion. The Republican Senators, led by Sumner, and the Secessionists, led by Mason, sought to defeat a vote by proposing amendments, and consumed time by debates and discussions.

The compromise party, led by Douglass, opposed their tactics and sought to bring on a vote. All night. (March 3 and 4), and until six in the morning, the battle raged. Such a scene I shall probably never witness again. Finally, at 6 a.m., March 4th (just six hours before the inauguration of Abraham Lincoln), the resolution passed by 24 to 12, the necessary two-thirds vote. All these compromises and efforts to adjust the slavery question paved the way for the slaveholders' rebellion, the emancipation of the slaves, and the regeneration of the nation.

ANDREW JOHNSON.

It was during this visit to Washington that I first heard Andrew Johnson speak. Mr. Johnson was a self-made man, a natural orator and as courageous a man as ever lived. One of the Southern Senators, during a debate on a Homestead Bill, had the bad taste to twit Johnson of his early trade— that of a tailor. Mr. Johnson's reply was one of the most thrilling bursts of eloquence I ever listened to.

He said: "When, after years of painful struggles to earn a livelihood at my humble trade, with the young wife I had brought from my native place in North Carolina, and the little family which had grown up around us, I was enabled to purchase a small plot of ground in Tennessee and build a cabin upon it which I could call my own, I remember the feeling of triumph and exultation with which we looked upon the poor little shed, and knew that at last we had A HOME OF OUR OWN. And then, long years ago, I made up my mind that, if ever I had the power, every poor man, struggling as I was, should be enabled to obtain a home—should have one spot of earth, however small, one cabin, however rude and scanty, which, in the light of heaven and the face of man, he should be able to call his own."

An ominous rustle in the galleries followed this

K

outburst, but subsided on a growl from Senator Mason. Senator Johnson continued inflicting a severe rebuke on the insolent object of his invective, and finally closing with a magnificent eulogium on the Union. On this, the pent-up feelings of the spectators could no longer be restrained. A tremendous cheer arose. Senator Mason instantly moved that the galleries be cleared. A few hisses were heard—then a stentorian voice shouted, "THREE CHEERS FOR THE UNION!" They were given with a will. Not only did the men cheer and shout, but. the ladies screamed and waved their handkerchiefs. Never since the first meeting of the Senate, did that body endure such an insult. For some minutes the din was overpowering.

"The sergeant-at-arms will clear the galleries!" commanded Senator Mason, fiercely.

It was easier said than done. There were at least five hundred excited men in the galleries. For some moments it was a question whether the Senate would clear the galleries, or the galleries the Senate. But finally the galleries were cleared and the doors locked.

INAUGURATION OF PRESIDENT LINCOLN.

The inauguration of President Lincoln took place on March 4. This was the proudest day of my life, for on this day I witnessed the inauguration of an

honest man, a sincere Republican, a lover of freedom and a lover of his country. Through the kindness of Mr. Sumner I obtained a good point of
elevation, from which I witnessed the interesting
and on this occasion important ceremony.

Most of the leading Secessionists had left for the
South, to begin their work of destruction—supplied
with means, stolen from the general Government, by
the secretaries and officials of the Buchanan administration.

PRESIDENT LINCOLN'S PROSPECTS.

The prospect before Mr. Lincoln was anything
but encouraging. The Slave States were in open
rebellion, and the leading democrats of the Northern
States were in open sympathy with the Southern
rebels. The small regular army of the United
States had been dispersed to far distant territories,
and the ships of the navy were sent to European
waters; the arsenals in the North were empty, and
traitors held positions in every department of the
Government. It was under these circumstances that
President Lincoln entered upon that mighty conflict
between freedom and slavery, between justice and
crime, which resulted in the triumph of liberty and
the overthrow of human slavery in the United
States.

ABRAHAM LINCOLN.

Within a few weeks after the inauguration of Mr. Lincoln, I was introduced to him by Charles Sumner, and the opinion I formed of Mr. Lincoln at that interview, ripened into conviction as I became better acquainted with him, for I met him on several occasions during the war, under varied circumstances, and as I had no personal favors to ask of him, I was in a position to study him from a favorable stand-point. Personally and politically a more honest, generous, straightforward man never lived : and as the great and terrible war raged and progressed he grew in strength and wisdom and noble purpose, until he at last signed the emancipation proclamation, an act of justice which should have been performed three years earlier. But, if he was slow, he acted honestly, according to his best judgment. He was very cautious, slow in making up his mind, but reliable and firm when his decision was made. He was a good judge of men, rarely mistaken in his estimate : being of a kind, generous nature, he was often led to grant favors to undeserving men. In personal appearance, Mr. Lincoln was about six feet two inches in height, tall, thin, rugged, angular and awkward ; his step unmeasured and unprecise ; his feet and hands large, strong and bony : his face, long, thin and rugged ; his head, large, and broad between

the temples; his eyes, blueish gray—beamed with
kindness and wisdom: his language, well chosen
and forcible, and always accompanied by appropriate gesture.

HORACE GREELEY.

I was in New York shortly after the presidential
contest of 1872, and called upon Mr. Greeley.
Clasping my hand in his, he said, pathetically, " I
am glad to see you, my dear friend, for the end is
near; I cannot stand this strain much longer, it is
killing me by inches." I was shocked and pained
by his appearance, all the old-time cheerfulness was
gone, his countenance haggard and distressed, his
eye had a hopeless and sad look. "For twenty
days," he said, " I have not slept: I shall never sleep
again, I pray for death." He trembled like a leaf:
his beautiful hands were pressed against his dome-
like brow, as if he were suffering intense pain. His
skin had a pale, sickly appearance. I did all I could
to cheer him up, but his destiny was on him: he
could talk of nothing else but death, which he said
he longed for and prayed for. His pitiful condition
reminded me of his great grief years before, when
in speaking of the death of his little son Pickie, he
said to me (in substance): " If I felt sure that I
should know and be with Pickie in the other world,
I would prefer to die now, for life cannot efface the
sorrow I feel." I never shall forget the scene, the

most distressing I ever witnessed. A great mind
wrecked and stranded. When I bade him good-
bye, he said, " My good friend, I shall never see you
again in this world ; the end is near." From that
horrible scene I retired as if stunned by the approach of some terrible calamity. In less than
three weeks from that day he died. He was a
precious man. When in good health his face was
shining and soul-lighted ; beaming with kindness
and goodwill. Intellectually, he was a giant, a king
above princes ; his brain was fine, large, and tire-
less. He loved and was loved by the common
people ; he was their friend and counsellor. He
was one of the ablest minds, one of the purest
characters, one of the hardest workers, and the
most widely useful man of his generation. Of
Horace Greeley it may be said, " The common people
heard him gladly."

CHARLES SUMNER.

From New York I journeyed to Washington, and
there met many old friends and acquaintances of
by-gone years. One of my first visits was to the
beautiful home of Charles Sumner—there I found
him, among his books, pictures and lofty thoughts,
much changed in appearance since I first saw him.
He was older, grander, more stately and gracious.
His noble countenance was marked and scarred by
many conflicts with the slave power. His voice

had the same grand tone as of old, but softened somewhat by time. His hair was well mixed with grey, and his face bore the impression of internal pain and suffering. He told me that at times he suffered the most acute agony in the region of his heart. He had many sorrows that the world knew nothing of, and his heart was heavy with the fierce strife of a generation.

Mr. Sumner was a man of rare and extensive culture and accomplishments, but, better than all, he was an honorable man, a man of noble impulses and lofty aims. He was an honest, consistent and virtuous statesman, and one of the main pillars and support of the Republic during the slaveholders' rebellion. Mr. Lincoln honored, loved and trusted him implicitly. The last days of Mr. Sumner were embittered by many troubles. His own beloved State had judged him unkindly, and, as he felt, unjustly, while the conduct of President Grant toward him was not only cruel but base. I spent several hours in his company on this occasion, talking over the great struggle for freedom and the future of the Republic, and when I left he accompanied me to my hotel and bid me farewell.

LUCRETIA MOTT.

On my return homeward from Washington, I stopped for a day in Philadelphia, to visit my dear friend, the sweet Lucretia Mott. Wending my way through the quiet city, I went to " Roadside," the serene home of this gifted and pure woman. She received me, as always, with a loving smile and sincerely kind welcome. She was nearly eighty years old, but her face still bore the charm of delicate and regular features. She was dressed, as usual, in a simple dove-colored Quaker dress, with a pure white muslin handkerchief crossed at the neck. On her head was a pretty little Quaker cap. She led me to a seat in the plain but extremely neat little sitting-room, and expressed her pleasure at meeting me again. During this visit, which lasted for two hours, she never ceased her knitting, except for a moment, at times when deeply interested. Her intellect was clear and her memory so retentive that she recalled many incidents that occurred sixty years before, and seemed never at a loss for a name or date. She still retained her brilliancy of mind and sympathy of nature as of old. If ever any woman inherited the earth, it was this blessed Quaker woman. Blessed, indeed, for the example of her industrious life, for the influence of her gentle teachings, for the honor that she conferred upon all womanhood. No misrepresentation or abuse, for she had both, ever deterred her from doing her duty. Her pure, sweet life made Lucretia Mott queen of the realm of humanity.

Mrs. Mott was small and slight of stature; her forehead broad and high; her eyes, dark blue, beamed with kindness and goodness; her hands small, delicate, and finely shaped. Her home was the abode of peace and harmony. Mrs. Mott lived to be 87 years old, retaining all her faculties to the last. She died as she had lived—in peace.

RALPH WALDO EMERSON.

From my early manhood I had been a diligent reader and warm admirer of Ralph Waldo Emerson. I had also corresponded with him for several years, but had never met him or seen him. I had received frequent and pressing invitations to visit him, but could not find time; finally there came a letter so urgent and pressing that I decided to gratify my long-felt desire to meet this god-like man.

INVITATION FROM CONCORD.

" My Dear Dr. Ross,—* * * I hope you will make your first visit to Massachusetts and Concord, the rather that my family and friends are finding that I am losing my mother tongue and have to look to them for words. Perhaps that is the reason I have not written to the dear little Garibaldi. Let me have good news of you soon, and bring them yourself. Please let your visit cover the last Saturday of the month, so that I may make you acquainted with some very good people in our Saturday Club, which dines on the last Saturday of every month. With best hope and affectionate regards."

R. W. Emerson

VISIT RALPH WALDO EMERSON.

A few days after the receipt of the above letter, I left Canada for Concord. On my arrival there I found Mr. Emerson at the depôt, waiting to receive me. I recognized him at once from a photograph I had seen, but no picture can give the impression of his personal presence. He came toward me with his hand extended, saying, "You are Dr. Ross." The expression of his countenance was so pure and sincere, his manner so gentle and magnetic, his every act so cordial, that I was charmed with my reception. There was no vigorous or impulsive hand-shaking, but the serene light of cordiality that emanated from his features as he gave me his greeting, and held my hand in a warm and steady clasp, was impressive and made me feel at home with him at once.

He was tall, slender, and somewhat bent with years, his hair grey and thin, his nose long and prominent, his mouth was somewhat large, his lips closed with a firm, interested smile, his eyes were blue, straightforward and honest, and seemed to look at you from out another world; his ears were large and impressed me as being his only connection with the world of sensation. He walked with his head bent slightly forward, and appeared to me to be unconscious of what was passing around him.

He partook of food in a methodical manner, as if in philosophic obedience to the need of eating. His features were sharply cut and very intellectual; his voice had a strange power which affected me more than any other voice I had ever heard—it was a purely intellectual voice, the music of spiritual utterance; it was a clear, keen, penetrating, sweet voice, a fit medium for the utterances of his commanding mind. At times it had an impersonal character, as though a spirit was speaking through him.

My visit was on Friday, and the evening was spent in his library, where we (or rather he, for I was a willing and charmed listener) talked until midnight, when I was shown to my bedroom, the same, I understood, as occupied by John Brown, Mrs. Stowe, Wm. Lloyd Garrison, Thoreau, and many other kindred spirits. On the morrow (Saturday) we dined at the Saturday Club, where I met Mr. Longfellow, whom I had known previously, and who said: "Do not fail to call upon me before you return home." I was introduced to many excellent persons whose names I now forget. I was treated with marked kindness and consideration by all, and at the table was seated with Mr. Emerson on my right and Mr. Longfellow on my left.

In my cherished interviews with Mr. Emerson, I was made to realize the superiority of the spiritual over the physical part of man. It was only by personal intercourse with him that the singular force, sweetness, elevation, originality, and comprehensiveness of his nature could be appreciated.

I parted from him with feelings of sincere regret, but while I live I shall never lose the spiritual peace that emanated from the presence of this godlike man.

DEATH OF EMERSON.

His health had been breaking down for a year or more past, while his consciousness that his memory was giving way, led him to seek seclusion. The funeral of his old friend Longfellow, however, called him to Cambridge, and despite the inclemency of the day, he followed the procession to Mount Auburn, and stood at the verge of the grave. His feebleness attracted attention and aroused fears that it could not be long before his last day must also come. It has come, and the scholarship of the world mourns the death of Ralph Waldo Emerson. Emerson was the supreme representation of the highest type of manhood. Simplicity and purity were the bases of his character and thought, his temperance was like his religion, unconscious of itself—natural. He was a white soul—the purest and sweetest of our time.

VISIT THE POET LONGFELLOW.

From Concord I went to Cambridge to visit Mr. Longfellow. I was shown into his library, a fine

large room, the floor of which was covered with a
rich Persian carpet, and the walls panelled with
dark oak. At one end of the room stood lofty
oaken book-cases, framed in drapery of crimson
cloth. Easy chairs were scattered about, giving the
room an air of comfort. In the centre of the room
was a large table littered with books, pamphlets, and
papers. I had time to make the above observations
when Mr. Longfellow entered and greeted me warmly. He was a very different personage from Mr.
Emerson. He impressed me as a cultivated English
gentleman of fortune and ease. His dress was very
becoming. His hair was fine, and as white as snow.
His skin had the peculiar pallor that comes of old
age. He was active in his movements and very
talkative, making many enquiries about Canada.
Mr. Longfellow had a fine head, the forehead was
broad, indicating intellectual power. His eyes were
beautiful, large and lustrous, from which the fire of
youth seemed not to have fled. He spoke in terms
of love of Emerson, saying: " he (Emerson) is a full
soul." Of Charles Sumner he also spoke with re-
verent feeling, and showed me a fine bust of him.
When I rose to take leave, he said, "I must show
you the great tree," and, while he stood underneath
its giant arms, admiring the majestic elms of which
he was so proud, he gave me a brief history of the
old mansion which he occupied, which was once the
headquarters of General Washington during the
revolutionary war.

VISIT THE QUAKER POET.

From Cambridge I went to Amesbury, the home of dear Whittier, and was delighted to find him in excellent health, and the same warm-hearted, sincere shy man as of old. He said he wrote but little now, as he felt the weight of his years. He seemed pleased to converse upon the Anti-slavery contest and the exciting incidents of that period. In speaking of John Brown, he said, " I regret that I never saw him. In my little trifle, 'John Brown of Osawatomie,' 1 allude to his act of kissing a negro child, which I am told is apocryphal, a poetical license." In speaking of Emerson, he said, " Of all Americans, living or dead, he is *the only one* that will be remembered one thousand years hence. Emerson will take rank with Plato and Socrates." Of Lucretia Mott and Mr. Garrison he spoke in terms of loving kindness, adding, " Thee should not return home without seeing Mr. Garrison, he often speaks of thee and thy labors in words of praise."

CALL UPON WM. LLOYD GARRISON.

Bidding the good Quaker farewell, I returned to Boston, and called upon Mr. Garrison, whom I found in poor health, but mentally he was as active and industrious as ever. He was a remarkable man, the most determined, brave, persistent enemy that ever assaulted the institution of slavery He did not possess a particle of the spirit of compromise. He never for one hour relaxed his warfare, until his object was accomplished, and slavery abolished. In speaking of the great event, he said, " neither you nor I, nor any other abolitionist expected to live to see this unparalleled transformation—the entire four millions of slaves set free from their bonds and raised to the rights of American citizenship."

While in Boston I had the good fortune to meet Lydia Maria Child ; she was very old and feeble, but cheerful and happy. Her life and labors were drawing to a close, but her mind was active with the stirring events of by-gone years, on which she loved to dwell, recalling many interesting occurrences of anti-slavery days.

WENDELL PHILLIPS.

My good frien l Wendell Phillips was absent from the State at the time, which was a matter of deep regret to me, as I longed once more to meet this fearless and eloquent advocate of freedom.

With Mr. Phillips I had been on terms of warm personal friendship since 1856, and had always found him a never-failing tower of strength, courage and inspiration He was a faithful friend and wise counsellor; a natural orator, agitator and reformer; an honest, fearless and uncompromising

opponent of tyranny and injustice, whereever it
existed.

    " He had his faults, they said, but they were faults
    Of head and not of heart—his sharp assaults,
    Flung seeming heedless from his quivering bow,
    And heedless striking either friend or for,
    Were launched with eyes that saw not foe or friend,
    But only, shining far, some goal or end,

    " That, compassed once, should bring God's saving grace
    To purge and purify the human race.
    The measure that he meted out he took,
    And blow for blow received without a look,
    Without a sign of conscious hurt or hate,
    To stir the tranquil calmness of his State.

    " Born on the heights and in the purple bred,
    He chose to walk the lonely ways instead,
    That he might lift the wretched and defend
    The rights of those who languished for a friend.
    So, many years he spent in listening
    To these sad cries of wrong and suffering.

    " It was not strange, perhaps, he thought the right
    Could never live upon the easeful height,
    Nor strange, indeed, that slow suspicion grew
    Against the class whose tyrannies he knew.
    But, bitter and unsparing as his speech,
    He meant alone the evil deed to reach.

    " No hate of persons winged his fiery shaft,
    He had no hatred but for cruel craft
    And selfish measurements, where human Might
    Bore down upon the immemorial Right.
    Ev'n while he dealt his bitterest blows at power,
    No bitterness that high heart could devour."

DR. R. T. TRALL.

Dr. Trall was one of the most gifted men in America. He was quite a young man when I formed his acquaintance. I was attracted to him by his earnest appeals for medical reform. To him we are indebted—more than to any other man—for our present knowledge of hydropathy and hygienic therapeutics. He was an able and effective writer in the cause of medical reform. Many of his works on hydropathy and hygiene have become class-books, and surpass all others in clear, precise, and faithful delineation of hygeo-therapeutics. He founded and organized the first hygeio-therapeutic college in the world, of which he remained the active head until his death. His students and graduates have gone forth as ministering angels to afflicted humanity. The present successful College of Hygienic Physicians and Surgeons of St. Louis is the product of his teachings and labors.

DR. J. EMERY CODERRE.

My staunch and most faithful supporter and friend, during my warfare against compulsory vaccination in Montreal (in 1885), was Dr. J. Emery Coderre, Professor of the Medical Faculty of Victoria University, and physician to the Hotel Dieu. Dr. Coderre was a veteran in the cause of human

L

freedom.   In 1837, he labored with persistent fidelity under Papineau and Dr. Wolfred Nelson, against the tyrannical government of that day.   He was arrested and imprisoned on a charge of high treason. Dr. Coderre possessed a most kind and gentle disposition, but where the rights and liberties of man were concerned, he was as uncompromising and determined as man could be.   He joined me at a time when everyman's hand in Lower Canada was against me, when the medical profession and the clergy were engaged in circulating the most outrageous slanders and lies against me; when the press, without exception, joined the doctors in pouring out vials of abuse and hate upon me.   This required a high order of courage, backed by pure moral principles—qualities Dr. Coderre possessed in a high degree.   He was a tower of strength to me in a trying time.   A nobler or braver man than Dr. J. Emery Coderre never lived ; he endured persecution, injustice, ostracism, poverty, and want, and died facing his enemies.

SENATOR BEN WADE.

My acquaintance with Benjamin F. Wade dated from 1850–51.   I first met him at the house of Doctor Baily (called " Coventry " by the democrats and slaveholders, because it was the resort of ultra whigs, abolitionists and others opposed to slavery). There have been few distinguished men who, in all their ways, and through all their career, have

been more thoroughly American than Senator Wade.
His sense of justice naturally made him an anti-
slavery man. He was always faithful to his liberal
principles. He was uncompromising in his opposition to slavery. He could not be intimidated or
cajoled. The slaveholders in Congress, who were
accustomed to brow beat and threaten Northern
members of weaker material, found Senator Wade
as firm as a rock, and as brave as a lion. Had it
not been for the treachery of a Kansas Senator,
Andrew Johnson would have been deposed, and
Senator Wade would have succeeded him as President of the U. S.

REPUBLICAN REFUGEES, NEW YORK, 1851.

The failure of their schemes had driven these
ardent republicans to take refuge in America, where
many of them were suffering extreme poverty.

General Garibaldi, late General-in-Chief of the
armies of the Roman Republic, was earning his
bread by daily labor; Gen. Avezzani, late Roman
Minister of War, was engaged in the cigar business;
while a Prussian colonel was selling beer by the
glass; a member of the French Chamber of De-
puties was a cigar vendor; and a French general of
cavalry was trying to sell walking sticks opposite
the Astor House.

Every Sunday night, these refugees from tyranny
met together in a little restaurant, near the Battery,

kept by a late official of the Roman Government.
On some evenings there were as many as thirty
exiles of different nationalities present, but usually
not more than twelve or fifteen ; General Garibaldi
was the central figure of the group—great deference
and respect was always shown him. The principle
theme of conversation was the political condition of
Europe. At these meetings I frequently met Felix
Pyatt, Hugh Forbes, Louis Blanc, Gen. Drouet, ex-
officer of the Imperial Guard of Napoleon, and many
others of less prominence whose names I forget—
among them French Republicans, English Chartists,
Italian Carbonari and German Communists. Nearly
all of these men were occupied in daily labor of
some kind, trying to support their unhappy lives.
Their peculiar dress, manner, language, spirit and
enthusiasm was interesting to me, while their history, sufferings and loneliness enlisted my warmest
sympathy for these brave men, who had endured
so much suffering and sacrifice in the cause of freedom. It was very gratifying to me, that I was pri-
vileged to enjoy their society, and to listen to their
conversations. On several occasions very exciting
scenes occurred. These men were well aware that
their steps were dogged by spies in the pay of
European governments, and strict precaution was
observed to prevent the intrusion of these servants
of despotism. On one occasion, a great uproar was
created by the discovery that a stranger was in the

room, who could not give a satisfactory account of himself. He was finally released, upon the assurance of Col. Forbes that he was all right. But the experience of subsequent years has satisfied me that Col. Forbes himself was a traitor, and the means of causing the imprisonment and death of several of these refugees. It was he who betrayed the confidence of John Brown to the U. S. Government and obliged Capt. Brown to hasten his assault on Harper's Ferry before he was quite ready.

GENERAL JOSEPH GARIBALDI.

I first met Garibaldi at the house of a mutual friend on Staten Island, New York. He had but recently arrived in America, from Italy. A few months before I met him he was dictator of Rome, with an army of 20,000 men under his command, now, a refugee without sufficient means to supply the necessaries of life. The tyrant of France "Napoleon the Little," had crushed the hopes of republican Italy under the feet of the French army, and Garibaldi, finding no safety in Europe, had taken refuge in the United States, until another turn in the wheel of revolution should recall him to his beloved Italy. From early manhood I had been an enthusiastic admirer of this heroic soldier of freedom, and my personal intercourse with him during several months increased my admiration and filled me with profound respect and love for this

great man, who, after many years military command
in South America and Italy, battling for freedom,
could lay down his sword and engage in the most
humble occupation to provide for his simple wants,
in preference to dependence upon his friends, who
would have esteemed it a favor to have placed their
fortunes at his disposal. General Garibaldi was at
this time about forty-three years of age, of medium height, large head and noble brow, his eyes
blueish gray, with a keen, intelligent and kindly
expression; his hair dark brown, whiskers inclined
to reddish, feet and hands small and well formed,
chest and shoulders broad, indicating great strength.
He was cool, quiet and self-possessed in his manner,
his voice low and musical in tone, his language con-
cise and to the point. He spoke the French, Spanish
and Italian languages with ease, and English indif-
ferently. He wore dark trousers, and a red flannel
shirt, and over this, when the weather required additional covering, a heavy grayish white cloak
lined with red flannel. During the general's residence in America I spent many happy days in his
company, charmed by his simple, unaffected manner
and kindly disposition, as much as by his heroic
services in behalf of freedom. He finally grew
restless and dissatisfied with the narrow life he was
leading, and engaged as captain of the Italian ship
"Immaculate Conception." Before leaving, he
changed the name to the "Commonwealth," and

sailed for South American and Chinese ports. He afterwards make several trips to New York, Philadelphia, Baltimore and Boston. On the occasion of his visit to Boston in 1853, as captain of a ship, I again met him. He had not changed much in appearance, except that his face and hands were bronzed by exposure. He was the same mild, quiet man, his voice as sweet and musical as when I first knew him in 1851. During his short stay in Boston, I saw him frequently and listened to his modest recital of incidents personal to his wonderful career. When I clasped his hand for the last time, as he was about sailing for Italy, he said :—"Dear Ross, if you are ever blessed with a son, do me the favor of giving him my name, and may it be a good augury for him." And when in the course of time his wish was complied with, he sent my little boy the following letter :—

Caprera, October 20th, 1873.

To my precious godson Garibaldi Ross:

MY DEAREST:—I think of you constantly and hope you will grow up a brave and good man. Remember that time is money, and to waste it is a crime. Embrace with ardor and steadfastness sound and liberal principles. *   *   *   *

I send you an affectionate embrace, and a father's wish for your future happiness.

Yours devotedly for life,

G. Garibaldi

On each succeeding birthday the general sent affectionate words of congratulation and kind wishes for his godson. In 1874, an Italian friend wrote me that Garibaldi was extremely poor, in fact, often without the necessaries of life. I at once wrote to the general, asking him to accept some assistance form me. He replied as follows:

Caprera, 1st September, 1874.

My Dear Ross:—

* * * I accept with gratitude your generous offer. I beg you to send me a draft on a European banker. * * *

A kiss for your little son.

I am for life your devoted

In acknowledging the receipt of my draft, he added, "A thousand thanks, my dear Ross, for this grateful token of your continued friendship."

In view of the ingratitude and neglect which the Italian Ministry had displayed toward this illustrious man, who made Italy free, and gave a kingdom to Victor Emmanuel, I deemed it my duty to make public the general's condition, which I did in a letter published in the New York *Tribune* of October 3rd, 1874. The letter was cabled to Rome, and appeared next day in all the leading newspapers of Italy, to the utter confusion of the Italian Ministry. Contributions for the general, from sympathizing friends in all countries, were sent to him. The parliament of Italy voted him a pension of $20,000 a year for life, and the people of Rome elected him a

member of the first parliament of united Italy that
sat in Rome. His heroic and persistent struggles to
free his beloved Italy from the yoke of the foreigner
have been crowned with success, and to-day the
name of Garibaldi stands before an admiring world
without a spot to dim the purity of his fame. From
Italy to Montevideo, from Montevideo to Rome,
from Rome to Sicily and Naples, and from the dictatorship of Naples to his humble home in Caprera,
and from there to the parliament of United Italy,
in victory and defeat, Garibaldi always displayed
the soul of the hero and patriot, never thinking of
himself, but always of the oppressed and down-
trodden.

The mere narrative of Garibaldi's life reads like
a mediæval legend, or a tale of heroic times. He is
at once the Achilles and Ulysses of the Italian
national epic. Long before his name was heard of
in Europe, his exploits both by sea and land had
made it a word of power in the new world. Having become involved in revolutionary intrigues, he
quitted Europe, in 1836, for South America, only
to return after twelve years' exile, the story of
which, with its stirring adventures, both of war and
peace, is as wonderful as any subsequent portion of
his extraordinary career in Europe. He experienced many vicissitudes during his exile in South
America. At one time commander-in-chief of an
army, then a guerilla chief, then captain of a war

vessel, then a prisoner, then a private soldier, a
dealer in cigars and jewellery, a school teacher, a
peddler, a teacher of French, then again a commander of an army; such are a few of the changes in
his wonderful career.

BRIEF SKETCH OF GARIBALDI'S CAREER.

Garibaldi was born at Nice of humble parents, on
the 4th of July, 1807. At an early age he embraced
his ancestral calling of a sailor, ! and was for
several years engaged in the coasting trade in various parts of the Mediterranean. At the age of
twenty-four he became acquainted with Mazzini,
with whom he was concerned in a successful conspiracy against Charles Albert, the king of Sardinia. Compelled to leave his country, he eventually made his way to South America, and soon
after his arrival in that country engaged in the
privateer service of the revolted republic of Rio
Grande against Brazil, and experienced the various
vicissitudes of victory, defeat, imprisonment, ship-
wreck, and escape in the revolutionary war. Amidst
his dangers by land and sea, he found comfort in
his marriage with a Brazilian lady named Anita, to
whom he was devotedly attached, and who fully returned his affection. In battle, whether by sea or
land, Anita was at his side, aiding with sword and
gun, and dauntless courage, her lion-like husband.
In peace or war, in good or ill fortune, she was al-

ways his truest and best friend. During the siege of Rome, the fighting was continuous night and day, she never left Garibaldi's side, and when the fortunes of war compelled him to withdraw from the city, disband his army, and become a fugitive in the marshes, she never left him, until overcome with fatigue and exhaustion, she laid down and died. She was a heroic wife of a heroic man.

In 1847, hearing of the elevation of Pius IX. to the Papacy, and persuaded of his liberal tendencies, Garibaldi offered him his services, but they were not accepted. He then offered his sword to Charles Albert, then in the field against Austria, and upon being repulsed by that monarch he repaired to Milan, where he was commissioned by the provincial Government to organize Lombard volunteers for the war for freedom. After the flight of the Pope, Garibaldi visited Rome, where he found the people rejoicing over the proclamations of a republic, under which he was elected to the Constituent Assembly. He received orders to watch with his troops the movements of the King of Naples, but was called from this duty in order to resist the French army, which was then proceeding to invest the Roman territory. A severe battle took place on the 30th of April, in which Garibaldi, after a hard struggle against superior discipline and numbers, drove the French soldiers from the field. This victory was followed up by another over the Neapolitan army on the 9th of May. Rome, however, after a terrible struggle, which raged without intermission from the 23rd to the 28th of June, fell into the hands of the French, and on the 2nd of July, Garibaldi, with 5,000 of his volunteers, took his departure, to carry on the war against the Austrians and the King of Naples. But misfortunes overpowered him. Many of his soldiers surrendered to the enemy, and his faithful Anita, who had shared all his dangers, yielded up her life a victim to anxiety and fatigue.

Then came the episode of his life in America, on Staten Island, and then a brief return to his old business as a trader in Southern and Chinese seas. Having amassed a little capital, he purchased half of the small island of Caprera, off the coast of Sardinia, where he settled down as an agriculturist, determined to await events.

The opportunity came, in 1859, when he was summoned by Victor Emmanuel to Turin, to concert the plan which he was to play against the Austrians then threatening Sardinia. He received a commission as Lieutenant-General, and found himself at the head of a choice band of 3,000 volunteers, with which he left Turin, on the 20th of May, and carried on a guerilla warfare, which greatly harassed the Austrians. His followers soon increased to 17,000 men. He took Varese, Camerlats, and Como, and was successful at Bergamo, Brescia, and Rezzato.

After the hasty treaty of Villafranca, which put an end to the war, leaving Venice in the hands of the Austrians, Garibaldi retired from his command, and resigned his rank in the Italian army, in order that he might be free to engage in his long-meditated expedition for the liberation of the two Sicilies from the misrule of Francis II.

When all was ready, he embarked from Genoa for Sicily, on the 5th May, 1860, and landed on the 10th, at Marsala, where he proclaimed himself Dictator of Sicily, in the name of Victor Emmanuel, and proceeded to take Palermo and Messina. He then crossed the straits, landed in Calabria, and possessed himself of Naples, which he entered on the 9th September. There he proclaimed Victor Emmanuel King, amidst general enthusiasm and rejoicing. The Neapolitan army was defeated on the 1st of October; on the 21st, the people of Naples voted in favor of annexation to the Sardinian States; on the 7th of November, Victor Emmanuel entered Naples, and on the 27th, the army of Garibaldi was disbanded.

Garibaldi now retired to Caprera, where he matured his plans for the ill-advised and unsuccessful expedition against Rome, in which Victor Emmanuel was obliged to take part against him. In 1864, he paid a short visit to England, where he was received with great enthusiasm, and again retired to Caprera. He took an energetic part in the campaign of 1866, which gave Venice to Italy, but still restless under the exclusion of Rome from the kingdom, he began an agitation, in 1867, for the annexation of the

Papal States. This brought him again into collision with the Italian government, and he suffered arrest and imprisonment. He succeeded, however, in escaping, and entered the Pontifical States at the head of a small force. After a few unimportant successes, he was defeated by the combined French and Papal forces at Mentana, on the 4th of November. On the evening of the same day he was arrested, and conducted to the fortress of Varigano, near Spezia. Owing to a severe illness, it was deemed expedient to transport him to Caprera. With the exception of the brief service in France during the Franco-German war, Garibaldi's military career was now ended. He lived to see the desire of his heart fulfilled, in the restoration of Rome as the Capital of United Italy, and although he would have preferred a republic, he gave a loyal support to monarchy, as offering the only practicable solution of the great problem of Italian freedom and unity.

Garibaldi's last letter to the author:

CAPRERA. July 29th, 1880.

MY DEAREST ROSS;—

Give a kiss for Manlio and me to my precious godson, Garibaldi (my son), and a loving salutation to all your family.

Yours for life,

G. Garibaldi

DEATH OF GARIBALDI.

Garibaldi died at Caprera, on the evening of June 2nd, 1882. The window of the apartment in which he lay was open, and just before he died a little bird alighted on the window sill where it remained twittering. Garibaldi saw it and exclaimed, "How joyful it is." These were his last words. The funeral of Garibaldi at Caprera was not less romantic than his chequered life. Never was hero buried under such novel circumstances. Practical difficulties, combined with the expression of Italian opinion to prevent his body being burned as provided by the General's will. Amid a furious storm, the remains of the dead Liberator, borne by survivors of the Thousand of Marsala, were consigned to a temporary tomb beside the remains of his children, Rosa and Anita. He wanted to be burned as Pompey was, so he put the matter into his will to give his purpose sacredness. "Having by testament determined the burning of my body," he wrote, "I charge my wife with the execution of this will, before giving notice to anyone whomsoever of my death." He had even collected and cut up into convenient size a quantity of spicy woods, to be used for his funeral pyre. This was poetic, but of no avail, as the following letter from his widow explains :—

SARÁCCHI, PIEDMONT,
July 12th, 1882.

MY DEAR DR. ROSS.

The cruel misfortune which has deprived me of a most loving husband and my children of a kind and affectionate father, has crushed me to despair. I cannot help thinking that he might have been spared to us if he had been on the mainland where he could have had medical skill. In his will he expressed a desire that his remains should be burned ; dear soul, so much was he desirous of it that he charged me, in his last testament, not to let anyone know of his death until after his body was consumed. His wishes were overruled, and his remains now lie near his children, Rosa and Anita. My dear husband often spoke to me of your long friendship for him, and charged Manlio (his youngest son) and me never to forget your faithfulness during many years. My daughters and Manlio join me in tender regard to you and your little Garibaldi and all your family. * * *

Affectionately and devotedly,
FRANCESCO GARIBALDI.

No name in the history of modern Italy shines with a more brilliant or purer light. The sturdy old patriot was a hero of a noble type. No one did more for the welfare of his country than he, and despite the criticisms called fourth by the apparent inconsistencies of his later life, the good he wrought was fairly appreciated. That is not the happy lot of some patriots. Garibaldi was earnest and sincere, thoroughly honest and unselfish, true in his friendships, and a good hater toward those who wronged him. In parliament he was silent and obscure ; his place was in the field leading a fight for liberty. Garibaldi has been much condemned because he was content to accept finally a monarchy for his country, instead of a republic, but therein he showed more political wisdom than at any other time of his life. A republic then was impracticable. The acceptance of a pension by him from the King cannot be considered as a bribe, or as the wages of silence. His native land, and, above all, Victor Emanuel, owed him a comfortable old age. A confirmed invalid, it is a pleasure to know that the old hero was able to spend his last days in peace and quiet on his island, where he was most at home and happiest. Garibaldi loved Italy above all other earthly objects; but his great heart throbbed in sympathy with struggles for freedom in any part of the world. The patriot and hero died, beloved not only by the great mass of his own countrymen, but by lovers of freedom in all parts of the world.

GARIBALDI'S DREAM.

"One day I fell asleep in my cabin on board the *Carmen*, and dreamt that I was in Nice, where all nature bore a lovely aspect. In my dream I saw a sad procession of women carrying a bier, and they advanced towards me. I felt a fatal presentiment, and struggled to approach the bier, but I could not move, I was under the influence of nightmare; and when I began to move and felt beside me the cold form of a corpse, I recognized my mother's blessed

M

face. The mournful howling of the wind and the groans of the ship aroused me. On that day, and at that hour, my precious mother died."

The portrait of Garibaldi's mother always hung near his bed. It represented an old lady wrapped in a crimson shawl, and with a mild, sweet countenance. Garibaldi's veneration for his mother was intense. If he saw anyone looking at her picture tears would start to his eyes. He often expressed remorse at having by his adventurous life been a source of cruel anxiety to her. She was a woman of remarkable goodness and inexhaustible charity.

HOW HE WON ANITA.

One evening, while his vessel lay off the coast of Brazil, he saw a group of women and girls at work on the shore. At first their forms passed unnoticed before him, but by degrees, his eye, and perhaps his heart, fixed upon one, and he stopped to contemplate her. She was a young woman, in the bloom of health and strength. She was the ideal woman that Garibaldi was in search of. Before he had spoken to her, or heard her speak, he loved her. She, also, had remarked the leonine blonde head of the foreign sailor who watched her day after day, and had already given her heart to him. One evening Garibaldi resolved to delay no longer, and went to the girl's home. At the door he met her father, who invited him in to take a cup of coffee; he would have entered without invitation. Without hesitation he said to the girl, " Maiden, will you be mine ? " to which she replied only by a look, which contained the promise of unutterable love; a few evenings after, he returned and carried her off, and put her on board the safe refuge of his vessel and under the protection of his cannon and his sailors. He swore before Heaven to make her his wife, and they were married at Montivideo soon after. Her name was Anita Riberas; her father had promised her to another, for whom she had no love. Her marriage to Garibaldi distressed her father very much, but Anita had not broke faith with her father's choice, as there was no engagement (or marriage, as has been frequently said). " If there was any wrong done, I only am to blame," Garibaldi said.

JOSHUA R. GIDDINGS.

Joshua R. Giddings was the " bravest of the brave " among old time abolitionists; neither friends nor enemies could check his onslaught on slavery. He was the leader in the House of a little band of Free Soilers that formed the nucleus of the Republican party of the future.

Mr. Giddings encountered obloquy and social outlawry at the Capital. His position was offensive,

because it rebuked the ruling influence of the time.
He was treated as a pestilent fanatic, because he
upheld the ideal of the Republic, and sought to
make it real.   He found solace for his social ostracism in the company of a few friends, who had the
courage of their opinions and who have lived to see
their principles vindicated.

Mr. Giddings served in Congress, in all, twenty-
one years.   From his first appearance in the House
he was distinguished for constant devotion to the
principles of liberty.   He was so unceasing in his
opposition .to slavery that he aroused the bitter
hostility of the pro-slavery party.   Indeed, so intensely was he feared and hated in the Slave States
that a prominent newspaper of Richmond, Va., contained a conspicuous advertisement, offering ten
thousand dollars to any one who would bring the
person of Mr. Giddings alive to Richmond, or five
thousand dollars for his head.   On one occasion,
while he was delivering a speech in the House that
wounded the tender feelings of the slave-holders a
southern member approached him with a terrible-
looking bowie- knife in his hand, and ordered Mr.
Giddings to cease speaking or he " would cut his
damned abolitionist heart out there and then." Mr.
Giddings gave the cowardly assassin such a look of
defiance and scorn that he turned and slunk back
to his seat utterly discomfited.   When I asked the
old patriot how he felt when threatened with in-

staut death, he said, "I knew I was speaking for liberty, and I felt that if the assassin killed me, my speech would still go on and triumph."

Mr. Giddings was conspicuous for the courage with which he attacked slavery, and in all discussions on this subject, he took the broad ground that slavery was a mere local institution, which the general government could not, and ought not, to recognize.

He stood shoulder to shoulder with John Quincy Adams, the old man eloquent, in resenting the tyrannical demands of the slave-drivers.

As a public man, Mr. Giddings was pure, honorable, and conscientious. As a speaker, he was forcible, pertinacious, and courageous. In all his acts he showed personal courage and a determination to maintain the right at all hazards; and during the long struggle with slavery he never flagged in the fight, although he was ostracised by all men, except half-a-dozen, at the national capital, and denied the common civility and friendship of social life, but he fought on, and fought on, until in his last days he saw the triumph of the principles for which he had endured so much and labored so hard.

In personal appearance (in 1850) Mr. Giddings was a magnificent rugged specimen of physical strength. He was fully six feet in height, powerfully and compactly built; his head was large, and covered with dark brown hair, slightly mixed with grey, and inclined to curl; his countenance, when denouncing the wrongs of slavery or excited by the heat of discussion, was truly grand and lion-like, and presented a picture of herculean strength, backed by moral power; his eyes were blue, and expressed kindness and honesty; his nose large and pugnacious; his mouth and chin indicated firmness and tenacity.

In the social circle he was a charming and entertaining companion, his disposition most kind, gentle, and thoughtful. Mr. Giddings was one of the most welcome guests at the house of my good friend, Dr. Bailey. He was fond of active out-door sports, and exhilarating games.

In 1861, President Lincoln appointed Mr. Giddings Consul-General to the British North American Provinces, with his official residence at Montreal.

Here our acquaintance was resumed, and soon ripened into a warm friendship, which terminated only with his life. For several days before his death I was with him almost continuously, and, from his remarks as well as his manner, I am convinced he was impressed with the nearness of death. Three days before he died he handed me a package containing letters addressed to President Lincoln, Secretary Chase, and Elihu B. Washburn; he requested me to deliver these letters after his death. Many other little incidents occurred during these last days of his life on earth which convinced me that he was preparing for death. The many happy hours passed in the company of this noble old statesman will ever remain bright spots in my memory. His conversation during his last days evinced a spirit full of love and charity for all mankind, and especially for those misguided men who were fighting to destroy republicanism on this continent, and to erect in its place a government with human slavery for its chief corner-stone.

Few names will rank above that of Joshua R. Giddings, when the history of the long conflict with slavery is written down, and justice done to those who fought for the inalienable rights of man. He died suddenly, while amusing himself with a game of billiards. Only an hour prior to his death he said to me during a conversation on national affairs, " I have but one desire to live longer, and that is to witness the complete triumph of the cause to which I have given the energies of my life; but I am ready whenever the summons comes; I have no fear of death, it is only a short journey, from this life to the next."

> " Giddings, far rougher names than thine have grown
> Smoother than honey on the lips of men ;
> And thou shalt aye be honorably known,
> As one who bravely used the tongue and pen
> As best befits a freeman."
>
> —*Bryant.*

The following is Jefferson Davis' erroneous conception of Mr. Giddings' character :

"I never saw a more remarkable man, nor one who was inspired by a spirit of more concentrated bitterness. He was very old and infirm, but his hatred for the South and for slavery glowed like the hot fire of youth in his veins and seemed potent enough to vivify his exhausted frame. The hoarded hate of a lifetime gleamed in his sunken eyes, and gave ferocity to a voice that was like the growl of a tiger about to spring upon its prey. I used to watch him with a sort of fascinated interest which the display of strong and sustained passion is sure to create, and I remember how the alertness of his attitude and the suppressed passion of his face used to suggest to me the idea of some fierce creature crouching for a spring. To this day I believe it would have given him pleasure to behold the South desolated with sword and with famine and with pestilence, until neither man, woman, nor child remained. He had poured out so much tenderness upon the slaves, that there was not a drop of pity in his heart for even the innocent babes of the slaveholders."

Jefferson Davis did not *know* Joshua R. Giddings, or he would never have uttered such a libel against one of the purest hearted and most affectionate men of this country. His love for children was a marked characteristic. He was a noble, good man.

WILLIAM LYON MACKENZIE—CANADIAN PATRIOT.

My acquaintance with Mr. Mackenzie was formed after he had returned to Canada from his exile in the United States. Long before I met him I had imbibed feelings of respect and admiration for his character as a man, a patriot, and a statesman. In

personal appearance Mr. Mackenzie was small in
stature, and active and energetic in his movements.
His head was very large and massive; his brow
broad, high and projecting; his head high from the
ears to the crown, indicating firmness and self esteem; his jaw was broad, square and strong; his
nose large and inquisitive; his eyes thoughtful, sad
but keen; his language good and to the point; his
face broad, with rather prominent cheek bones; his
mouth strong and decisive. Like most radical reformers, he was poor and remained poor all his life.
Mr. Mackenzie was not a magnetic man, in the
sense in which it is applied to politicians, but he
was a very attractive man to those who admired
mental and physical courage of the highest order.
He dared to look the devil of tyranny, arrogance
and selfishness square in the face and smite it. He,
before and above all his adherents and followers,
had the courage of his convictions. His love for his
adopted country was sincere, and his motives unselfish and patriotic. For loving liberty and justice
more than selfishness and pelf, he was proclaimed
on outlaw, a price placed upon his head; he was
hunted from place to place, as if he were a wild
beast; he was persecuted, imprisoned and exiled, as
if he were an enemy of mankind. But, the time
is not far distant when the name of William Lyon
Mackenzie will be hailed as that of "Canada's
truest and best friend," and when that day comes,

as come it will, the names of his maligners and per-
secuters will be forgotten or unpleasantly remembered.   Once, while speaking of his career, he said,
" Well may I love the poor, greatly may I esteem
the humble and lowly, for poverty and adversity,
were my nurses, and in youth want and misery my
familiar friends."   It is sad to relate, but true, that
poverty and adversity and want and misery remained his companions and accompanied him to his
grave.

GEN. SAM. HOUSTON.

During my residence in Washington I became
intimately acquainted with General Houston.   His
fondness for the society of young men, and the
warm interest he evinced in their prosperity, together with his fame as a soldier and statesman,
made him an object of attraction to the young.

His genial disposition, simple habits, and the halo
of romance which surrounded him, made him one of
the most distinguished personages in the Senate.
He possessed a great fund of anecdotes connected
with men he had met during his eventful career.
He had known General Jackson, General Harrison,
Colonel David Crockett, Colonel Bowie, the Indian
Chiefs Red Jacket and Black Hawk, and many
other men of prominence and celebrity of the early
days of the Republic.   He delighted to talk (to an
interested listener) of the hardships and trials of

his early life and manhood. His father died when he was a child of twelve, and the support of his mother devolved upon him. He accompanied his mother through a trackless forest from Virginia to Tennessee, where they made a home, and where young Houston won the respect of his neighbors by his honesty, industry, and pluck. When the Cherokee war broke out, he joined the regular army as a private. His conspicuous daring and courage attracted the attention of General Jackson, and he was made a lieutenant, and subsequently a captain of the regular army. When the war was over he returned to Tennessee, studied law, and was made a member of the bar. He became Attorney-General of the State, member of Congress, and Governor of Tennessee. In 1834, a rebellion broke out in Texas, having for its object the independence of that State. Houston raised a band of seven hundred volunteers and went to Texas to assist the people in their efforts to cast off the Mexican yoke. At San Jacinto he met the Mexican army of five thousand men, commanded by the President, Santa Anna, and several prominent generals skilled in the art of war. General Houston addressed his little band and gave them for a battle cry, " Remember the Alamo," (the place where Crockett, Bowie, and three hundred American volunteers had been surrounded and brutally butchered in cold blood by the Mexicans, only four weeks before.) The battle of San Jacinto was one of the most hotly contested battles that ever took place on this continent. Houston was victorious; two thousand prisoners were captured, including the President of Mexico and three generals. Fifteen hundred Mexicans were killed and many driven into the river, where they were drowned. Only a few hundred Mexicans escaped. The independence of Texas was recognized, and Houston became its first president. He was subsequently elected for two terms and finally brought about the annexation of Texas to the United States. He was elected United States Senator for Texas for several terms, and was Governor of Texas when the slaveholders' rebellion broke out. He remained true to his allegiance, and refusing to join the rebels he was deposed and Texas was forced into the Confederacy. In personal appearance Gen. Houston was a man of marked physique. He was fully six feet six inches in height, straight as an arrow, of massive frame and gallant bearing. He had a large, long head and face, and his fine features were lit up by keen, eagle-looking eyes. He was a man of strong practical sense. A more honest statesman than Sam. Houston never sat in the Senate. He was a brave soldier, a kind father and husband, and a faithful friend. When Texas was coerced into the Confederacy he retired to his modest little home at Independence. The old hero was broken in health and spirit by the misfortunes of his state and country. His wounds, received in his many battles, broke out afresh, and in July, 1863, while the country was in the throes of a war he had tried to prevent, he laid down and died broken-hearted. To the shame of Texas be it said, his body yet lies in an unmarked grave.

GERRIT SMITH.

Gerrit Smith was one of the purest and noblest men it has been my lot to meet. He possessed a noble, generous, chivalrous heart, lion-like port, and uncompromising conscience. His charities became almost as familiar to men's thoughts as the gifts of rain and sunshine. When the cry of distress was put forth, his ear was always one of the first to hear it, and his hand one of the first to succor. His most controlling passion was that for the abolition of slavery, which he rightly considered to embrace the deepest national honor, and the largest sum of human misery and degradation. He was an ever faithful friend to the cause of freedom, and bore his part of the burden with princely generosity. He was a large man, mentally and physically; his mental impulse was great; he was always alive and awake; his wealth was his opportunity; he spent nothing on pleasure, nothing on amusement, and but little on dress; he bought no luxurious ornaments or trinkets. His affections were ardent and constant. His cheerful sympathies imparted heartiness to his manner and mellowed the tone of his rich, full voice. He had great fondness for children; he made the christian life his law—the Sermon on the Mount contained the sum of his philosphy, and the Golden Rule was his motto. He was a brave, beneficent . man, who lived not for ease but for duty.

GENERAL WILLIAM WALKER.

During one of my journeys through the Slave States I became acquainted with General William Walker, who claimed to be the legal president of Nicaragua. He was engaged in recruiting a force to regain his position from which he had been driven by the forces of Costa Rica, in alliance with the old government of Nicaragua, and by the treachery of some of his own officers. His prospects were at a very low ebb at this time, as the United States government were closely watching his movements to prevent another expedition leaving for Nicaragua, he was obliged to observe great caution and prudence. I found him a very intelligent and agreeable companion, and became fond of his society. Naturally he was taciturn and uncommunicative, but when his confidence was won he was fascinating and interesting. He had enlisted about three hundred men and was drilling them into soldiers under experienced officers, among whom were Col. Rudler and General Henningsen.

It was not until after a fortnight's acquaintance that I was allowed to accompany the General to his barracks—an old sugar house. The men met at eight p.m. every night and were drilled until ten, when they left in small parties. I could not refrain from laughing aloud when I first saw his army; a more ragged or rough collection of cut-throats I never saw before, some were without boots, others without hats, and the majority looked capable of perpetrating any outrage, and yet these ragamuffins proved brave fighters, and defeated three times their number of regular soldiers, gaining many victories, and finally reconquering Nicaragua. General Walker was very desirous that I should accompany him in his next expedition, and gave me the position of surgeon. But the obstacles thrown in his way delayed his expedition so long that I returned North and to other duties.

Among the inducements held out to me to join his expedition was one that highly commended itself to my mind. His intention was to establish a thoroughly liberal system of public education for the people of Central America, for his ambition was not confined to Nicaragua, but included all the states of Central America. A few weeks after my return home I received the following from the General:

"DEAR DR. ROSS,—I had hoped that before this you had got over any disagreeable impression made by seeing bad news or abuse of your friends in the daily papers. Pray do not let them annoy you with their senseless despatches and foolish letters. The president (Buchanan) is bitterly hostile, but he will be forced to abandon what he ambititously calls his foreign policy. He knows as much of the people of Central America as he does of the Eskimaux, or, for fear he may know something of these last, I will add, of the inhabitants of the moon. Congress, however, will drive him from the road he has marked out for himself, and force him to pay more attention and respect to the constitution and laws, as well as the opinions of other people, than he seems disposed to do. * * *

Very truly your friend,

W. Walker
of Nicaragua

General Walker was in many respects a remarkable man, a physician and lawyer by education, and a liberator by choice and force of circumstances. He was five feet, six inches in height, slender and somewhat delicate in frame. His countenance when in repose, was marked by severe earnestness and stability. His head was large (twenty-four inches around), and presented the appearance of being flat on top. His forehead was high and broad ; his eyes bluish-grey, and remarkable for their brilliancy and penetrating power; his chin square and strong; his lips were full; his mouth (the only unpleasant feature) not well-formed; his hair thin, fine, light brown, and closely cut; his nose, large and thin; his face, beardless and long. His manner was self-possessed. I never saw him laugh, and seldom smile; his usual appearance was that of a serious, thoughtful man. While talking, his head would incline toward the person addressed, and when he desired to persuade, he was really fascinating, eloquent and effective. He was ascetic in his habits, and utterly indifferent of acquiring wealth. He possessed great physical courage and determination, and had bravely faced death on twenty battle-fields. In disposition, he was modest, simple and retiring. From my personal knowledge of General Walker, I believe his motives were pure and good. He desired the welfare of Nicaragua, and if those who invited him to Nicaragua to defend her soil from invaders had proved true to him, his rule would have been a lasting benefit to that interesting country, and to the whole of Central America as well. General Walker, in his last general order, said, "From the future, if not from the present, we may expect just judgment. That which is ignorantly called 'filibusterism' is not the offspring of hasty passion, or ill-regulated desire; it is the fruit

N

of the sure, unerring instincts which act in accordance with the laws as old as the creation. They are but drivelers who speak of establishing fixed relations between the pure white American race, as it exists in the United States, and the mixed Hispano-Indian race, as it exists in Mexico and Central America, without the employment of force. Whenever barbarism and civilization, or two distinct forms of civilization, meet face to face, the result must be war. Therefore the struggle between the old and the new elements of Nicaraguan society is not passing or accidental, but natural and inevitable." In 1860 I met General Walker for the last time; he was in Washington interviewing the Southern senators in reference to another expedition to Nicaragua, and received so much encouragement in Washington that he embarked from Mobile with two hundred men on what proved his last effort. Through some misunderstanding with his friends on the coast of Central America, he landed on the coast of British Honduras, and was forced to surrender to the captain of a British sloop-of-war, who perfidiously handed him over to his enemies, who brutally shot him in cold blood. Thus died one of the bravest and most unfortunate men that ever lived. In his death, Nicaragua lost her best friend. The seed sown by Walker will ultimately result in a rich harvest of blessings for Central America. The following are the closing words of his last letter to me, written on the day he left Mobile, on his last expedition to Central America :—

DEAR DR. ROSS,— * * * *

We may perish in the work we have undertaken, but if we fall, we feel it is in the path of honor. And what is life, and what is success in comparison with the consciousness of having performed a duty? * * *

Truly your friend,

Wm Walker

of Nicaragua.

> " Success had made him more than king ;
> Defeat made him the vilest thing,
> In name, contempt, or hate can bring ;
> So much the leaded dice of war
> Do make a man of character.
>
> " I simply say, he was my friend
> When strong of hand, and full of fame ;
> Dead and disgraced, I stand the same
> To him, and so shall to the end."

INTER-STATE SLAVE TRADE.

The great rivers of the Southern States were the lines of transport over which the inter-state traffic in slaves was carried on. The boats on the Mississippi, Ohio, Tennessee, Alabama, Black Warrior, Tombigbee, and Red River of the South, carried cargoes of cotton and slaves to New Orleans, the

great slave market of the South ; and returning,
carried slaves and merchants' supplies to the interior states. Usually the slaves were chained together in coffles, or hampered by heavy chains on the
ankles. The poor wretches were forced to appear
satisfied with their condition in the presence of passengers. At times, however, they would be overcome with sadness and depression. Then the snap
of the driver's whip, and his command, "Be lively,
boys, give us a song," would force them to sing,
urged on by the snapping of his whip, and the
stamping of his foot. The steamers going up the
river from New Orleans, usually carried as passengers, numbers of gamblers who victimised the planters of the products of their sales. Gambling was
openly practised on all the river boats in those days.
Towards midnight the results of strong drink and
losses at gambling would be manifested by fights
and broils, in which the bowie knife and derringer
would play an active and often fatal part. Sometimes a plucky planter who had lost all his money
would wager his slaves on the game, and when these
were lost, would put up his watch as a last venture.

A SLAVE PEN.

On one of the streets running off Canal-street, in
New Orleans, there stood, in 1857, a large two-story
flat building, surrounded by a stone wall, ten or

twelve feet high. This building was one of the largest slave pens in the city. I have seen as many as three hundred slaves, men, women, and children, at one time in that vile place. In a small room off the hall could be seen at the time many curious instruments of punishment and torture, " Wire whips," " toe and nail pincers," " iron collars with spikes so arranged as to prevent the wretched victims from resting their heads," iron branding irons," " chains for the neck and waist," and other horrid appliances of punishment and torture. Here in this building from morning till night came planters, traders, and lecherous speculators to buy, sell, or gratify their sensual curiosity. Here slave girls were stripped of their clothing, and subjected to the gaze and obscene examinations of vile men. Here families were separated, and the poor creatures classified into field hands, artisans, servants, and mistresses. No tie of blood or family relation was respected. I have seen little babes torn from their mothers' arms and sold for a few dollars, or exchanged for whiskey or groceries. In a special room of this building, slaves were received to be whipped by order of their master or mistress. On one occasion I saw a young girl sold at this house, who was probably not more than fifteen years old. She was quite white, with blue eyes and long auburn tresses, and a very intelligent face. When placed on the block to be sold she was told to "look cheerful," but I never saw a

more broken-hearted look on the face of a human
being. The sale began by the auctioneer calling
attention to the girl on the block by saying, "Gentlemen, here is the finest girl I ever offered for sale
in this city. She has good health and a mild temper, and has only just turned fifteen. How much
am I offered? 'Five hundred dollars?' only five
hundred dollars for such a likely girl as this? Why,
gentlemen, look at her, look at the article you are
bidding on. A real octoroon, fit for any gentleman
in the South. She is virtuous and pure. Her late
master tells me she is a Christian, and very obedient.
How much for her? 'Seven hundred,' 'eight hundred,' 'ten hundred;' keep on, gentlemen, she's
worth a lot more than that. I tell you she is pure;
'twelve hundred,' 'fourteen hundred,' 'sixteen hundred.'" And for this sum of sixteen hundred dollars, she was sold to a dealer in human flesh, who
took her to his sodomic house in that city as a
source of income. O! the cloud of these dark, devilish days comes over me at times like a nightmare,
as I recall the scenes I witnessed in that foul land
of horrors.

CHAPTER VIII.

MORAL AND PHYSICAL REFORM.

"A WORK OF NECESSITY AND MERCY."

Extract from the Official Report of the Medical Superintendent of the Toronto Lunatic Asylum.

"Would that one-tenth of all the zeal and intelligence and stirring eloquence which has been expended on other and not unimportant reforms, could be enlisted in the exposition and amelioration of this enshrouded pestilence! But who will venture on such a work? *Whoever would most certainly and most largely benefit his fellow-beings in this Province, may find his work in this sphere of moral reform.*"

Twenty-five years ago my attention was directed to the prevalence of a particularly sad type of insanity produced by sinful and unphysiological habits

215

secretly practised by the youth of Canada. A careful and earnest study of the tables of " Causes of Insanity and Imbecility " in the official reports of Medical Superintendents of Asylumns for the insane in Great Britain, Germany, France and America, as well as my own observation and experience, forced me to the sorrowful conclusion that fully ONE-THIRD of all the insane have brought this blighting curse upon themselves by indulgence in an unphysiological habits practised in ignorance of the results.

And, notwithstanding the alarming prevalence of this sin, and the shocking consequences that follow it, not a voice of alarm was raised in all the land to warn the poor victim of his fate. Not a word of warning from the pulpit of the preacher, the desk of the teacher, or the mouth of the physician. Here was a worm eating at the core of society, and doing more injury than all other diseases combined, yet there was no warning cry to or from the objects of pity.

I consulted with clergymen, professing christians of all denominations, and men of influence in different walks of life. but, while all agreed as to the necessity of the work, *not one* was willing to identify himself publicly in this work of necessity and mercy. It is easy and pleasant to labor in popular works of charity, to win smiles of approval from the rich, the powerful and the fashionable, but to identify one's self publicly and earnestly in a work of reform that conflicts with the conventionalities of society is to commit social suicide. No matter how beneficent or merciful the work may be, no matter if the health, happiness and lives of thousand of our race are jeopardized, all must be sacrificed to the social Moloch of false delicacy and moral cowardice. I felt *then*, and feel *now*, that this work of moral and physical reform would enlist the active sympathy of Jesus, were He on earth to-day.

The solemn question appealed to my conscience. Is it not a crime for you to withhold the knowledge you possess on this subject, is it not YOUR DUTY to proclaim it broadcast throughout the land? Impressed me deeply, and I resolved to do what I conscientiously believed to be MY DUTY, and from that hour to the present I have labored quietly and persistently through good and evil report in circulating information and advice to the youth of our land.

The subject is a very delicate and difficult one to handle effectively. The press and pulpit, muzzled by false delicacy, and the medical profession, wrapped in false dignity and criminal indifference, disdainfully refuse to discuss the subject or acknowledge the right of an individual member to act according to the dictates of his own conscience.

My experience has taught me that whoever loves TRUTH, and means conscientiously to pursue it, will find peace in his own bosom, but abundant storms, calumny and unkind treatment outside.

But, I am persuaded, that TIME and the HONEST VERDICT of posterity will approve of every act of mine in the discharge of this unpleasant, but IMPERATIVE DUTY.   To be one with TRUTH is a majority.

CRUSADE AGAINST VACCINATION.

TELLING UNPOPULAR TRUTH.

Telling unpopular truth to the public is not pleasant, still unpopular truth should be told ; for good may follow, though one cannot tell how or when.   It may be contradicted, or it may find here and there a disciple ; or the author of it may be reviled, persecuted, imprisoned, or held up to the scorn and ridicule of the public.   In one or other of these ways attention may be drawn to the subject, and a spirit of enquiry excited which may result in the overthrow of the existing error.

FILTH AND DISEASE.

In March, 1885, my attention was called to a report that several cases of small-pox existed in the east end of Montreal. Knowing something of the filthy condition of certain localities, I made a careful sanitary survey of all that part of the city east of St. Lawrence Street, and south-west of McGill and St. Antoine Streets.   What I saw I will attempt to describe—what I smelt cannot be described !   I found *ten thousand seven hundred cess-pits* reeking with rottenness and unmentionable filth— many of these pest-holes had not been emptied for years—the accumulated filth was left to poison the air of the city and make it the seed-bed for the germs of zymotic diseases.   Further, I found the courts, alleys and lanes in as bad a condition as they possibly could be—decaying animal and vegetable matter abounded on all sides.   Everywhere unsightly and offensive objects met the eye, and abominable smells proved the existence of disease-engendering matter, which supplied the very conditions necessary for the incubation, nourishment and growth of small-pox.

Knowing well the fearful consequences that would result from the presence of such a mass of filth in a densely populated part of the city, I gave the widest publicity to the subject, hoping thereby to rouse the municipal authorities to a proper appreciation of the danger that menaced the health of the city. But I was called an alarmist ; my advice went unheeded, and the filth remained as a nest for the nourishment of small-pox, which grew in strength and virulence rapidly, until it swept into untimely graves, from the very localities I have mentioned, *thirty-four hundred persons !*—victims of municipal neglect. Instead of removing the filth and putting the city in a thoroughly clean defensive condition by the enforcement of wise sanitary regulations and the adoption of a rigid system of isolation of small-pox patients, the authorities were led by the medical profession to set up the *fetish* of vaccination and proclaim its protective virtues through the columns of an ignorant, tyrannical and time-serving press   Day after day the glaring, snaring headlines of '' Vaccinate, vaccinate," "Alarm, alarm," appeared in morning and evening papers. A panic of cowardice and madness followed, and tens of thousands of people were driven (like sheep to the shambles of the butcher) to the vaccinators, who reaped a rich but unrighteous harvest.

The truth of my predictions was amply and sadly verified by the sickening and mournful fact that *thirty-four hundred* persons, mostly children under twelve years of age, died from small-pox in the very localities I pointed out as abounding in filth, while in the West End, west of Bleury and north of Dorchester streets, where cleanliness prevailed, there were only a few cases, and these sporadic. I do not hesitate to declare it as my solemn opinion, founded upon experience acquired during the epidemic, that there would have been no small-pox epidemic in Montreal if the authorities had discarded vaccination, and placed the city in a thoroughly clean and defensive condition when I called upon them to do their duty in April, 1885

CRUSADE AGAINST VACCINATION.

During my crusade against vaccination in Montreal, I had to contend against a powerful and solidly-united medical profession, supported actively or passively by every clergyman and every newspaper in the country, aided by the auxiliaries of ignorance, bigotry, cowardice, prejudice and indifference of the people. The seed I have sown has already taken firm root. Thousands of intelligent people who never questioned the virtue of vaccination before I began my warfare against it, are now opposed to it. Each of these converts will disseminate their views in the circle in which they move, and in a few years an intelligent public opinion will be arrayed against the absurd and filthy right of vac. cination, which will compel the profession to abandon it, as they have already abandoned other fallacies, such as bleeding, mercury and arm to arm innoculation. Medical fallacies die hard, and this fallacy of vaccination, being a munificent patron, will be no exception to the rule. When I began my crusade against vac-·cination I expected obloquy, slander, lies and persecution. I expected the lineal descendants of Ananias, Sapphira and Judas would unite their efforts to crush me — I have not been disappointed. I have sacrificed money, peace and many friendships in this cause, and still I think the cause worthy the sacrifice.

WHAT I TAUGHT THE PEOPLE.

(1.) That epidemic diseases are the creation of municipal and personal neglect of cleanliness. That any medical theory which sets aside the laws of health, and teaches that the spread of natural or artificial disease can be advantageous to the community, is misleading and opposed to science and common sense.

(2.) That exemption from cholera, smallpox and other filth diseases is not to be found in vaccination, but in the enforcement and extension of wise sanitary regulations, such as better habitations for the people, perfect drainage, pure water in abundance (and free to the poor), wholesome food, and inculcating amongst all classes of the community habits of personal and domestic cleanliness.

(3.) That vaccination is *utterly useless*, and affords *no protection whatever* from small-pox. For proof, I refered to the official reports of the Montreal small-pox hospitals, showing that hundreds of thoroughly vaccinated people were stricken with small-pox and that scores of them died, having on their bodies *one*, *two*, and in some cases *three*, vaccine marks. And further, the fact that the ravages of the epidemic were confined *exclusively* to that section of Montreal noted for uncleanliness and non-observance of sanitary regulations.

(4.) That vaccination (during an epidemic of small-pox) is an active and virulent factor in propagating small-pox by creating a susceptibility to the disease.

(5.) That vaccination is not only *useless*, but absolutely dangerous, as it frequently causes troublesome swellings of the arms and glands, and filthy diseases of the skin, blood, hair and eyes.

(6.) That compulsory vaccination is an outrage on the natural and inalienable rights of man, and should be resisted by physical force if peaceful means fail. The legislature has no more right to command *vice* and *disease*, than it has to forbid *virtue* and *health*.

WHY I OPPOSE COMPULSORY VACCINATION.

The theory of vaccination has its peculiarity, that the more firmly it is established the less justification does it afford for the plea that compulsion is essential to public safety. For the theory is that vaccination protects against small pox. Very well; if that is so, then every man has the opportunity of protecting himself and his children against the neglect of his neighbors. What justification has any one in that case for coercing his neighbors to adopt his belief? If it is said that his neighbor's children may take the small-pox and thus endanger those who are already "protected" by vaccination, they surrender their claim that vaccination protects. Of two things, one: either it protects, in which case the vaccinated are not endan-

gered by the unvaccinated ; or else vaccination does not protect,
and in that case what right has anyone to compel another to run
the risk of so dangerous and useless a *rite*.

RESISTANCE TO OPPRESSION.

The right to resist injustice and oppression is inalienable, and
its exercise in no way depends upon the nature of the authority
wielded by the oppressor.   A majority can be as tyrannical as an
autocrat.   Injustice does not become just or tolerant because it
has been countersigned by a majority.   No one has a right to
oppress, that is, to treat unjustly ; no, not even if the oppressors have a majority of nine hundred and ninety-nine to one.

*I stand for the right of every citizen, rich or poor, high or low,
black, brown or white, male or female – the individual's right above
all others to maintain the purity and integrity of his person as
against all theory or practice of unsettled and unsought defilement,
his right to resist, by all means in his power, the enforcement of
vaccination on his own person or the bodies of his children.*

CONSEQUENCE OF TELLING UNPOPULAR TRUTH.

When I entered upon this anti-filth and anti-vaccination
crusade, I knew that my convictions were exceedingly unpopular, I knew they were perilous of utterance, that they were sure
to be misconstrued.   I knew that the members of the medical
profession to a man would oppose me—not with reason, but with
personal abuse, persecution and misrepresentation.   I asked only
that it may be allowed that I was sincere, but the medical profession and its subsidized press declined to permit that.   They
declared that no intelligent physician, no honest man, could
entertain the views I expressed against vaccination.   I was ridiculed, maligned and persecuted, made the victim of a conspiracy
of medical and vaccination lies ; threatened with imprisonment
and outrage, and publicly charged with being responsible for the
death of those who died from small-pox.   Such was the treatment I received for giving expression to my honest convictions
on the subject of filth and vaccination.   (See Appendix.)

MEDICAL REFORM.

The medical practice of to-day is a reproach to our civilization and a disgrace to science. It is to-day what it has always been, a colossal system of humbug and self-deception, in obedience to which mines have been emptied of their cankering minerals, the intestines of animals taxed for their filth, and poison bags of reptiles drained of their venom, and all these—and many more abominations—have been thrust down the throats of credulous and long suffering human beings, who, from some fault of diet, organization or vital stimulation, have invited disease. In truth, the prevailing medical practice has no foundation in science, truth, philosophy or common sense. Multitudes of intelligent people in America and in Europe, express utter want of confidence in physicians and their methods. The cause is evident: erroneous theory, and, springing from it, erroneous, often—fatal practice !

Nearly all the medical literature of the world is a medley of inconsistencies, absurdities and incoherent ideas. Every day develops new views, teaching us that much of what we before thought immutable truths, are baseless theories. On these theories which have usurped the place of truth, a system of routine, or empirical, vacillating and uncertain practice, has grown up based on conjecture and improved by sad blunders, often hidden by death.

Before the prevailing fallacious and destructive medical practice can be abolished, and a system introduced at variance with established usuages, in direct antagonism with the general habits, customs, education and prejudices of the people; in utter contempt of the teachings and practices of the present predominant medical profession, it will be necessary to establish a medical doctrine founde l upon facts in harmouy with and sustained by the unerring laws of nature, and of the vital organism.

Unreasoning faith in physicians and their toxic and poisonous drugs—an heritage from a barbaric and ignorant age—is fast fading away. A new era is dawning upon the medical world, based on a systematic study of natural agencies for the prevention of sickness and the restoration of health. The realm of the *vis medicatrix naturæ* is both broad and comprehensive, and every year's experience adds to the conviction, that the remedial forces of nature are the foundation and crown of all curative and restorative processes. This new theory bids fair to emphasise an epoch in the history of medicine.

Natural Medical Principles.

1. That HEALTH-EASE is the natural condition of man. It is the result of all functional action working in perfect harmony; it is the natural condition of every living thing; it is the natural result of conformity to the laws of nature.

2. That DIS-EASE IS NOT AN ENTITY ; it is not a thing to be cured, STAMPED OUT OR EXTIRPATED , it is an effort of the system to purify itself; it is REMEDIAL ACTION, working to expel impurities, poisons, and extraneous matters from the body ; it is ease-restoring, because it aims to reproduce the conditions of health. Physicians often speak of *dis-ease* when they mean, or should mean the action of the living system in getting rid of its impurities and poisons. When we are sick there is a torpor of functional action in the various organs of the body ; this means retained secretion : the system becomes clogged with its own impurities. Then comes a rallying of the vital forces TO THROW OUT THESE IMPURITIES. How are we going to aid this REMEDIAL ACTION ? By swallowing drug medicines ? By adding impurities? CERTAINLY NOT ! Drugs of whatever kind, are ANTAGONISTIC to the vital organism, and therefore injurious to human life and health. We should aid the vital forces in this work of elimination by supplying right conditions. We should control, regulate, and direct the REMEDIAL ACTION, until the system is purified and health is restored. To effect this object—the healing of the sick—the self same agents are to be employed that administer to health. When the body is disordered by sickness, its natural tendency is to right itself ; its most stable and comfort-

able state, is a state of EASE, and to that equilibrium it gravi-
tates naturally, when not hindered by MEDDLESOME MEDICINE.

To further illustrate. A healthy person allows his system
to become clogged and poisoned with impurities from unnatural
food and drink, and the vital powers, make a strong effort to
expel the accumulated filth through the pores of the skin. This
is *inflammatory or high fever.* If the infected person were more
feeble the remedial effort would be less vigorous toward the sur-
face, or to a greater extent directed toward the other outlets,
constituting the slow or *nervous typhoid fever.*

Again, if the system is very gross and full of putrescent materials when the remedial effort occurs, the *putrid form of typhus
fever* will be present.

And as the impurities have accumulated in the system more
rapidly or more slowly, will be manifested the different forms
of fever as to periodicity.

Hence the *natural condition of cure* consists in modifying and
regulating the *remedial effort,* by supplying favorable conditions.
And thus, all the mysterious problems connected with the various
forms and features of disease are easily understood.

3. THAT ALL HEALING POWER IS INHERENT IN THE LIVING
ORGANISM. That for violated physical law, nature has provided
PENALTIES, NOT REMEDIES.

4. That the REMEDIAL FORCES OF NATURE are the foundation
and crown of all curative processes. That there is no "law of
cure" in the universe ; and the only condition of cure is obedience
to the laws of nature.

5. THAT LIVING MATTER ACTS ON DEAD MATTER, and not dead
on living. This may be illustrated by the so-called action of drug
medicines, though an equally good illustration is found in the
digestion of foods. If food is taken, the "action" from the time
it enters the mouth till it is finally assimilated in the tissues, is
not on the part of the inert substance (food,) but on that of the
living organism. The hand carries it to the mouth, where it is
masticated, insalivated and swallowed ; and after it is received
into the stomach, duodenum, and small intestines the gastric

O

and other juices digest it ; then it is taken up by the absorbents, conveyed to the various tissues, and by them appropriated. This is NORMAL VITAL ACTION : the bread all this time, does nothing ; it is simply done unto,—or acted upon. But suppose something abnormal is taken ; for example a drug medicine. It be may by an emetic; in this case the muscles of the stomach will contract and expel it. Or if a purgative has been administered, the bowels undertake the work of elimination ; if a diaphoretic, then the skin must throw it out, if a diuretic, the kidneys, if an expectorant, the lungs ; if a cholagogue, the liver takes an abnormal activity ; and so on, to the end of the chapter. In every case it will be seen that the so-called action is always on the part of the living organism, and never on the part of the thing taken ; that as soon as a foreign substance is recognized by the vital instincts, REMEDIAL ACTION begins, and sooner or later, one or more of the excretory organs will (if possible) expel it. THIS IS ABNORMAL VITAL ACTION—DIS-EASE.

NATURAL MEDICAL PRACTICE.

NATURE'S PROPHYLACTICS AND RESTORATIVES consist of FOOD, WATER, AIR, REST, HOPE, PEACE, TEMPERATURE, EXERCISE and other NATURAL AGENCIES. The right use of these agents will balance VITAL ACTION, thus enabling the system to rid itself of poisons, execute repairs, and build itself up. By this system of healing the VITAL FORCES are neither weakened nor destroyed, and after the remedial process is ended, the different organs of the body resume their normal functions. THIS NATURAL MEDICAL PRACTICE stands out boldly in the sunlight of truth ; it tolerates no warfare against the vital forces of nature ; it sees no philosophy in clogging up their beautiful machinery with *posionous drugs* ; it acknowledges Nature as the best of all physicians.

PREVENTION BETTER THAN CURE.—The work of the physician of the future, will not be merely to heal the sick and mitigate the penalties af violated law, but to banish sickness by teaching the people how to live better, purer and more natural lives, and thus ensure health, and promote happiness and long life. When that time comes, as it certainly will in a few years, people will appreciate the advantage of employing a physician to PRESERVE THEIR HEALTH. His duty will be to regularly inspect the sanitary conditions of the house and its surroundings, and to act as health adviser in all matters of dietetics, hygiene, and habits of each member of the family. There are thousands carried to untimely graves every year, who have been the direct cause of their own death (some from ignorance of the simple laws of health, and others from inattention to those laws), and there are millions who live weak and sickly lives, who might be strong and healthy if they had proper instruction in the laws of health.

HUMANITY HAS A DEEP INTEREST IN THIS SUBJECT OF MEDICAL REFORM. The people will gain immensely by its adoption ; both in health, happiness and prolonged life.

MEDICAL FREEDOM.

A PATERNAL GOVERNMENT IS AN INFERNAL GOVERNMENT.

If a man may not choose his bodily physician, why should he have the right to choose his spiritual physician ? Is his spiritual health of less importance than that of his body ? Why should the State be called upon to direct and control the individual in one case and not in the other ? The argument is, that the public must be protected against their own ignorance. If this is true of bodily health, why is it not true as to spiritual and other matters ? The same principle if carried out, would set up a paternal government, including religion, etc. In other words, it would be the knell of individual liberty.

The laws of Canada secure to our people the right to their respective religious opinions and practices, why should the people not have an equal right to their medical opinions and practices ? There is a boundary which no discreet legislature should overstep, lest they provoke the justifiable opposition of every independent and right thinking mind, and that this boundary has al-.

ready been overstepped by medical legislation in Canada cannot
be denied. For the State and its selected doctors have not, and
never can have, any right to compel submission to a medical
creed or dogma, any more than to a religious one, whatever may
be the salvation which each may offer.

DESPOTISM OF STATE MEDICINE.

Under the treacherous guise of *protecting the people*, the legislatures of Ontario, Quebec, New Brunswick, Nova Scotia, and
Manitoba, have been hoodwinked by doctor craft, into enacting
certain unrighteous, selfish and despotic laws, which absolutely
deprive the people of one of their most precious natural rights—
the right, in the hour of sickness, and in the presence of death to
choose whatever method of *healing* they please.

Life is precious, and the right to preserve it, the most sacred
of the rights of man. No legislature has a rightful power to invade or trespass upon that right. But, that is just what our
provincial legislatures have done in passing these infamously
despotic " Medical Acts." The people never asked for protection ; the people do not need it ; their own good common sense
is their best protection. By enacting these tyrannical laws, a
greedy and heartless " Medical Combine " has been established,
which outrages the most sacred rights of the people and enriches
a monopolistic medical oligarchy.

The only persons protected by these laws are the needy *unem-
ployed* physicians who organized the " combine " and lobbied
these infamous laws through the legislature. Under these despotic laws, no one (not a member of the "combine,") no matter
how competent or skilful he or she may be in the art of healing
the sick, dare exercise this humane and natural right—without
pain of fine or imprisonment. Talk of Russian despotism ! why,
there is no tyranny in the empire of the Czar to equal this medical tyranny in Canada !

MEDICINE NOT A SCIENCE.

Medicine is not a science, but an aggregation of different theories, which are being changed and modified. While surgery has

made marked advances in recent years, therapeutics, or the application of remedies, is really in a more backward state, as far as any definite system is concerned, than it was two thousand years ago, when Hippocrates declared : *Natura sanet, non medicus*—nature cures, not the physician. After two thousand years of experiments, there is not one single remedy which is recognized throughout the medical world as a certain cure for any single disease. Not only do schools of medicine differ, but the latter change their practice from time to time, as new remedies come into fashion. Describe your symptoms in identical words to a dozen doctors and you will get on an average at least nine different opinions and remedies. Is this science?

No systematic or theoretical classification of diseases or therapeutic agents ever yet promulgated is true, or anything like truth, and none can be adopted as a safe guidance in practice. And yet it is this theoretical classification that has been imposed on our people by medical trickery, and legislative stupidity and cowardice. Every man must put his life, and the lives of his children, at the mercy of one of these untrue systems, or else go without medical assistance altogether.

It is a fearful thing to think that this invasion of our dearest rights is the law of the land. Every legislator who voted for it struck a blow at one of the clearest rights of the individual—the right to protect his own life, and guard his own health in his own way.

Is it just to the people to compel them to imperil their health and lives by employing physicians of such a dangerous and unreliable system of healing as above described by the leading men of that system?

A conclusive reason against protecting any form of medical practice is that the so-called science has no standard. It is all uncertainty, ever shifting or changing. To fix a legal boundary, marked by a sheet of paper called a diploma, to a business of this nature, can hardly be considered a sensible act. It is only physicians of small calibre who have faith in the certainty of medical knowledge. The great men of the profession agree that it is all groping in the dark beyond certain contracted and commonplace limits. Some of the greatest would practically agree with the witty Voltaire, when he says, "the art of medicine consists in amusing the patient, while nature cures the disease."

In fact, there is no profession in which restraining laws are so out of place as in that of medicine. Shall the law restrain, by fines and imprisonment, the mother from seeking such means as she believes will cure her dying child, whether it be "faith cure," the "laying on of hands," or a spoonful of mullein or cat-nip tea ? Do we, with all our knowledge, know that such means will not cure in a given case. Are all psychical and therapeutical agencies so well understood that we can invariably say what will and what will not cure them? Any law which thus inter-feres with individual freedom of thought and action is an out-rage on human rights, and subversive of personal liberty.

FOOD REFORM.

HEALTH is the natural condition of every living creature. All creatures living in their natural condition live out their natural term of life and die a natural death.

NOT ONE PERSON IN FIFTY THOUSAND lives a natural life, or dies a natural death ! A very large proportion of the human race commit suicide with their teeth—they eat unnatural food and drink unnatural drink ; they live unnatural lives, generate unnatural offspring and die unnatural deaths.

TO LIVE A NATURAL LIFE is to live close to nature. To eat only man's natural food—the grains, roots, fruits and legumes. To drink only man's natural drink—pure water. To breathe pure air by day and by night. To observe habits of personal cleanliness. To take sufficient bodily exercise to promote diges-tion and excretion, and to avoid worry and fret.

HE WHO LIVES SUCH A LIFE will enjoy perfect health and a long and happy life. It is true many are handicappped by the inheritance of penalties for parental sins, but even such may at-tain a large measure of the blessings resulting from natural living.

MORE THAN ONE HALF OF THE SICKNESS which embitters the middle and latter part of life is due to avoidable errors in diet. More actual sickness, impaired vigor and shortened life is caused by erroneous habits of eating and drinking than all other causes combined.

IT IS LARGELY IN OUR OWN POWER to induce or banish sickness, to live happily or miserably, to lengthen or shorten our lives ; and the food we eat is the principal factor in either case. As soon as we begin to live we begin to die, and would die if we were not sustained by nourishing food. Every thought, word, breath or action causes waste of part of the body and tends to its destruction. Hence we are continually wasting away, and consequently require to be renewed or rebuilt, or we would die. Now comes the important question—what food is best suited to repair the waste, nourish the body and promote health and long life.

IT IS MY FULLEST CONVICTION that man's natural food consists only of the natural fruits of the earth—the grains, roots, fruits, legumes and water. It is useless to apply to medical authority concerning what you shall eat or drink, because each physician will order or forbid that which is the fashion to order or forbid. Each seeker after health, happiness and long life must of necessity be his own judge as to the quality and quantity of the food best suited to his particular case, but the source from which he selects *must* be the original and natural source—the vegetable kingdom.

THE PROPAGATION OF THESE IDEAS will no doubt for a time be ridiculed by the medical profession, and all who are engaged in making money by trafficking in animal flesh for *food*, and tea, coffee and intoxicating liquors for *drink*. But vegetarianism in its whole nature is so simple, pure and true, that, in a not distant future, there will come a revolution in its favor, that will banish the flesh of animals as *food*, and the use of tea, coffee, intoxicants and all other substitutes for water as *drink*, from every refined and cultivated community. The time is coming when the eating of flesh and the drinking of unnatural liquids will be held as evidence of a gross, depraved nature. Then will come an era of purity, health, and cleanliness, in which the Goddess of Health will reign supreme over a healthy and happy people.

DRINK REFORM.

Water: Man's Natural Drink.

NATURE is always *right*, and nature has provided no other drink than water, for mammals, birds or plants; and no animal but man seeks any other.

In the human body, as in external nature, the primary office of water is that of a solvent, and as such it is found in every tissue of the body, to a greater or less extent. The fluids of the body, on whose proper relation health so greatly depends, are simply watery solutions of various salts, in which float the corpuscles or particles peculiar to each one. Their physiological value is largely determined by their specific gravity, which depends to a great extent on the amount of water they contain. A deficiency of water in the system produces a nervous, irritable and tired feeling, with frontal headache, dry skin and brittle finger nails.

The physiological. therapeutic and hygienic value of water in the human system is in all cases in proportion to its purity. Water is the only drink provided by nature for man and other animals, and no animal but man uses any other. In all animals provided with a stomach for receiving food, water is the medium by which the materials of nutrition are conveyed to all parts of the body. Water is the medium by which the waste material of the water is carried away. Water quenches thirst naturally and effectually. Water is a kind of food, and will sustain life for many days in the absence of other food. Water flushes the system, cleansing and washing away impurities. Water improves every tissue, and dissolves and removes the products of tissue metamorphosis. Water keeps the skin active and healthy. Water stimulates the kidneys to the removal of waste matter.

Water unloads the emunctories generally, and so leaves the cells in the best condition for functional activity, unclogged by surrounding débris. Water removes old worn out matter. Water paves the way for the reconstruction of new material. Water renews the system day by day, acting as a rejuvenant. Water is a natural tonic, increasing the vigor of body and mind. A pint of pure water drank an hour before breakfast, followed by brisk exercise, washes out the stomach, cleaning it from mucous which prevents the free secretion of gastric juice. It acts as a tonic to the gastric walls of the stomach and stimulates the action of the bowels. Water is a reliable purifier and cleans the bowels of waste matter. Water prevents the disintegration of the blood, protects the brain, and prevents the production of morbid matter. Water preserves the general health and strength of the body. Small pox and other contagious diseases are the product of filth. The free use of water, internally and externally, will prevent and limit the spread of filth diseases more effectually than any other means. If there is a universal remedy, whose effects are true, equal and harmless, that remedy is pure water. Considering that water taken into the stomach is quickly absorbed into the current of the blood and circulated through the body, its absolute purity is a matter of vital importance. Thirst warns us that the blood is too thick, or that it contains some acrid matter that should be washed away with that natural solvent and purifier, pure water. The one element we require to dissolve our food and give fluidity to the blood is water. Water is the only natural drink—whatever is mixed with it is food, flavor or poison. Our natural body as a machine is perfect, and has within itself no marks by which we can possibly predicate its decay; it is apparently calculated to go on forever, if supported by natural food and drink.

HEALTH BEATITUDES.

Blessed are you old men and women who from your youth have obeyed the laws of nature and lived natural lives; your good example shall enrich and bless many generations that follow you.

Blessed are you husbands and wives who received proper physiological instruction in your youth and maturity, and who have lived in obedience to the laws of nature ; your children shall rise up in health and strength and call you blessed.

Blessed are you children whose parents were wise in their day, and began your physical and moral training years before your birth ; your days shall be many and happy in the land in which your parents have placed you. Every child has a primal right to be well born, not handicapped, by the uncertainties of chance, or parental ignorance of the laws of reproduction.

Blessed are you boys whose parents or instructors withheld not from you a knowledge of the dangers and disasters resulting from unphysiological habits in youth ; verily ! you have reason to rejoice and be glad.

Blessed are you girls whose mothers forgot not to instruct you in knowledge essential to your health, beauty and purity ; both you and your children shall reap a rich reward in health and happiness, in consequence thereof.

Blessed are the people who know the laws of health and faithfully obey them ; health and prolonged life shall be their portion.

Blessed are you who covet not your neighbor's riches ; riches are often a burden—sometimes a curse, and are quite unnecessary to the attainment and enjoyment of health, from which all other blessings flow.

Blessed are the people whose laws restrict not, or conflict with the inalienable personal rights of man—to life, liberty and the pursuit of happiness ; rejoice and be glad, for great are your opportunities.

Blessed are you young men who have learned to labor and wait ; one pound of PLUCK is worth a ton of LUCK.

Blessed are you who are engaged in the noble work of lifting men up to a grander conception of this present life, its duties and responsibilities ; a generation ago it was a subject of constant solicitude how to save the soul ; to-day people take more interest in saving the body and improving the mental, moral and physical condition of man.

Blessed are you physicians who have risen superior to your environments and thrown aside the therapeutics of a dark and barbarous age, and cast off the shackles of false dignity, the artifices of the pretender, and the humbug, deceit and fetishness of the charlatan ; verily ! the people shall greatly profit in health and pocket thereby.

Blessed are the people who have learned to live upon man's natural food—the first fruits of the earth—and drink man's natural drink—water ; their lives shall be free from sickness, and their days prolonged upon the earth.

Blessed are you young men and women who live in this progressive age ; rejoice and be glad ! for great are your privileges ! mighty elements are in process of development, and great problems in social and political economy and the arts and sciences are being worked out which will ultimately become accomplished facts and utilized for the benefit of mankind.

Blessed are you young men who have not yielded to the blandishments of the evil woman nor the use of tobacco and strong drink ; rejoice and be glad, for great shall be your reward in purity, health and happiness.

Blessed are you hygienists and sanitarians ; the practical utilization of hygienic and sanitary knowledge is not only purging the world of contagious and infectious diseases, but obliterating the evil effects of centuries of wrong living, wrong thinking and wrong doing.

HEALTH COMMANDMENTS.

I. Thou shalt not eat the flesh of any animal, for the flesh of animals is DEAD MATTER, containing the germs of disease, decay, corruption and death ; whoso eateth thereof shall suffer mental and physical impairment, and shall not live out all his days.

II. Thou shalt eat only the first fruits of the earth ; the grains, nuts, pulses, fruits and roots ; all of which are LIVING MATTER, containing the seeds or germs of vitality and renewed life ; and all of which are rich in nutriment and capable of sustaining life ; repairing waste, making pure blood, bone, tissue and nerve.

III. Thou shalt not drink anything but nature's drink—pure

water. Water is a kind of food; it alone will sustain life for many days, it quenches thirst, flushes the system, removes the worn-out matter, bathes every tissue, keeps the skin active and healthy, and gives renewed life to the body.

IV. Thou shalt not drink any of the pernicious substitutes for water—tea, coffee, cocoa, chocolate, or any spirituous, distilled or malt liquors, for all these artificial drinks injure the health, shorten life, and make invalids, criminals and paupers.

V. Thou shalt not use tobacco in any form, for whoso useth thereof shall suffer mental and physical impairment, which may be transmitted from generation to generation.

VI. Thou shalt not take into thy body any drug medicines composed of minerals or herbs or any other substance; all drug medicines are unnatural, antagonistic to the human system, and destructive to health and life. All healing power is inherent in the living organism; the remedial forces of nature are the foundation and crown of all curative processes.

VII. Thou shalt not be vaccinated, nor permit thy children to be vaccinated. Vaccination does not protect against small-pox, and it frequently causes foul diseases of the blood and skin which may be transmitted to future generations—an ever abiding curse.

VIII. Thou shalt safely protect thyself and thy children from all filth diseases if thou dost faithfully obey these commandments and observe habits of personal and domestic cleanliness, and keep thy dwelling and its surroundings in a perfect sanitary condition.

IX. Thou shalt not make haste to be rich; nor incur a debt; nor covet thy neighbor's property, his social or political position; nor anything that is his.

X. Thou shalt not live for thyself; thou shalt love thy neighbor as thyself; thou shalt do unto others as thou wouldst have others do unto thee.

If thou dost faithfully observe these commandments thy life shall be healthy, happy and long in the land in which thy progenitors have placed thee.

What Whiskey Does.

Whiskey enters the pulpit with the preacher, shuts his mouth to the truth, and makes him a coward. Whiskey stupifies the brain of the physician, and takes the life of his patient. Whiskey enters the church with its members, and closes their ears to the heart-broken appeals of wives, widows and orphans. Whiskey enters the halls of legislation, and makes the legislators cringing cowards. Whiskey enters the sanctum of the editor, and makes him weak, cowardly and treacherous to the dearest interests of humanity. Whiskey mounts the bench with the judge, lowers his dignity, and extinguishes his sense of justice. Whiskey deadens the conscience of the lawyer, and makes him the thief of his clients' interests. Whiskey compels church members to vote licenses to men who make drunkards and criminals. Whiskey makes cowards and sneaks of our members of parliament. Whiskey rules the Church, the State and the People. Whiskey has its victims in every jail, poor-house, insane asylum and penitentiary. Whiskey enters the mouth, the stomach, the life of the parent, and poisons the blood of the unborn. Whiskey drives its victims into dens of dissipation and prostitution. Whiskey debauches manhood and womanhood, and degrades and drags childhood from its throne of purity and innocence. Whiskey has at its command millions of dollars and armies of slaves. Whiskey enslaves our mayors, aldermen and officials, and makes them cowardly and base. Whiskey makes men sluggish, stupid, and indolent. Whiskey has twenty times more groggeries than religion has places of worship. Whiskey drives thousands into untimely graves, and other thousands into poverty and disgrace. Whiskey makes criminals, paupers and invalids. Whiskey stamps the unborn child with idiocy, insanity and love of intoxicants. Whiskey darkens the mind, injures the nerves, and destroys the will of its victim. Whiskey is the factor and ally of crime and debauchery. Whiskey destroys homes, breaks hearts, and blights the happiness of thousands. Whiskey is the direct cause of more poverty, misery and suffering than all other causes combined. Whiskey is the greatest scourge that afflicts humanity, it fills the world with more wretchedness, misery and woe than war, pestilence or famine.

A Few Words to those who Uphold the Traffic in Intoxicating Liquors.

You PRAY "thy kingdom come," and then *vote* to grant licenses to men who *prey* upon the hearts and homes of mothers and children. You PRAY "Thy will be done," and then *vote* to grant licenses to saloons and grog shops to graduate paupers and crim inals. You PRAY "Lead us not into temptation,". and then *vote* to place the worst of temptations in the way of others. You PRAY "Give us this day our daily bread," and then *vote* to legalize the sale of whiskey, which takes away bread from the mouths of mothers and children. You PRAY "Deliver us from evil," and then *vote* power to the liquor seller to place the worst of evils in the way of your neighbors. You BEG for money to send mis- sionaries to foreign heathen, and then *vote* licenses to whiskey dealers to send your brothers, sisters, and neighbors down to perdition. You GRANT licenses to sell whiskey which makes criminals, and then imprison and hang them for committing crimes while under the influence of whiskey. You SEND a few missionaries to the heathen on pretence of saving their souls, and then send cargoes of whiskey to damn both soul and body. You MAKE long prayers for sinners, and then cast your *vote* for a traffic which makes sinners. You GATHER your skirts up with holy horror and rejoice that you are not as other men are, and then re- ceive money from whiskey sellers whom you have licensed to de- stroy the most sacred things of life—home, family, virtue, truth, and character. You COURT the favor of the beer brewer and whiskey distiller, and give him the choicest seats in your sanc- tuaries. You receive his money as if it were not stained with the blood of widows and orphans. You KNOW that the ill-gotten money of the whiskey distiller, and beer brewer, represents the broken lives and homes of thousands of our people, and still you receive it into the same contribution box with the mite of the poor but honest widow. You know that by your *vote* or cowardly silent acquiescence, this accursed traffic in liquor has blighted thousands of lives ; that thousands of homes are blasted with misery and ruin ; that thousands of widows and orphans are to-day suffering poverty and disease as a direct consequence of this devilish traffic, and still you have the impudence to ask " Pardon our sins and transgressions." Tried by all the rules of justice, morality, virtue, and right, are you not worse than the heathen ? Are you not cowardly, pharisaical hypocrites ? Think of it.

WHAT I HAVE LIVED TO SEE, 1832-1892.

The revolution in Texas ; its independence under Gen. Sam. Houston, and its subsequent annexation to the United States. The introduction of friction matches. The rebellion in Canada ; and the civil and political liberty and material prosperity that resulted therefrom. The crowning of Queen Victoria in 1837, and the Jubilee of 1887. The misgovernment of Ireland for fifty years. The introduction of steam railways into Canada. The war between the United States and Mexico, and the annexation of California, Arizona and New Mexico to the United States. The foremost Christian nation of Europe sacrificing its blood and treasure to uphold the unspeakable Turks. The introduction of the electric telegraph. The introduction of envelopes. The introduction of postage stamps. The discovery of the sources of the Nile. The rise and fall of Louis Philippe, King of the French ; the rise and fall of the second Republic ; the rise and fall of the second Empire ; the rise and fall of the Commune, and the establishment of the third Republic in France. The rise and fall of the Roman Republic. The first settlement of the great States of Iowa, Minnesota, Nebraska, Neveda, Kansas, California, Oregon, and Dakota. The first settlement of the Great North-West Territories of Canada. The discovery of gold in California. The introduction of horse-cars.

The introduction of steel pens. Electricity utilized as a motor on railways, boats, and in many other useful ways. The introduction of coal, coal gas and coal oil into Canada. Four millions of human beings held in bondage in the American Republic. Every pulpit in thirteen of the great states of the American Republic upholding human slavery. Every pulpit in the northern or free states silently and passively upholding human slavery. Men, women and children bought, sold and driven in the American Republic just as cattle and swine are bought and sold to-day. American slave drivers hunting fugitives from slavery in the New England States. The John Brown anti-slavery raid on the slave states; the great civil war that followed, resulting in the emancipation of the slaves; the creation of the Southern confederacy; the downfall of the confederacy, and the restoration of the union. The discovery of kerosene oil in Canada. The introduction of bicycles. The Franco-German war; the fall of Napoleon and the unification of Germany. The discovery of the telephone. The Russo-Turkish war; and the liberation of Bulgaria, Roumelia, Bosnia and Herzegovina from Turkey. The United States Centennial Exhibition — 1876. The foremost Christian nation of the world continually at war with weaker and inferior nations. The rise and fall of General William Walker's government in Nicaragua. The emancipation of twenty-two million serfs by the Emperor Alexander II of Russia. The introduction of ocean steam navigation. The introduction of mowers, reapers, binders, and many other agricultural labor-saving machines. The laying of the first ocean telegraph cable. The introduction of ironclad steamships and gunboats. The discovery of photography. The continued misgovernment of Ireland. The confederation of the Canadian provinces and the creation of the Dominion of Canada. The Northwest Rebellion, and the impolitic and unjust execution of Louis Riel. The introduction of torpedo boats. The discovery of chloroform. The wonderful career of General Garibaldi in South America and Italy; the liberation of the Italian provinces, and the unification of Italy

under King Victor Emmanuel. The discovery of the phono-
graph. The introduction of sewing, knitting, type-writing,
type-setting, and other labor-saving machines. The introduction of breech-loading cannon and firearms. The partial acknowledgment that women are entitled to certain natural, personal, inalienable rights which men should be compelled to respect. The continued ignorance, superstition and fetishness of
the medical profession. A despotic but unsuccessful attempt to
enforce compulsory vaccination by fines and imprisonments in
Montreal, in 1885. A growing belief among intelligent people
that personal and municipal cleanliness is the best safeguard
against all zymotic diseases. A growing belief amongst all
classes of people that vaccination is a medical delusion, and
utterly worthless as a safeguard against smallpox. A growing
belief with all who think for themselves, that Hygiene is the
natural, hence scientific basis of medical practice. A growing
belief that tobacco and alcohol—twin curses of mankind—should
be banished from the earth.

WHAT I HOPE TO LIVE TO SEE.

A republic of the United States of Europe. The natural right
of every innocent human being to pursue life, liberty and happiness without medical, political and clerical interference. The
clergy discard their narrow, bigoted, uncharitable sectarian
views and become true helpers of men. The medical profession
give up its fallacies, delusions and humbug, and become honest
seekers after knowledge based on truth and justice. When
human rights shall prevail over all man-made laws. When
married women shall own and have absolute control of their own
persons. The full and complete extension to women of every
civil, political and professional right and privilege enjoyed by
men. Submarine navigation and aerial navigation accomplished
facts. When men and women shall go into physical and moral
training for the generation of superior children. The perfection
of the " electroscope," by which we may see distinctly what is
transpiring hundreds of miles away. When it will be considered

P

a crime for parents to produce weak, sickly, idiotic or malformed children. The perfection of the "telephone," by which we may converse with friends thousands of miles away. When drunkenness shall be sufficient cause for divorce. The perfection of the telescope and microscope, opening to our view the astronomical and infinitessimal worlds. Such an increase of knowledge that the secrets of the unseen world shall be as well understood by us as the ordinary things of to-day. The clergy engaged in educating the people to a noble conception of the present life, its duties and responsibilities. Physicians occupied in teaching the people how to preserve their health and prolong life by *right* living. The present hideous, hollow, obtrusive and absurd funeral and marriage customs and costumes abandoned. Cremation of the dead universally adopted. None but perfectly sound and healthy men and women allowed to marry. Parents, clergymen, and physicians, set an example of temperance, truthfulness and right-living in their homes. When public funerals shall be abolished. Parents teach their children the object and natural use of every organic function of their bodies, especially those connected with the digestion of food, and the reproduction of our species. Sun-power utilized for heating, and all kindred purposes. Food prepared in a condensed form, exactly suited to the wants of the human system. This will result in a great prolongation and vigorous enjoyment of life, while physical energy and brain power will be wonderfully developed. At present so much force is expended in the excretion of waste and injurious matter from the body that life is shortened. The abolition of disease by the extension of dietetic, hygienic and sanitary knowledge. Alcoholic drinks and tobacco—twin evils—banished from the earth. The day when a character for honesty, integrity and sobriety shall be the highest aim of every human being. The above enumerated changes are only a few of the mighty elements now in progress of development, and which will ultimately become accomplished facts, and utilized for the benefit and welfare of man.

THE PRESENT AGE.

The present is a wonderful age, an age of invention, discovery, development and progress, beyond any previous age in the history of the world. The most striking feature of this age is its intense activity in every department of human thought. Vital issues are coming forward for consideration and action as never before. To-day we stand on the thresholds of five wonderful worlds, and hold in our hands the crude weapons to be perfected for their conquest. The ocean world, the aerial world, the world of the infinitely little, the spirit world and the astronomical world. At present, we can only dimly see possibilities, which are as yet only dreams. Inexhaustible stores of powers exist all around us, useful now only for nature's interior operations, and openly visible only in the destructive outbreaks which may yet be made useful in mechanical labor, and may lift man to an individual eminence far beyond our utmost dreams at the present time.

" No seed is lost—in earth's brown bosom cast,
   No deed is lost—of all the deeds we do ;
Each grows to fruit—is harvested at last,
   Haply, in shape undreamed of, fair and new.
And though we die before the end be won,
   Our deeds live on, and other men will cry,
Seeing the end of what we have begun,
   Still lives the fruit for which flowers had to die."

RETROSPECT.

In looking back over the sixty years of my life now past, I rejoice that my lot was cast in a full period of mighty events and the fulfilment of great reforms that have proved a blessing to mankind. To have lived during this eventful period, and to have aided in the least degree in the accomplishment of these great reforms, is indeed cause for rejoicing and congratulation.

It has always been my lot to be on the radical side of medicine, politics and religion, in consequence of which I have suffered outwardly and pecuniarily, but I have preserved my independence and acted according to the dictates of my own conscience. Instead of servilely accepting and obeying conventionalities, I have questioned them and judged them from my own stand-point. I never could and never would look at things with other men's eyes, but through my own. I never could and never would accept formalities, either social or religious, as a substitute for a pure life. From my earliest boyhood I have hated oppression. I have renounced every friendship, I have withdrawn from every church and society where infringement of conscience or personal right was attempted.

If I know my own heart, I am conscious that my sincere desire has ever been to do some good in this world, to promote the welfare and true happiness of my fellow men. If my motives have been misconstrued and my actions misrepresented, I cannot help it—those who traduce me do not know me. I am quite conscious that my life has been marked by many errors and faults which I have amended as far as I could. I am also quite conscious of the purity of my motives, and that has sustained me, as has the conviction that my life, labors and pursuits have in some measure conduced to the freedom, happiness and welfare of others.

The sincere appreciation, affectionate regard and devoted friendship of a few good men and women have been a great comfort to me when grieved and pained by the injustice of those who judged me wrongly.

My life, thus far, has been busy and anxious, but not joyless. Whether it shall be prolonged few or more years, I am grateful that it has endured so long, and that it has abounded in opportunities for good not wholly unimproved.

> " 'Tis weary fighting all one's life,
> In one long, bitter desperate strife,
> 'Gainst hydra-headed wrong—
> To give up all life's joys, that we
> May humble banner-bearers be,
> And yet we choose the weary way,
> The fighting not the feasting day."

APPENDIX.

APPENDIX.

—

LETTERS FROM FRIENDS AND CO-WORKERS

IN REFERENCE TO THE AUTHOR'S

REFORM LABORS.

———◆◆◆———

Letters from Co-Laborers in the Anti-Slavery Cause—Letters
from Co-Laborers during the Slaveholders' Rebellion—Natural
History Labors, Opinions of the Press—Letters from Friends
in favor of Moral and Physical Reform—Letters from Friends
and Co-Laborers in the cause of Anti-Compulsory Vaccination.

From JOHN G. WHITTIER.

DEAR FRIEND ROSS,—* * * "Braver act was never done
than thine in thy raids of humanity. How very satisfactory it
must be to thee to know that the poor people whom, like another
Moses, thou leds't out of bondage, have proved so well worthy of
their freedom. God bless thee and thine.
"Thy fifty years nave not been idle ones, but crowded with good
works. I hope another half century may be added to them."

249

From Right Hon. W. E. GLADSTONE, *Prime Minister of England.*

HAWARDEN CASTLE, CHESTER,

January 14th, 1876.

DEAR DR. ROSS,—I have been reading some very interesting "Sketches of Anti-Slavery Men," and among them I find none more interesting than the sketch of your brave efforts to give freedom to the slaves of the American Republic. I conceive no one can deny the skill, forethought, and tenacity you exhibited in that pursuit, or withhold his admiration for signal courage, disinterestedness, and humanity, which formed the basis of your whole proceeding. * * *

From GERRIT SMITH.

MY DEAR FRIEND ROSS,—* * * No one knows better than I how deeply devoted you were to the cause of the oppressed, or with what heroic bravery, determination and success you labored to bring the poor slaves out of bondage. The descendants of those for whom you so often perilled your life, will "rise up and call you blessed." * * * Heaven bless you my dear friend.

From WENDELL PHILLIPS,

DEAR ROSS,—* * * No higher heroism, courage or tenacity of purpose was ever displayed than by you in your chivalric efforts to help the slaves to freedom. That your days may be many and happy my *preux chevalier* is the sincere wish of your brother.

Wendell Phillips

From OLIVER JOHNSON, *one of the founders of the American Anti-Slavery Society.*

DEAR ROSS,—* * * What joy it must be to you to revive the memory of your self-sacrificing labors and success in freeing the slaves. I pray that the blessing of heaven may rest upon you.

———

From LUCRETIA MOTT.

MY DEAR FRIEND,—* * * Thou hast my sincere admiration for the noble and courageous part thee acted during our struggle with slavery. Thou hast made the world better by thy life and labors. * * * Thy sincere and devoted friend.

———

From GENERAL JOSEPH GARIBALDI, *the Italian Liberator.*

DEAR ROSS,— * * * It is more than a quarter of a century since our friendship began in the little house on Staten Island. * * * * * I am proud to number among my dearest friends one who has done so much for the cause of human freedom as you have. * * *.

Yours for life,

G. Garibaldi

From the HONOURABLE HENRY WILSON, *Vice-President of the United States.*

DEAR DR. ROSS,'— * * * When the history of the great conflict waged by the Abolitionists against the Slave Power is fully written out, no name will take higher rank than yours, for devotion, courage and faithful service in the cause of freedom.

From VICTOR HUGO.

Accept, sir, the homage of my respect and sympathy for your brave and successful labors in the cause of human freedom.

Victor Hugo

From HONORABLE BENJAMIN F. WADE. *Vice-President of the United States.*

MY DEAR ROSS, — * * Never in the history of the world did the same number of men perform so great an amount of good for the human race, and for their country, as the abolitionists, and it is my duty to add that no one of their number submitted to greater privations, perils or sacrifices, or did more in the great and noble work than yourself; long may you be remembered, and may God be praised for your success.

——

From the Can. Illus. News, March 19th, 1881.

"Dr. Ross' fame as a naturalist is world-wide; but his claims to public recognition are not confined to his achievements in that field. His labors, perils, and successes as an active, earnest worker in the great anti-slavery struggle in the United States, which culminated in the liberation from bondage of four millions of slaves, won for him the praise and friendship of his co-workers in that great struggle. There is no risk now in denouncing the sin and injustice of human slavery; but it was another thing to denounce, and to seek individually to release its victims from bondage twenty-five years ago, when it was upheld by the law, the church, and self-interest in the Slave States; yet that is just what Dr. Ross did on many occasions. The little band of radical abolitionists with whom he was laboring, were despised, hated, and ostracised by the rich, the powerful, and the so-called higher classes: but Dr. Ross has always possessed the courage of his convictions, and prefers the approval of his own conscience to the smiles or favors of men. The subject of our sketch is a native of Canada and a highly esteemed citizen of Montreal."

From WILLIAM LLOYD GARRISON, *the Pioneer Abolitionist of the United States.*

MY DEAR FRIEND, —I have not forgotten you nor your brave crusade in behalf of the poor bondsmen. It must be a source of unalloyed pleasure to you to call to mind the active and zealous part you took in our great struggle, particularly in reference to enabling slaves to escape from their Southern house of bondage, and procuring for them aid and succour on their way to Canada, and after their arrival on that side of the line. That you did not fall a victim to your humanity, in view of the perils which, everywhere at the South, beset your pathway, but were permitted to see the four millions of slaves set free from their bonds, and raised from the chattlehood to the rights of American citizenship, is indeed cause for equal wonder and congratulation. Neither you nor I, nor any other abolitionist, expected to live to see this unparalleled transformation. At times, however, it seems almost like a dream, rather than a bright reality. * * *

Yours, for universal freedom,

Wm. Lloyd Garrison.

From HARRIET BEECHER STOWE.

MY DEAR DR. ROSS,—Your welcome letter carries me back to the time when my brother, Henry Ward Beecher, and myself, just returned from a Western life and come to live in Eastern cities, were shocked and outraged by finding, both in church and state, a universal bowing down to the Fugitive Slave Law. I re member his coming then to lecture up in the State of Maine, where I was then living, and of our meeting and sitting up at night to ask each other, What can *we* do for a testimony against this wrong. He was going to preach and lecture through the land ; and I said, " I have begun a set of sketches in the *National Era*, to illustrate the cruelty of slavery ; I call it Uncle Tom's Cabin." " That's right," he said, " write it, and we'll print it, and scatter it ' Thick as the leaves of Vallambrosa.' "

That was the beginning, and since then " What hath God wrought ? "

Whenever since then I have been tempted to be low-spirited or desponding, I think, well ! thank God for one thing, I have lived to see slavery abolished ; and God only knows what a comfort that is. Never let any one despair that has lived to see that. What a comfort to you must be the reflection that you have saved so many from these horrors. I congratulate you. With sincere respect and sympathy.

From LYDIA MARIA CHILD.

DEAR DR. ROSS,—* * * You deserve the respect and gratitude of every friend of freedom for your earnest and efficient efforts to bring the oppressed out of the house of bondage. The present generation cannot realize how courageous, as well as cautious, a man must have been to carry on such a mission as you did during several years. It seems so strange that those exciting times in which we lived and labored with soul-thrilling incidents, constantly urging us on, have now become mere records of history ! And how inadequate the record will be to convey a true idea of the time, money, talent, and zeal so lavishly expended to right a great national wrong ! With feelings of profound thankfulness for your heroic help during our struggle to throw off the virulent disease that was poisoning the life-blood of the nation. * * *

From the New York Evening Post, September 2nd, 1875.

Dr. A. M. Ross, the Author and Abolitionist, devoted himself for the five or six years that preceded the war to the work of assisting slaves to escape. Anybody familiar with the temper of the Southern people just before the war will easily guess the fate of a man who should have been detected in what Dr. Ross proposed to do, and did.

From the Irish Canadian, Toronto, July 7th, 1875.

We know Dr. Ross to be the devoted friend of the slave. His sympathy for the oppressed of all climes and colors is as boundless as the impulses of his noble heart, and the exact color of a man's skin, or the particular race to which he may belong, is no barrier in his estimation to the right to freedom which God intended from the beginning should be the birthright of all the human family.

The following extracts from letters received by the Author during the great rebellion, are published with a view to illustrate the varied hopes and fears that animated leading Abolitionists during the con-·test between freedom and slavery.

From WENDELL PHILLIPS.

BOSTON, September 4th, 1864.

DEAR ROSS,—* * Mr. Lincoln may, probably does, wish the grand result, freedom to the negro, but he is too much a *border statesman* in his opinions. Hence the negro is not to him a *man* in the full sense. Hence he overrates the prejudices and comfort of the slaveholders. Consequently, though he desires the result, he hesitates at the MEANS. Public opinion has bayonnetted him up to his present position, and may yet save us through him, or rather in spite of him ; but it is a very dangerous risk to run. SETTLEMENT is a more dangerous hour than war. Hence I oppose Lincoln's re-election ; prominent Republicans dread it. The leading Senator of New England said lately, " Lincoln's election would be destruction ; McClellan's would be damnation." So the leaders are making an effort to induce Lincoln to withdraw, and unite all earnest men on a better candidate. If we effect that, we are safe.

The task we have to do is a very great one. Davis made a rebellion ; it was all he could do. Lincoln, by tampering, delay, indecision, and long tenderness for slavery, has made a Confederacy—united, proud, with friends, and military strength. * * *

With great regard and many thanks for all you have done for us.

Wendell Phillips

From HORACE GREELEY.

OFFICE OF THE TRIBUNE,
NEW YORK, May 19th, 1863.

DEAR FRIEND,—Since the outbreak of our terrible war, I have made it a rule to be rarely ever away from our city for any distance. I should like very much to meet you and Mr. Giddings at Gerrit Smith's next week, but it is not possible for me. When this bloody conflict ends, I shall take a breathing spell ; then, I hope, you will spend a week with me, and we'll talk over the events of the past ten years in which you have borne so active and noble a part. Don't pass through New York without dropping in to see me. * * *

Yours faithfully,

Horace Greeley,

From JOHN GREENLEAF WHITTIER (*The Quaker Poet.*)

AMESBURY, 27, 5th mo., 1865.

DEAR FRIEND ROSS,—It gives me great satisfaction to see the friends of freedom in Canada and England acting in behalf of the freedmen of the United States. * * *

The tears which both nations are shedding over the grave of our beloved President are washing out all the bitter memories of misconception and estrangement between them. So good comes out of evil.

> Oh, Englishmen! in hope and creed,
>   In blood and tongue our brothers;
> We, too, are heirs of Runnymede,—
> And Shakespeare's fame and Cromwell's deed
> Are not alone our mothers.

> Thicker than water in one rill,
>   Through centuries of story;
> Our Saxon blood has flow'd, and still—
> We share with you the good and ill,
>   The shadow and the glory.

Thine truly,

John G. Whittier

From WILLIAM CULLEN BRYANT.

ROSLYN, LONG ISLAND, June 3rd, 1865.

DEAR DR. ROSS,— * * * I am glad to know the cause of the United States has so strenuous a defender in Canada. Your zealous and patriotic labors merit the thanks of all who desire the prosperity of this country. * *

Faithfully yours,

W. C. Bryant

From GENERAL GARIBALDI.

BRESCIA (Italy), September, 1865.

* * * I rejoice with you over the destruction of slavery in the American Republic. * * * Cloisters and prisons are not His work. God made liberty—man made slavery.

Ever yours,

G. Garibaldi

From GERRIT SMITH.

PETERBORO', August 31, 1864.

MY DEAR FRIEND,— * * * I had strong fears from the first that you would be baffled. We thank you for your noble and benevolent purpose, and accept the will for the deed. I believe the Heavenly Father means that my country shall live ; she has more to fear just now from Northern demagogues than from Southern rebels. * *

* * * I am glad to learn that your heart is set on Lincoln's re-election. * * * This nation will live. It has given ample proof that it can withstand both foreign and domestic foes ; both Northern and Southern rebels. Yes, this nation will live to see herself and the whole continent free from oppressors—not from slaveholders only, but from Imperial despots also. As life is the

Q

law of righteousness, so death is the law of wickedness ; and the wickedness of the Democratic party is nearing that extreme limit, where wickedness dies of itself. Be of good cheer—God is for us. Your friend,

From WENDELL PHILLIPS.

BOSTON, June 12th, 1865.

DEAR ROSS,—* * * I mail you, with this, my last two speeches and evening talks on Lincoln's death, from which you will obtain a view of my present position.

I will only add that since these speeches, I have become more and more anxious and doubtful about the policy our President (Johnson) will pursue. The Cabinet are about equally divided on the question of negro suffrage. But we hope to make an active use of the interval before the next session of Congress, to manifest (I say manifest, because it already exists), such a determined public opinion as will awe the Government into following that radical course in which the masses are abundantly ready to support them. Time will show what we can do. Politicians are slippery reliance in war times as well as in peace. Thank you for your active and zealous efforts in our behalf.

From GERRIT SMITH.

PETERBORO', July 1st, 1865.

DEAR FRIEND,— * * * Slavery has received its death blow ; but it is by no means certain that our nation will be saved or still united. We may first have to pass through a war of races. I am not satisfied with the course our Government (Johnson's) is pursuing in the matter of " reconstruction." My poor, guilty country cannot be saved so long as it hates and persecutes the black man. Our nation is lost if the Freedmen are denied the ballot.

Your friend,

GERRIT SMITH.

NATURAL HISTORY LABORS.

Opinions of the Press.

From the Canadian Illustrated News, Oct. 3rd, 1874.

" We have much pleasure in presenting to our readers this week a portrait of Dr. A. M. Ross, the distinguished naturalist. Dr. Ross is forty years of age, a Canadian by birth, of Highland Scotch descent. For many years he has devoted himself to the collection and classification of our native Flora and Fauna. His Ornithological, Entomological, and Botanical collections, are undoubtedly the most extensive and complete ever made by one individual. Dr. Ross has embodied the results of his labors in several valuable and interesting works from his pen, which have met with a cordial and appreciative reception in Canada, and by naturalists in Europe and America. Dr. Ross' labors, as a naturalist, have been highly appreciated by the leading *savants* of Europe.

It is matter of congratulation that we have resident among us a gentleman whose achievements in the fascinating sciences of Ornithology, Entomology, and Botany, have made him a standing authority throughout the scientific world.

From " Men of the Times," Routledge, England, 1878.

Dr. Ross has been engaged in collecting and classifying the Flora and Fauna of British North America. He has collected and classified 570 species of birds that visit Canada ; 247 species of mammals, reptiles, and fresh-water fish ; 3,400 species of insects belonging to the orders of Lepidoptera, Coleoptera, and Neuroptera ; and 2,200 species of Canadian flora. Dr. Ross has, by his labors, enriched the Natural History Museums of Paris, St. Petersburg, Milan, Rome, Athens, London, Constantinople, Tiflis, Teheran, Brussels, and Dresden, with valuable contributions of Canadian flora and fauna. Several of his literary productions have been republished in France and Italy ; his chief publications are : " Birds of Canada," 1872; Butterflies and Moths of Canada," 1875; "Flora of Canada," 1874; "Forest Trees of Canada,"·1874; "Monographs on Architecture of Canadian Birds' Nests," "Food of Canadian Birds," "Migration of Canadian Birds," "Remains of the Elephas Americanus and Mastodon Giganteus found in Canada," 1875; "Recollections and Experiences of an Abolitionist," 1875; "Mammals, Reptiles and Freshwater Fish of Canada," 1878.

From the University Journal, Athens, Greece, Dec. 9th, 1876.

"With pleasure we announce to our people that the illustrious Canadian naturalist, Alexander Ross, has enriched our Museum by a magnificent and precious gift of many rare objects of Canadian natural history, and a complete set of his published works. The celebrated Canadian has by this kindly gift taught our people to study that far-off land and its wonderful natural productions."

From the Opinion Publique, Montreal, April 23rd, 1876.

"The *Italian Illustrated*, published in Milan and Rome, Italy, contains in a recent number an excellent portrait of Alexander M. Ross, the celebrated Canadian naturalist, and an interesting account of his labors and successes.

"The fame of Dr. Ross belongs to Canada as one of its most brilliant men. No other scientific man in America has received more evidence of the esteem of his fellow-men, nor any such decorations on the part of the sovereigns. He has been made a member of nearly all the scientific societies of Europe. The King of Italy has made him a Chevalier of the Crown of Italy; the King of Portugal, Chevalier Commander of the Military Order of the Conception; the King of Greece, Chevalier of the Redeemer; the King of Saxony, Chevalier of the Order of Albert; his Imperial Majesty the Emperor of Russia, Chevalier of the Imperial and Royal Order of St. Anne; Denmark, Belgium, Austria, and Egypt have bestowed medals and diplomas of honor. Some of his numerous writings have been translated into French and Italian, and their reproduction has spread in all Europe the most useful ideas of the inexhaustible resources of Canada." We are happy to offer a portrait of the doctor taken from a recent photograph.

LETTERS FROM FRIENDS

IN REFERENCE TO THE AUTHOR'S

CRUSADE IN BEHALF OF MORAL AND PHYSICAL REFORM.

By the REV. JAMES COUTTS, *Kemptville, Ont.*

I have been moved to write the following brief sketch of Dr. Ross' labors from feelings of gratitude, admiration and justice; having been fully cognizant of his labors and sacrifices, in this great work of moral reform, from the first.

Dr. Ross took the ground that "THE PEOPLE SHOULD KNOW" of this evil in its enormity, and in its far-reaching devastation and ruin. Strange to say, in attempting to give this information, he met with bitter opposition from many members of the MEDICAL PROFESSION. Said the late Dr. John Rolph, of Toronto, to him, on asking his advice regarding entering on the work: "Don't touch it, unless you are prepared to be ostracised and hated by the medical profession, and slandered and persecuted by society at large; but, if you are willing to face these obstacles, you can do more real good than all the preachers, teachers and physicians have done on this subject during the last century."

In the prosecution of the work, Dr. Ross found the above statement to be a prophetic declaration. It has been fulfilled to the letter. He has suffered persecution, ostracism, slander, misrepresentation and personal sacrifice while engaged in this Christ-like work; but he went *right on* with his work, in the face of all this opposition, bravely and persistently doing his duty, not even stopping to reply to his persecutors and slanderers. This required *determined* purpose and *singleness* of aim, both of which are found as factors in the character of Dr. Ross. Such men are *bound* to succeed in what they undertake.

During these eighteen years he has, at his own expense, circulated *six hundred thousand documents*, filled with words of warning to the rising generation of young men and women. This itself is a grand work accomplished,

Dr. Ross has given the best years of his life to this work. He has thrown all the ability, energy and earnestness of which he is possessed into it. In short, here is the work of a real philanthropist.

From Rev. John Ellison, Chaplain to His Grace the Archbishop of Canterbury.

Addington Park, Croyden, Eng.

Dear Dr. Ross,— * * * You have doubtless heard of the death of the Archbishop of Canterbury on Advent Sunday. Nothing but his long illness prevented him from taking an active part in your great work. I should be glad to be the means of distributing your little tracts if you would kindly send me some.

From His Grace Archbishop Lynch, of Toronto.

My Dear Dóctor Ross,—I am very glad that you have taken up this matter. I have striven to combat this vice all my life, both publicly and privately, and I shall be most happy to distribute your tracts.

From Dr. Daniel Clark, *Medical Superintendent of the Toronto Asylum for the Insane.*

My Dear Doctor,—I wish you all success in this much needed work. I published 600 copies of my "Report" upon my own responsibility and distributed them where I thought they would do the most good.

From John G. Whittier, *the Quaker Poet.*

Dear Friend,—I thank thee for thy kind note, and enclosed report of a much needed labor in the cause of the moral and physical health and happiness of the community. Thy friend.

From Wendell Phillips, *the Orator of Freedom.*

Dear Old Friend,—Thank you for the gallant fight you are making in the good cause ; you expected obloquy and persecution. Persevere! The ideas and principles you are maintaining are richly worth the sacrifice. Cordially your brother.

From Rev. Prof. Scrimger, *of Montreal.*

I sympathize very strongly in the object you aim at. I have reason to know that the vice is much more common than most people suppose. It is also an exceedingly difficult matter to deal with in any effective way. If you could send me say 100 copies of your tracts, I would like to place them in the hands of the young men and lads under my pastoral care. I hope your efforts will do much good.

——— ——

From Rev. Dr. W. S. Rainsford, *New York City.*

I wish you all success in your thankless task. I am convinced that many are more and more coming to recognize the need of plain statement and more offensive attitude with regard to this widespread evil. Send me some of your tracts suitable for my confirmation classes.

————

From Rev. W. W. Andrews, *Sackville, N. B.*

I desire to express my sympathy with your crusade against that moral pestilence that walketh in darkness. In our High schools it is almost an epidemic, and many who would recoil from other impurities are caught in this net of Satan. Go on, Doctor! You are fighting an enemy that marcheth not with banners or with plumes, and that requires the greatest courage, but yours will be a nobler victory and the brighter crown.

————

From Rev. James McAlister, *Thessalon, Ont.*

I desire to pen a few words of sympathy and encouragement, praying that they may be the means of strengthening you in the grand and holy work in which you are engaged. You are employed in a work the prosecution of which, in its grand effects, will continue to roll down the ages yet to come, scattering light in its glorious way, and causing thousands of human beings to call you blessed.

————

From Rev. F. A. Cassidy, *Woodstock, Ont.*

I tender you my most hearty and prayerful sympathy in your good work. Believing that your life and labors have already been made a blessing to our country, I hope you may long be spared to prosecute your truly philanthropic labors; and that you may save many a youth from an untimely grave, and many a mother from a broken heart.

From REV. CHARLES W. HOLDEN, *Napier, Ont.*

Thousands will, with feelings of inexpressible gratitude, remember the name of Dr. A. M. Ross, who began, and is carrying on so successfully this work of moral reform. Through the labors of this great reformer many are being enlightened and saved for lives of usefulness.

From REV. C. E. MANNING, *Toronto, Ont.*

When there seemed no eye to pity the ignorant victim of this sin, God in His love moved upon the heart of Dr. Ross to originate and carry out the greatest moral reform of this age.

From REV. H. G. FRASER, "McMASTER HALL," *Toronto, Ont.*

What more noble, what more philanthropic work, than that in which Dr. Ross has been the pioneer and worker? God speed his work! must be the wish of all who know its nature and results.

From REV. HENRY IRVINE, *London, Ont.*

I am glad the stamp of men who are willing to be ostracised, and branded if need be, for the sake of right and truth, still live. "To those whose names are cast out for the truth's sake, it is a small thing to be judged of man's judgment."

From REV. A. INWOOD, *Parma, Ont.*

Spread the information broadcast over the land, and under the light of knowledge this hideous evil will be stopped. It is yours to battle for the TRUTH, to fight against WRONG in the face of opposition. I pray for your success in your noble crusade against vice.

From REV. JOHN E. HOCKEY, *Victoria University, Cobourg, Ont.*

I wish you every success in your enterprise for humanity. You may be persecuted by an ignorant and ungenerous generation, but a grand future awaits you amongst future generations of men, when your worth will be appreciated and your name enrolled with the noble and good of all ages.

From REV. W. R. WOOD, *Woodstock College, Woodstock, Ont.*

Dr. Ross is doing the work of a true philanthropist; not only has he been the means of saving the lives of hundreds who have proved useful, but he has awakened thousands to the enormity of this sin.

From REV. WM. PRICE, *Stratford, Ont.*

I enter most heartily into your plan with regard to this crying evil, and will be glad to assist in your labor of love to fallen humanity. "Cry aloud, spare not, lift up thy voice like a trumpet, and tell the people their transgressions."

Crusade against Compulsory Vaccination.

WORDS OF SYMPATHY FROM EUROPE.

"*I regard compulsory vaccination with mistrust and misgiving.*"
—RIGHT HON. W. E. GLADSTONE.

"*I am strongly opposed to compulsory vaccination.*"—HERBERT SPENCER.

"*The London Society for the Abolition of Compulsory Vaccination.*"

LONDON, ENG., Jan. 5, 1886.

DEAR DR. ROSS,—I am desired to forward to you the subjoined copy of a Resolution moved by our President, William Tebb, seconded by W. S. Beurle, Esq., and carried unanimously at the meeting of the Executive Committee, held on Wednesday, Jan. 2nd.

Yours very truly,
WILLIAM YOUNG,
Secretary.

" Having heard with deep regret of the illness of Dr. Alexander M. Ross, of Montreal, brought on by his arduous and self-sacrificing labors in resisting the vaccination tyranny :—RESOLVED, that the sympathy of the Executive Committee of this society be, and is hereby tendered to Dr. Ross, with the hope of his speedy restoration to health, coupled with an expression of their high appreciation of his successful efforts for the promotion of rational and scientific methods of preventing disease."

From BARON GRYZANOWSKI, *Doctor of Medicine.*

LIVORNO, ITALY.

MY BRAVE CONFRERE,—I hasten to express my cordial sympathy with your aims, which are our aims, and your sufferings, which are greater than our sufferings. If the fallacy of the vaccination doctrine were a scientific one, it might not be so very difficult to prove it ; but the *onus probandi* lies on the vaccinators, and they have long since confessed that vaccination has no scientific basis. Your heroic fight has been watched with deep interest in this country—one man with truth !—against a million with error !

From J. MACKENZIE, M.D., F.R.C.S.E.

EILENNACHE, SCOTLAND.

DEAR DR. ROSS,—I have been in active civil and military service since 1824, and no subject has ever met me carrying to the thoughtless public anything approaching in folly or crime, the load of lies that vaccination has had, and has, to bear from its votaries and victims.

Myself vaccinated in childhood, yet attacked by smallpox, and myriads of the vaccinated daily dying from smallpox, besides those who suffer from scrofula and other diseases everywhere, though once denied, but now admitted, as being introduced to our bodies by vaccination, it is really shocking to see numbers of medical men still busy extolling to their dupes that smallpox is extinguished by vaccination. How they ever can touch vaccination fees without holes being burned in their vile hands, astonishes me.

From EDWARD HAUGHTON, M.D.

LONDON, ENG.

DEAR DR. ROSS,— * * * I trust your generous advocacy of Truth and Liberty has not got you into any personal difficulty ;

and I desire hereby to record on behalf of many others, as well as myself, that we in this country deeply sympathize with you in your—at present—unequal contest with a time-serving press.

From the RIGHT HON. LORD CLIFTON, M.P., *England.*

MY DEAR DR. ROSS,—I need not say that I deeply sympathize with you in the gallant fight you have been making in Montreal against a despotic profession and a prostitute press. No words can be too strong to express my abhorrence at the attitude taken by the Montreal press, to say nothing of English and American journals.

The cruel and despotic tone of these hired quill-drivers would lead one to suppose that one was living in the darkest ages of superstition and tyranny. I am very glad that we anti-vaccinationists, who are denounced by a sordid and lying press as men of only *one single idea*, can yet number in our ranks such a well-known and tried slavery abolitionist as yourself.

From HER EXCELLENCY THE COUNTESS DE NOAILLES, *Sussex, England.*

DEAR DR. ROSS,—I must thank you most heartily for the great work you are doing in Montreal. You have many warm friends and admirers in England who have watched your brave contest with deep interest.

From J. J. GARTH WILKINSON, M.D., LL.D.

4 FINCHLEY ROAD, ST. JOHN'S WOOD, LONDON, ENG.

MY DEAR DR. ROSS,—I hope I need not tell you how deeply I sympathize with you, a lone rider and a horse of battle, in the midst of the vast pack of vaccinating wolves. The treatment you have experienced is unspeakably infamous. The profession which has inflicted it has cast the last remains of conscience out of its heart. It used to be a medical canon that in or during small-pox epidemics, vaccination should not be resorted to. Why is it abandoned now? Because epidemics are panic times; and at these times there is more power to coerce the unwilling and a readier seduction of the wavering and the willing to submit to the foul, false rite. The abolition of this canon, founded upon real knowledge, is an act of public baseness on the part of the medical body. How has vaccination destroyed our poor profession ; its power of thought, its skill, its common honesty. How is it made the ready prostitute of Pasteurism and all its congenerate Sodoms ! We will fight on under God, and His time will come for purging the nations of this immeasurable iniquity. With deep respect and admiration for your brave stand for your people, I am yours fraternally.

From PROFESSOR (*Emeritus*) FRANCIS W. NEWMAN, *of Oxford University, England.*

DEAR DR. ROSS,—I feel it my duty to send to you an expression of my sympathy with you in your gallant fight against compulsory vaccination.

No physician knows what is put into the blood by vaccination, so-called ; but the sin of it is to *alter* the blood, forsooth, to improve it by artifice ! No legislator has a right to assault a healthy body. A physician who accounts a healthy child "dangerous to society" is a fool. Those who advise re-vaccination because the force of vaccination is evanescent, indicate that they wish to keep us in permanent cow-pox or calf-pox, or some other pox—they care not particularly which. This will suffice to show how warmly I esteem your labors.

I read with deep interest that in the slavery age of the United States, you in Canada personally played so noble a part on the side of freedom. I sincerely thank you for what you *then* did, and for what you are *now* doing. In Roman fashion I would say to you, *Macte virtate esto.* You will certainly never repent of it, whatever your sacrifice.

From DR. GOTTFRIED SCHUESTER, *Professor of the University, Zurich, Switzerland.*

"I desire to thank you for your crusade against vaccination. You have many sympathising and admiring friends in this country. Vaccination is not compulsory in Switzerland."

From LINDA GILBERT, *the Prison Reformer, New York.*

MY DEAR DR. ROSS,—I am in hearty sympathy with your work as regards anti-vaccination. God bless you !

From BARON PAUL WALEWSKY, *Councillor of State, Staff Surgeon of the Imperial Russian Army.*

To DR. ALEXANDER ROSS of Canada,—I have heard of the battle you have fought and won against the enemies of cleanliness and common sense. You have my cordial thanks for the brave stand you maintained in the face of so much opposition. Vaccination, is not compulsory (except in the army and navy) in Russia—but Canada is a free country (?). *   *

From DR. DON JOSE SANTA PIETRA, *Naval Surgeon.*

DEAR DR. ROSS,—Information has reached me from England of your gallant fight against vaccination; I rejoice in your success and congratulate you, *Ex animo.* *   *

From PROFESSOR P. A. SILJESTROM, *Rektor of the University.*

STOCKHOLM, SWEDEN.

DEAR DR. ROSS,—I wish you every success in your struggle for our common cause—that great cause the importance of which, from a sanitary point of view, only few persons duly appreciate. I am astonished to see the absurd and tyrannical rite of vaccination kept up, as it appears, with still more severity on the other side of the Atlantic, than in the Old World, and it is really depressing in our days to witness a spirit of persecution which recalls past ages of religious persecution, and from which yourself have suffered in a most odious way. If there were wanting any further evidence of the falsity of the vaccination theory, this sort of persecution is certainly one. True science never applies to such means. But we may hope for better times, and undoubtedly a time will come when the claim of the medical profession to save our bodies from small-pox by the aid of fines and imprisonments, shall be read with the same feeling with which we now read of the persecution of the church in former times, —to save souls by halter and stake.

From DR. WILHELM RITTER VON FRANKENBURG, *Vienna.*

DEAR CHEVALIER ROSS,—I was much surprised to learn that vaccination was compulsory in a free country like Canada. You, my good friend, are deserving of praise instead of persecution, for the brave fight you have made against such terrible odds. I hope for your success.

————

From ALFRED MILNES, ESQ., M.A., *Fellow of the Statistical Society of London.*

DEAR DR. ROSS,—If words of friends are helpful in your hour of need, I would that words of mine could come clothed in power beyond speech. I am not so presumptuous as to suppose that anything can be said by the raw recruit to cheer you, the veteran of a hundred fights. Men and women have breathed the air of liberty, who but for you had died in thraldom. And, now, the fight is won for the parents of an oppressed race, it has to be fought out for the children of all races. Nor is the struggle quite so unequal as it seems. Your purpose is single and your aims are weapons of precision. Toil on, then, undaunted; you are sowing seed that our little ones may reap, nor fail to bless the sower.

————

From DR OIDTMAN, *Staff Surgeon of the Imperial German Army, and Chief Physician to the Hospitals at Verdun and St. Quentin, during the Franco-German War.*

RURICH CASTLE, PRUSSIA.

MY DEAR FRIEND AND COLLEAGUE,—The Count Hompesch wishes you all success from his heart, and I do also. Our congratulations on your success! Your brethren in Germany are having success. Chancellor Bismarck has taken our side. With all wishes for your success.

————

From DR. ALFRED R. WALLACE, *co-discoverer with Darwin, of the Principle of Natural Selection.*

FRITH HILL, GODALMING, ENGLAND.

DEAR DR. ROSS,—You are doing an excellent work, and the result will, I trust, be the repeal of the most iniquitous compulsory vaccination law. The reckless way in which false or one-sided statements are promulgated by pro-vaccinators is surely an indication of the badness of their cause. A good and really scientific practice never needs bolstering up by exaggerations and lies. I stepped out of my special path to strike a blow at this wretched superstition as soon as I became thoroughly convinced of its errors, and of the cruelty and danger arising out of its compulsory enforcement. With best wishes for your success.

––––––

From LADY E. DE MORGAN.

CHELSEA, ENGLAND.

DEAR DR. ROSS,—You are waging a noble warfare, against prejudice and ignorance. Be of good courage, " *Blessed are ye when men shall reproach you, and cast out your name as evil.*" May God bless your labors.

––––––

MODERN REFORMERS.

" The world has had reformers, men who were sternly just,
Who smote the thrones of wickedness and laid them in the dust ;
Meek, tender men, made mighty by mankind's blood and tears,
Strong men, whose words were thunderbolts to smite the wrong
    of years.

Were all these stern reformers of a breed too weak to last ?
Did all the great wrong-smiters wane and perish in the past ?
Did they fight a losing battle ? were they conquered in the fray ?
Why are there no reformers fighting in the world to-day ?

Well, 'tis but a thing of labels ; the reformers have not gone,
But they're mixing with the people with misleading placards on ;
For we placard them "Fanatics," "Visionaries," "Cranks,"
    and "Fools,"—
Men denounced by clubs and churches, by the journals and the
    schools.

There are men who bear these placards daily in the market-place,
Heroes of the ancient lineage, kings and saviours of the race,
Yet we never see their greatness through life's trivial events,
But our children's sons will read it on their granite monuments."

FINIS.